A Ring WITHIN A Field

C.S. MCKINNEY

Illustrated by S.L. McKinney

This book is dedicated to my sisters.

The two best siblings I could ever ask for.

"You don't flirt with the important things in life; you marry them."

—Coach Williams

The IFF Series:

A Setting Summer

If and Only If

A Ring Within a Field

For more information, visit:
www.csmckinney.com

CHAPTER 1:
An Invitation

The small white car zigged and zagged along the familiar road. She only let off the gas slightly as she passed the now-faded black marks, all that remained from a night that once haunted her. Sarah peered in the rearview mirror, only momentarily, as she began to count her blessings. She sighed heavily and then looked onward toward the crest of the hill. The sunken heart she once possessed was now filled with a sense of excitement. The past month had been one she could never forget.

Packed in the back of her car lay her clothes, but in the passenger seat rested two boxes and an envelope. The small, black, velvet-lined snap top held the diamond earrings she had received from her parents on Christmas Eve. Beside the jewelry, in the cardboard gift-wrapped carton, sat a gift for Emily.

Over Christmas break, Sarah had turned twenty-two on New Year's Eve, and even though Emily's birthday was another few weeks away, they decided to exchange gifts when they returned to school. Sarah laid her arm across the seat as she rounded a curve to secure them snug in place. As she guided her hand back to the steering wheel, a smile crept across her face.

In the years past, the eve of the New Year and her birthday were much the same. Family would visit at night for the fireworks, and the earlier day was spent with presents instead of poppers. This year, Emily had visited an extended two days, unlike the few hours they spent together on Christmas. The wheelchair was still her mainstay, but they had not allowed the restraint to hinder their fun. With the help of her dad, Carter, Emily could transition to the floor or another chair without issue. After a few card games and Jenga crashes assisted by Matty, the struggles of the past semester felt stale.

She could not recall when they fell asleep. Well after midnight, Sarah and Emily's mother, Cora, had assisted Emily in changing into flannel pajamas before lifting her onto Sarah's bed. With the two settled for the night, laughter still proceeded from her room until the last of the family had left. 3:00 a.m. was as close as she recalled, but that had been the last time she noticed the clock.

The following day was spent with a late breakfast after a delayed awakening. Sarah had not bothered to change out of her pajamas, partially as assurance that Emily need not to fret over the hassle, but also, she felt like relaxing into the afternoon. Emily heeded to Sarah's lead, staying nestled in her pajamas as her parents slid her into the car. Seeing her friend like this, Sarah knew Emily's senior track season was lost. Selfishly, she thought what that meant to her, but only momentarily before reality crept in.

Sarah's smile slowly faded as she thought on the situation that awaited at school, but transitioned to a grimace at the afterthought of what happened when Emily left.

Collapsing on the couch for an afternoon nap, Sarah's inner conscience was catapulted to life with a sudden, rapid knock on the door. The sleep that hung in her eyes only emulated excitement as the door opened to a familiar face.

"Happy belated birthday, Sarah!"

"Caroline!" Sarah threw her hands around the friend she had not seen since summer break. "What are you doing here?"

"You didn't think I would go without seeing you for another semester, did you?" Without waiting for Sarah's response, she continued, "I heard about you being in the hospital, although I was more worried since it came through the grapevine."

"Oh, I'm so sorry. I really, I mean, everything has been a blur since then, and I—"

"Sarah, don't worry about it. I know. Ever since college started, we haven't gotten to hang out."

Sarah took the long pause to interject a brighter conversation. "So, what brings you by today? I wasn't even sure if you came back for Christmas."

"I flew in on Christmas Eve, but I'll be leaving out tomorrow. Here, I brought you something."

Sarah took the time-weathered cardboard box in her hand, smiling at the sentiment. She already knew what it was. "I can't believe we have kept this going for so long, Caroline."

"Well, I've had it since June, so now it's yours, until I get home this summer."

Sarah laughed, then unhooked the worn edges, and pulled back the tissue paper. A small plastic mood ring shown a bleak black from within the wrapping.

"How old were we when we started passing it back and forth on our birthdays?"

"Early high school; so, whenever that was," Caroline laughed.

Sarah slid the ring onto her right hand with little effort. "Perfect! It still fits after all this time. Why don't you come in and have some cake?"

"I would love to. Can't stay long, but cake sounds great."

Shutting the door behind them, Sarah went to the kitchen for two plates and slices of cake. "Coffee?"

"No, thanks. I'll grab some milk though," said Caroline, helping herself to the cupboard. "Where are your parents and brother?"

"They took Matty to a friend's house for the afternoon. They should be home in just a bit if you want to see them."

"I really can't stay long," she said, settling in a chair across from Sarah. Biting into a small piece of cake, she chewed for a moment, as if mulling over her thoughts. With a hard swallow, she continued, "Sarah, there's something I need to tell you."

Sarah lowered her fork to the plate, quickly chewing the cake so she could address Caroline.

"What is it?" Sarah looked hard into her friend's concerned eyes, waiting for clarity.

"We have been friends for a long time, right? Well, I don't know how to tell you this, so here . . ." Caroline pulled an envelope from her pocket and shoved it across the table.

Sarah studied Caroline's face before proceeding to lift the lip of the sleeve and pulling out the cardstock inside. Her eyes read over the calligraphy-etched announcement:

Mr. and Mrs. Bascomb

Request the honor of your presence at the marriage of their daughter,

Haley Rena Bascomb

To

Wesley David Parker

On

Saturday, March 7th

At

Oak Valley Church

719 Main Street

7:00 p.m.

And at the Reception to follow.

Please R.S.V.P by January 17th

Sarah raised her eyes to Caroline's worried face.

"I'm sorry, Sarah. I know it has got to be tough when your first love gets married. And to top it off, Bryant is the best man, so I'll have to go." A perplexed brow rose on her forehead as Sarah began to smile. "Sarah, are you okay?"

"I ran into him on Christmas Eve. Him and Haley."

"Oh . . . how did that go?"

"Really well actually. They seemed like the perfect couple."

"More perfect than you two were?"

The question resonated with Sarah, bringing forth the distant memories, some of which she had suppressed after they broke up. "Uh, well, I hadn't thought of it like that, but they were happy. And honestly, I'm happy for them."

Caroline rolled her eyes. "Please. No one is ever happy for their ex. But more importantly, what are you going to do?"

"What am I going to do? Nothing . . . I've moved on, dated other guys. There's nothing I want to do."

"No, no, I mean are you going to the wedding?"

"I wasn't invited," laughed Sarah. "He was the same old Wesley when we spoke, even gave me a generous hug, but when he introduced Haley, neither said I should come to the wedding. I didn't realize it was so soon though."

Caroline took a large gulp of milk and then a bite of cake. Not waiting to finish eating, she softly said, "That's not what I got from Bryant."

"What do you mean, Caroline? What did he say?"

"He asked if I had talked to you, wanting to know if you would be staying at the same hotel. That way you and I could go to the venue together since he will be with the wedding party."

Sarah shook her head trying to recount her conversation with Wesley, considering she might have missed something. "No, he definitely didn't invite me. Mentioned it, yes. Besides, I didn't receive an invitation."

Caroline shrugged, failing to offer more insight, but additional questions. "Do you think he still has feelings for you? Do you have—"

"No, Caroline, and don't finish that sentence. That would be a no as well."

"Okay, don't shoot the messenger," she laughed.

"I'm not, pigeon," Sarah said, followed by a cuckoo.

Caroline flapped her arms as she rose from her chair and then proceeded to take her plate to the kitchen.

As Sarah took her last bite, she heard the sink turn off, then silence.

"Umm, Sarah . . . come in here please."

Sarah was still enjoying the taste of the mouthful of cake as she entered the kitchen. As she saw the envelope in Caroline's hand with *Sarah Mills* printed across the top, her mouth dropped, almost choking as she coughed while attempting to pull the cake back into her mouth.

"Now do you believe me?" Sarah's failure to grasp the idea only sunk in as Caroline handed her the card. Caroline raised her hand, wiping the fragments of cake from the side of Sarah's mouth. "So . . . What are you going to do?"

Pulling into the parking lot outside of their apartment, Sarah left her bags in the car, only grabbing the belongings in the front before rushing inside.

"Emm! I'm here." A sheet draped across the middle of the living room jerked back as Emily's head emerged from behind. "Ha, what's this?"

"Dad thought it would be best to set up my room downstairs. I don't have much strength, so going upstairs all the time was out of the question."

Sarah looked behind the makeshift wall, envisioning how she might help make the temporary placement more homely.

7

"You have a good start, but let me help and we can really make this look like your room, beginning with a rug to add some color." Sarah drew her attention back to Emily as she noticed a bag placed in her lap. "Oh, I almost forgot, here's your birthday present."

"And here's yours," said Emily lifting the purple gift bag.

"You first, Emm."

Without delay, Emily tore the paper from the box and pulled back the four edges. Inside lay another box that opened to a pair of shiny silver stud earrings. "Oh, Sarah, I love them."

"I bought them for you when I was still borrowing your diamonds, but then Mom and Dad gifted me a pair for Christmas. They should make great everyday earrings if you want."

"You're right. I can just keep these in." She slid the backings off each stud and threaded them through her ears. "How do they look?"

"They're perfect for you, Emm."

"Open yours, Sarah."

Sarah dug through the tissue paper, removing her hand upon clutching her fingers around a plastic baggy. Inside, a looped chain was linked together at a golden cross. "I didn't think you had one, and well, given everything, I thought you might like it."

"Thank you, Emily. It's beautiful." Sarah stretched the links out in front of her. "Do you mind?" Emily took hold of the ends as Sarah turned around and kneeled beside her. Lifting her hair off her neck, Sarah bunched the strands between her fingers. Carefully, Emily leaned forward, weaving the metal between Sarah's arms and around her neck, before clasping the ends together. Sarah positioned the cross, allowing it to lie on her chest.

"There you go, Sar." Sarah pivoted before returning to her feet. Looking down at the necklace, then at Emily, she realized, there was something she needed to ask of Emily.

"Say, Emm."

"Yeah, Sarah?"

"What are you doing the first weekend in March?"

Emily laughed but ceased as she noticed the plea that was gazing from Sarah's eyes. "Oh, sorry. Nothing that I know of. Do you need me for something?" she said, straightening in her chair.

"Well, kinda. That's if I go."

"Go? Where are you going?"

"I received a wedding invite."

"Whose wedding?"

Sarah paused, trying to determine how she might explain her thoughts. "That's the problem. It's my ex's . . . Wesley and his fiancé," the last word sticking to her tongue.

"Ah, I remember you talking about him a lot when we first became friends, but you haven't brought him up recently."

Sarah's mouth bunched with her cheeks at the thoughts of the past semester. "Yeah, I had moved on. I mean, I've moved on now, but I ran into him before Christmas. We just briefly spoke, but it was a friendly conversation. Anyways, a few days ago, I received an invitation in the mail, and I know, it's likely a last-minute invite."

"Do you still like him?"

Without hesitation, Sarah continued. "No. Honestly, it's not like that. When I saw him with Haley, I was glad to see he was happy.

I just don't know what to do. I feel like I should go to be polite, but I'm not going stag."

"So, you want me to go and keep you company?"

"I know Caroline, a friend I ran with in high school, will be there. She wants me to stay at the same hotel as her and Bryant's, but I really don't want to be the single girl who came to her ex's wedding. At least saying I have a plus one sounds better."

Emily laughed. "So, you want to be the single girl who brought a girlfriend to the ex's wedding?" She stopped giggling as she saw the concern on Sarah's face. "Just don't go. That's what I would do. Tell him you can't because of track."

Sarah thought over Emily's words. "I'll think about it. I rather not just decline or accept too soon."

"That sounds like a plan. Oh, and Sarah, I need to ask you for something too . . ."

"Sure, what's up?"

"I hate to be a bother, but I can't drive right now . . . Would you mind taking me to my physical therapy sessions?"

Sarah smiled as the curiosity cleared her mind. She looked down at Emily's stationary position, legs bent to fold up onto the footrest of the chair. "Emm, I'd take you to the moon and back if I had to."

Emily's laughter cut the seriousness of the remark. "Oh, and one more thing."

"What's that?"

"Be sure to bring your bathing suit with you."

"Ha, my bathing suit?"

"Yeah, they want to do exercises in the pool. You know . . ."

"Okay, but on one condition. We have to go shopping for new ones. I'm pretty sure mine doesn't fit."

"Deal."

"I'm going upstairs to unpack. Do you need anything?"

"Nope, I'm fine. I might take a nap while you work."

Sarah left briefly to grab her bags from the car before heading upstairs. Inching up the last few steps, she paused for a second.

The door opened to an eerie feel. The last time she had stepped foot in her room was before spending the night with Emily at the hospital. Given the burden of worry and fear had since lifted, Sarah could now resettle into a familiar place.

The clothes Sarah brought from home were mainly the laundry she hurriedly fetched the prior semester. Setting the folded jeans and shirts out across the bed, Sarah flattened out any creases before putting them away, then stored the hamper to the far side of her bed. A remaining box that housed her earrings was the final item to find a home for. She hated to put them out of sight, but on a last thought, she found a fitting place next to her Bible.

An hour or so nap wouldn't be a bad idea at all, she thought. However, as she reached to untuck the covers, she paused. An instant of hesitation was followed by the same urge which drew her from bed during break. She was done sleeping her life away, even if it was not for pity.

Throwing the bedroom door open, she bounced down the stairs to Emily's sectioned area. Still sitting in her chair, Emily looked up from examining her nails. "Oh good, you're still up. Do you want to go shopping now instead?"

"I was hoping you'd be down soon. I'm tired of sitting in this chair."

"So, how is this going to work? Can you get in and out by yourself?"

"I probably could, but Dad helps me move to and from the car, while Mom assists with showers and stuff."

"Oh, yeah. Your shower is upstairs." Emily's sheepish grin waited for Sarah to continue. "Well, I guess one trip up the stairs a day won't kill us. We'll just have to utilize your legs a little more."

"And, Sarah."

"Yeah?"

"I forgot to mention something earlier." Her eyes filled with worry as she formed the next few words. "Paul. Do you mind if he rides with us to therapy? I know that might be weird—"

"Emily, it's okay. I rather see you two together than not see either of you at all."

CHAPTER 2:

Returning

The small parking lot's capacity bulged at the seams as Sarah and Emily pulled alongside the curb. Some students packed the nearby grocery store, loading buggies full of supplies for the coming months, while others looked to stock up for a final party before school.

"Park in the handicap," Emily instructed, pointing toward the blue painted emblems. "Here," she continued, pulling a card from her purse to hook along the rearview mirror. "It took me a while to get used to the idea, since I technically can still walk, but after seeing all of Mom and Dad's work, I decided not to fight it."

Sarah realized Emily's life had changed, but now she would be taking on the responsibilities of her parents. "Hold tight while I get the wheelchair." Sarah stepped out of the car, pulling her shirt down over her jeans as she shut the door. Leaning over the trunk, she examined the compressed seat and rather large wheels. Getting the bulk into the trunk had proven challenging enough, but she lacked the power to freely lift it up. Carefully, she pulled at the rims, inching them over the rubber seal of the trunk. The careful maneuver worked until realizing the bumper would scratch if she continued.

"Need any help?" Emily called from the front.

"No, I'm fine. Just stay where you are."

Sarah stood with her hands resting in the small of her back as she examined the base pivoting on the edge. On an initial attempt, she leaned her back over the bumper and pulled on the frame. With more strain on her back than lift, Sarah quickly dropped her grip on the chair. Hearing Emily shuffling around and afraid she would attempt to crawl outside, Sarah bent down to the ground. Her knees landed hard on the asphalt, but without delay, she lifted the wheels over the bumper, before resting them on her lap. Balancing the frame, she stretched to reach the handles and, with a strain, pulled the backrest up and outside. Once all the weight rested on her thighs, she rolled the wheelchair off to the side.

"Alright, Emm, I'm coming." Sarah pulled the collapsed seat apart before rolling to the side of the car. "Here, I'll help you."

"Let me try first. I've got to learn to use them at some point," she laughed.

"If you insist, but I'll brace my arms underneath you, just in case." With Sarah positioned, Emily rocked forward onto her quivering legs. The shift in weight instantly bore on Sarah's arms. "I've gotcha, Emm, just try to stay on your feet." Slowly, Emily rose enough to rotate from the passenger seat and inched a few steps to the wheelchair before collapsing.

"Well, that was fun," Emily joked. "I guess Mom and Dad have been lifting more than I thought. Maybe you should try on bathing suits alone and I'll wait on you to model them for me."

"I'm not letting you off that easy. We can still do anything we've done before, just a little differently for the time being."

"You're right. We'll just take it one step at a time."

Sarah flipped down the footrest before swiveling Emily around to head inside the store. As the entrance doors automatically slid open, Sarah soon noticed odd stares directed at them. Judging from Emily's reaction, she was clueless to the perturbed glances. Sarah shot a few narrow-eyed stares back, which drove the lingering eyes away.

"I believe they have a rec section in the rear."

"Oh yeah," said Sarah. Directing her attention again on Emily, she pushed her along the aisle toward the far end of the store.

Tucked behind the basketball and gym equipment, there remained a few small racks from the summer sales dedicated to swim attire.

"What size are you thinking, Sarah?"

"All my stuff is a small, so I'll have to try for a medium I suppose. You're still a small, right?"

"Maybe for bottoms, but the top is going to be an extra small now."

Sarah thumbed through the hangers, eyeing the mishmash of tags. Threads of larges were only broken up by the occasional small, the same sizes that always seemed in stock after season. Halfway down, a purple top coupled with bottoms stood out as mediums. "Here we go, Emm. Hold these."

Across from her own selection hung the uncoupled pieces. "I don't think we'll be able to find you anything that matches, Emily."

"That's alright. Just as long as they don't fall off."

"Here are some small black bottoms. And how do you feel about a pink top? It's the only extra small I see."

"That's fine. Toss them to me."

"Do you know where the changing rooms are?"

"There's just the one over in the corner. They do have two stalls."

"I guess we can share the big one," suggested Sarah.

Pushing Emily through the swinging door, Sarah turned to secure the latch. She butted the handles against the wall, facing Emily toward the mirror. "I'll try mine on first, then I can help you." Sliding her shirt over her head, Sarah handed it to Emily before unbuttoning her pants. She shimmied the denim down her legs, kicking her feet out of the holes. Sarah took the bathing suit from Emily as she unhooked her bra and replaced it with the purple one. As she pulled the bottoms up over her undies, she turned to face the mirror. "How does this look?"

"I wish I had your chest. You're going to be getting eyed at the pool for sure," Emily laughed.

"Very funny. I think they fit great. Not loose, but probably nowhere near as tight as your extra small."

"You're about to see what I mean." Emily pulled her shirt over her head, sliding the bra off as well. "See, I didn't even have to unhook the clasp." Sarah understood what Emily meant, given the reduction in cleavage. "I'm probably down a cup size, but I haven't bothered to buy any new underwear. The weight will come back, so why bother?"

"They don't look bad. Mine actually hurt my back a bit, so I guess we either have one problem or the other." Even though it was a fib, and Emily likely knew better, the two still enjoyed a laugh that echoed over the walls.

"Now for the other half. Lift up your hips and I'll slide your pants off." Emily braced her hands on the arms and hoisted her pelvis a few inches out of the chair. Sarah quickly tugged the waist down, allowing Emily to relax. However, the two quickly realized the awkwardness of the situation. "Umm, where's your underwear, Emm?"

"Ha. I forgot I wasn't wearing them. I figured I'd have to go to the bathroom on my own, and well, you know, one less thing to worry about." Sarah shook her head as she helped her to put on the bottoms.

"Emily, only you would think of that." Sarah laughed as she unrolled the seam around Emily's stomach.

Leaning back, Sarah's eyes took notice of red splotches that peaked out from underneath Emily's legs. "What are those?" she questioned, pushing Emily's knees aside.

"These? They're what the doctor called bed rashes. Apparently, they form from lying down for extended periods, but they eventually go away. I'm more worried about my leg hair. I haven't bothered shaving my legs but a few times since getting out of the hospital." Sarah released her grip, still looking over the marks. "So how does this look?"

"Huh? Yeah, they look good to me. Do they feel like the right fit?"

"They'll work for now." She reached for her pants draped over the handrail. "I'll spare you the view this time."

"A warning would have made a big difference," she laughed.

Sarah turned to undress herself as Emily worked her way out of the swimwear and back into the jeans. She could hear the struggle from behind, but Emily was insistent on dressing herself. Only after a few minutes of wrestling around did she hear a sigh.

"How do you feel about getting dinner after that work out?"

"Sounds great, but let me buy yours."

"Emm, no it's—"

"No ifs, ands, or buts. It's the very least I can do."

"But, Emm, I didn't say any of those."

"Well, you did now, so there," she laughed.

Sarah gathered their belongings and placed them in Emily's lap before heading toward the checkout. Only once they returned outside did the chilly wind detour their thoughts of swimming as a shiver traversed down their spines. Sarah strode to the car, offering Emily help into the passenger side. Zipping her coat against a tugging wind, she raced the chair to the back while folding the pieces together. With a quick, agile lift, she hoisted the weight up and over the bumper, allowing it to fall freely into the trunk. *A few more like that and I'll have the hang of it,* Sarah thought.

Her moment of triumph faded minutes later as she lugged the chair once again from the car. This time her knees met the cold and now-damp pavement as a light drizzle moved in. Lifting herself up, Sarah opened an umbrella before returning to the passenger side. Emily held the rod, attempting to keep the rain off of them, but the vein effort left both girls soaked upon entering the Mexican restaurant.

Through the dimly lit room, the attendant motioned for them to pick a seat and he would serve them after finishing a phone call.

Sarah removed one of the chairs at a stand-alone table, placing it in a corner to make room for Emily.

"The last time we were here, we ended up stumbling home," Emily recalled.

"Yeah . . . I never told you, but afterwards, I got sick in my bathroom. It was a mess."

"Oh, Sar. I didn't realize that."

"It's fine. I just rather not repeat it today."

"Well, you can't anyways. I mean you still have some time before track practice starts, but you drove."

"Are you drinking, Emm?"

"No, the last thing I need right now is to fall," she laughed. "Can you imagine me explaining that to my parents?"

Sarah's laugh was cut short as a slight twinge rolled in her abdomen. "I'll be right back. I need to run to the restroom." She looked over to the man who was still on the phone. "You know my order if he comes before I get back."

She left the table briefly before turning to retrieve her purse. Upon entering the stall, she hung the purse strap over the door hook before covering the seat with paper. As she turned and slid her pants down, she noticed a small splotch of blood. Running her finger between her legs confirmed the start of her period. *Not as regular as before, but it's about that time.* She settled back on the seat to relieve herself before leaning forward to pull a tampon from her bag. *This will be good news for Coach, seeing I should be able to join practice on time.* She shook her head, wondering what he might say when she informed him. *Umm, oh, yeah. Good work.*

Hearing the bathroom door open, allowing the lobby noise to flow inside, Sarah broke her trance. She discarded the applicator and wrapper before buttoning her pants and pulling her shirt tail down. Emerging from the stall, she was greeted by a smiling face. "Abby! It's so good to see you. How have you been?"

"I'm good, but what about you? I saw Emily outside and she said you were in here. I couldn't wait, so I had to come find you."

"Things are definitely getting better. I'm ready for school and track to start."

"So, you'll be able to run this season?" Abby inquired excitedly.

"Yeah, I believe so."

The conversation was interrupted by a bump on the door. "You gals in there?" Sarah jumped back from the sink to pull the door open.

"Sorry, Emily. We didn't forget about you."

"I just thought I would come join the fun. The waiter is still on the phone."

"Well, come on in."

Emily rolled herself through the door and up to the counter. She straightened her back as to get a fuller view of herself in the mirror. "I think I'm going to order two plates."

Abby looked to Sarah for an explanation.

"She thinks she has lost too much weight."

"Emm, look at me," said Abby. "I'm like a toothpick compared to you and Sarah," she laughed.

"It's my chest. It's shrunken down so small."

Abby sighed before she continued, "I'll tell you something, but it has to stay between us." Sarah and Emily's attention fell onto Abby as she now looked embarrassed.

"Of course. Did something happen?"

"Not really. A while back, Ralph and I were, you know, kissing."

"You mean making out," Emily interrupted.

"Yeah, well, that. Anyways, he was running his hand up my shirt and I stopped him. I didn't want to address my insecurity about my chest, but I guess I made it awkward. He started asking questions, so finally I told him what was bothering me."

"What did he say?" the two echoed.

"He said they were fine for him, but if we got married one day, he would pay for fake ones if it made me feel better." Abby lifted her eyes, and as giggles erupted, she soon began to smile.

"Did you take him up on the offer?"

"All I knew to do was kiss him again. That's what I love about Ralph. Whether he was serious or not, he knows how to make me smile."

Emily settled back in her chair. "That makes me feel better, Abby. However, I think I can still stomach two plates. Do you want to join us?"

The bathroom door opened again as an elderly woman entered. A distant voice from the lobby carried inside. "Auburn hair, about this tall . . ."

"Speaking of the plastic surgeon, I believe he's outside," said Emily.

Abby blushed. "Yeah, he's meeting me for dinner, but if it's okay, we can all get a table together."

Sarah caught the door as it was closing, allowing the other girls to go ahead. "I'll be right out. I forgot my purse." She turned and retrieved the bag before joining the others at the table.

Placing the purse strap around the seat, Sarah settled at the table across from Ralph.

"Hey."

"Hey, Sarah. On your period I see?" Sarah along with the others stared wide eyed as he continued, "What about you, Emm? Abby started hers yesterday, so maybe you all have synced up." Abby jabbed his ribs with her elbow to provoke his silence.

"If I could reach across the table, I'd probably slug you, Ralph," rattled Emily.

"What? I'm just saying. Isn't that something you women talk about? I'm not that dumb. Why else would girls think they need to take their purse to the bathroom?"

Sarah relaxed as the uncomfortable conversation drifted back to Ralph's usual logical processes. "Well, it's good to see some things never change, Ralph."

"I figured if I'm going to be the only guy, I might as well join in on the girl's conversation."

"Or we could talk about normal things," suggested Abby as she gave him a glaring eye.

"Fine. I'm not in tune with woman talk anyways. What shall we discuss then? School? Track?" Before any of the others could offer a suggestion, he continued, "Oh, I ran into Coach in town yesterday. He sounded pretty excited about this season."

"Did you already tell him you were coming back, Sarah?" asked Abby. Emily shot a confused glance in Sarah's direction.

"No. Not yet. I'm not a hundred percent sure I can. But as Ralph already mentioned, I've got my period again, so that means there's a good chance."

"That's just great and all, ladies, but I thought you wanted to change the subject?"

"Sorry, Ralph, go ahead with your story," said Abby.

"It's okay, love bug," he said, kissing her on the cheek.

"Get a room or continue with the story," pleaded Emily.

"Like I was saying. I ran into Coach yesterday. We started discussing track and he sounded hopeful for this season. I asked him if that meant Paul would miraculously return, but he said no, that part was doubtful. He did mention there'd be someone to step up and take the spot as team captain."

"Was he talking about you?" asked Sarah.

"Nope, someone else."

"Then who?"

"Nigel."

CHAPTER 3:

If Only

The rain beating upon Sarah's window broke the silence of the room. Interrupting her dream, the noise withdrew her from a tantalizing sleep. She had not slept so soundly in months. As the pattering drops grew louder, Sarah rolled over on her side and opened her eyes. Feeling the monthly cramps, she knew it would be another one of those days. A shower and change would be the first things before getting ready for class.

Sliding her legs over the flannel sheets, Sarah felt her way to the edge of the bed and placed her feet on the soft rug below. The brown strands of hair fell toward the top of her shoulders, almost grown out enough to cover her neck and meet the seam of her t-shirt. Sarah shut the door to the bathroom behind her and slowly shed the flannel boxers. Clasping at the hem, Sarah pulled the oversized shirt over her head, unveiling her plump breasts. Turning the shower handle, she tested the water before stepping inside and drawing the curtain behind her.

After refreshing herself, Sarah slipped into some dark red undies and a pair of fitted jeans. Finally, she strapped on a bra with a cami and long-sleeved blouse. She peered again into the mirror. Luckily, she felt cute. The rest of the week was going to be a painful few days.

Before creeping out the door, Sarah poured a cup of coffee and popped two aspirin. The first day of the semester was here, and hopefully a new start. Putting on her jacket, Sarah opened the door and quietly stepped out into the rain.

The clouds had covered the city for the past two days. Puddles formed along the walkways, with no clear sky in sight. Relieved that Emily's classes were not until later, Sarah enjoyed her drive in solitude, as they could forgo the first day without splashing Emily's chair in the rain.

With each passing of the windshield wipers brushing the water droplets from her view, she began to plan her return to the track. Coming back from an injury for an athlete was one thing, but Sarah knew her situation differed from most. Despite the setback, she would have one advantage over all the other girls. The winter months proved mainly dormant, aside from the few revitalizing runs that had taken place, so her legs felt fresh and itching for a new start.

After parking in an empty space beside the gym, Sarah headed down the flight of stairs and along the corridor of the athletic department. A single room radiated light from its open door. There was only one person who would be at work this early in January.

Sarah peeked in from behind the frame before finally stepping inside to offer a greeting that broke the silence.

"Good morning," she said. Coach Cavlere raised his eyes from his desk and a bright smile covered his face. He laid his pencil down along the sheet he had been working over and propped back in his chair.

"Sarah. It's so good to see you. How are things going?"

"Hey, Coach. Pretty good, I think. That's actually why I'm here."

"Come in and take a seat," he said, getting up to clear off a nearby chair stacked with boxes.

"Thanks."

"So, have you talked to the doctor?"

"Not yet. I have an appointment soon, but I wanted to see you first."

"What can I do for you?"

Sarah considered her words without making him uncomfortable. "I think the anemia is better. I've ran a few times and felt amazing. Also, my cycle is back."

"That's great. I knew I could count on your return for track. Of course, your doctor will have to clear you, but if everything feels good, then we are probably fine." He paused for a long sip on his coffee before continuing, "How is Emily adjusting?"

"So far so good. She has a makeshift room downstairs. I still help her around though. She'll be seeing a therapist, but as for now, her legs are pretty weak."

"Unfortunately, she and Paul will be out this season. However, I did receive some good news last week. Nigel will be joining us after all."

Sarah tried to hide her unrest at the words with a sense of curiosity. "Oh really? I thought he was going to be doing an internship."

"As did I. Apparently, that got pushed back a semester. Something to do with the number of students they needed shifted. Either way, that means track won't be a total forfeit."

"Did he say anything else?"

Cavlere paused, looking over to Sarah. She knew immediately the question uncovered the front she tried to portray.

"What do you mean?" he said with a sense of concern.

"Oh, just if he's disappointed about the job."

"I think he's still excited for track, besides I offered him a position as team captain."

Sarah's quickness passed off the concern she felt from her coach, but inside, questions still tugged at her. *Now that Emily and Paul are dating, would she and Nigel get together? Is dating even a good idea considering their history?* There were too many thoughts to consider. Seeing him at practice might trigger feelings between them, but for now, waiting seemed best.

"Right, Sarah?"

"Huh?"

"Abby. I think I'll pair you two together for training. You might not be up to speed, but I think she'll pull you along as you return to a normal schedule."

"Oh, Abby, of course," she agreed shaking her head. "Well, I appreciate the talk, but I better get going so I can grab breakfast before class," she said, getting up from the seat.

"One last thing before you go, Sarah. Happy belated birthday."

"Thanks, Coach," she said before turning to the door and heading into the hall.

The dining hall felt empty among the crowd. Emily was no doubt still asleep and would likely only join her for dinner that night. Moving her tray down the line, Sarah peered over the seats in hopes to find someone to sit with. Carrying her tray from the drink dispenser, she settled on a small table that was unoccupied.

Sarah ate each bite in solace. The weight gain had refueled her appetite and a likely cause of her quick recovery. Each hearty bite felt like binge-eating, but she could care less. Ingesting a mouthful of eggs, she glanced up at the door that led outside. A small group of guys, accompanied by Nigel, formed around the check-in. The lower part of Sarah's body tugged toward Nigel, while her upper logical half urged her to continue eating her eggs. She watched him from her peripherals, but never did he look in her direction. Eventually, the group gathered in a large booth with Nigel on the inside and out of her sight. Only when he was out of view did her mind regain control. *I hope that's just my menstruation reacting*, she thought with a sigh.

As she watched the surrounding guys laughing, a daring thought crossed her mind. Knowing she would have to see him at practice was one thing, but she rather not wait until then to determine their current situation.

Sarah gathered her tray and cup before heading to the wash drop-off. Turning in the direction of their table, she began walking toward them. Not until she approached the booth and almost walked past did Nigel notice her. Catching each other's eyes, she half smiled.

"Hey, Nigel," she said passively.

"Sarah. Hey, Sarah! Come back for a second." She stopped and returned to the tableside.

"Yeah, Nigel?"

"I was hoping to see you . . . I wanted to mention my internship was pushed back." He paused, expecting a response, but continued upon her silence. "The good news is I'll be running track this semester."

"Oh, good. I know Coach must be happy. See you at practice then?"

"Oh, what about you? Are you able to run?"

"Yeah. I'll start the season on time."

"Sweet."

"Well, I've got to run, but I'll see you later," she said, leaving without waiting for a reply. Sarah's insides still burned as she walked away. A lingering afterthought posed itself, making her wonder if any of the guys were watching her as she left. Only when she heard one of the friends comment on her figure did she smile with a sense of victory. *He may not want me, but he couldn't help but notice.*

Meeting the cold brush of damp air as she opened the door, a chill filled her body and calmed the fire that lay within. *When my body returned to regular, it sure didn't mind bringing a swing of hormones with it. I hope once I get back to running, that'll subside.*

Sarah unfolded her raincoat and slid her arms through each sleeve before departing from the awning in the direction of Boyd. With twelve hours scheduled for the semester to meet the final graduation requirements, the break had fallen at the right time. One upper-level math class remained, Real Analysis, but the ease of the other courses would buffer any additional load.

As she carried her thoughts through the building, she shed the now dripping coat. With only a handful of students occupying the classroom, like the others, she chose an empty seat to adorn with her rain-battered jacket and bags.

The professor wasted no time filing into the room, accompanied by the last of the students. With a dull piece of chalk, she carved three words onto the blackboard. Turning to address the class, Dr. Adeline pulled her notes from the clipboard she carried. "Today we will start the study of rings and fields and the process of finding a ring within a field."

Sarah's concentration faded from the gray and streaked windowpane. The only ring and field that she was concerned with lay outside on the track, but for now, she cleared her mind of running and Nigel.

The porch light glimmered in the frosty air as Sarah fumbled for the keys. "Hurry, Sar. It's freezing out here."

"There. I got it. I thought it was frozen shut for a second." Emily sped in to the warmth of their apartment, rubbing her arms feverishly before rolling into the living area. "Want to sit on the couch, Emm?"

"Yeah, let me see if I can get up. Just brace me so I don't fall." Sarah guided her arms under Emily's as they made their way to the sofa. Emily plopped down on the cushion as Sarah released her grip. Grabbing a nearby blanket, Sarah unfolded the cover and draped it across Emily before snuggling beside her. "Burr," Emily shivered. "Did I tell you I've gained three pounds already?"

"No, but that's great. I think you're really starting to make the turn on recovering."

"I hope so. I have my sessions scheduled twice a week in the mornings. That should give us time between classes and lunch."

"Yeah, that sounds like the best idea."

"So, you're sure you're okay with me and Paul dating?"

"Emm, it's quite alright. Speaking of, have you seen him recently?"

"Ralph dropped him off earlier today. He's getting a car once the insurance company sends a check. Apparently, the last person in the pileup is responsible for the entire wreck."

"That's good, at least from a bill's standpoint."

Emily let out a breath. "I was pretty worried until they told us. I wasn't sure how my family could afford all the medical bills that were piling up. It wasn't like I would ask Paul to pay for them."

"How's he doing now? Is he back on his feet?"

"He's way ahead of me. He walked slowly while Ralph helped him inside, but considering, I think he's progressing well. But, Sarah, the reason I ask, we were talking about doing something for my birthday, and well, going out may not be the best option. We thought it would be better if he came here instead."

"That's fine with me, I can stay busy upstairs."

"You can hang out with us if you want. I would invite some of the team, but I rather it be low key."

"Whatever you want, Emm, I'm there for you."

"Oh, I was thinking today. Have you thought anymore about the wedding?"

Honestly, she had not until then, but she knew what she wanted to do. "Yeah. If you'll give me the privilege, I'll go with you as my date."

"I'd be honored," Emily laughed. "However, I was going to ask, why don't you invite Nigel? Ralph said he is still here." A grimace drew over Sarah's face. "Oh, bad idea?" Emily recanted.

"No. Not really. I actually spoke to him today."

"Wait, you did? And why am I just now hearing about this?"

"I've actually tried to put it out of my mind."

"Why? He'd be perfect."

"I'm afraid . . ."

"Afraid?"

"Yeah. With our history, I think things might get carried away again, and I don't want that. Today when I saw Nigel, I felt a similar pull toward him, but more intense than the night we fooled around."

"Are you afraid he will hurt you again?"

"That's a big part of it. But also, I don't want to have sex with him just because we almost did or that it would be easy."

"No, I get it. Unless he puts a ring on your finger, I would say refrain from letting him get lucky. Guys can leave a relationship too easy to justify him scoring."

"What about the wedding?"

"We'll go to the wedding together. When you see Nigel, just keep it on the friend's level. If he asks you on a date, and you think you can contain him, then go. But if not then I would just give him a pass. Otherwise, I would forget about it. You have track to focus on, and honestly that should take top priority."

Sarah shook her head understandably, then a smile struck her face. "It's too cold for ice cream, but how would you feel about some fresh brownies?"

"Did I say three pounds this week? Let's make that five," she laughed.

"Hold tight, I'll get the oven going and mix the batter."

Emily pulled closer the extra cover that lay across the couch in Sarah's absence. Pans and spoons clanked in the kitchen as Sarah rushed to throw the mix together. Before her spot grew cold on the cushion, Sarah returned with a plop beside Emily.

"Sarah, you're supposed to put the batter in the oven."

"I know, but I saved some raw batter for us."

Emily took the wooden spoon and licked the drip of chocolate along the handle. "Here, the front side is yours."

"Geez, thanks, Emm," said Sarah as she stuck the whole spoon in her mouth.

Emily pulled the spoon away from Sarah, dipping it into the bowl before copying her. "We might as well share the same germs. If one of us gets sick, I rather it be the both of us," Emily replied.

"I like that."

"When are you going back to the doctor anyways?"

"I stopped by on my way home, hoping I could get a release form signed. The doctor said he still wanted to check everything, but he could squeeze me into an earlier appointment. It's before therapy, so I'll pick up Paul since he's on the way, then come back here for you."

Emily cleared her throat from the last of the batter as a ding echoed from the kitchen. "I'm ready for round two."

Sarah jumped up to fetch the brownies. "I hope you like them crispy on the edges," Sarah called.

"That'll be a good contrast to the gooey mess we just devoured."

When the last of the pan was empty, Emily lifted the covers, signaling it was time for bed. She raised her shirt over her belly, proceeding to poke out a small pudge that was forming. Rubbing her belly with one hand, she let out a yawn. "I think I ate enough for two tonight. At least my stomach is shaping out some. Help me to my feet if you don't mind."

Sarah grabbed her hands and mimed an overplayed effort to lift Emily from the couch. "I'll say you gained ten pounds today alone."

Bidding Emily goodnight, Sarah headed upstairs to her own bed. After brushing her teeth, she pulled on her pajamas laid out from earlier. With the last moments of the day, she said her prayers and snuggled into her bed.

The night remained quiet throughout the apartment and into the calmness outside. However, as dreams crept into her conscience, views of a man interceded her thoughts. From afar he walked closer, approaching a young woman. Sarah could see neither of them well, both appeared more as blurry outlines. As the man reached forward, he took the woman in his arms. Then, as he pulled away, a third image appeared as he coddled a baby.

CHAPTER 4:

Another Choice

A dark gloom, only interrupted by a streetlamp, still covered the sky when Sarah's eyes shot open. For the first time since the summer, she woke not to the sound of an alarm, but the beckoning to get moving. Leaving the coziness of her sheets and rushing into the morning air remained far from ideal, but the desire to run proved greater.

Lacing her shoes by the door, Sarah paused and listened to the softness of Emily's breathing from across the living room. Assured she was still asleep; Sarah creaked the door open and stepped into the frigid air. Pulling the door silently into place, she fell into a run without hesitation. Puffs of condensation blew from her mouth with each breath. Passing breezes stung her exposed face, while the bitter cold numbed her body.

No planned route hindered her thoughts, but her stride quickened as she neared the campus. Dorm rooms set void of life as darkness filled the windows. Warmth now filled her chest and legs, but a familiar ache tingled through her socks and gloves and into her extremities. Sarah cupped her hands around her mouth, but deep breaths only brought dampness to pass through the gloves' thin layers. Peeling them from her hands with her teeth, she tucked them into her waist band. With all sensation now gone, Sarah rubbed her frozen hands along her stomach before settling them under her arms. Not moving her arms in rhythm with her legs likely looked as awkward as it felt, but within a few minutes, they thawed enough for her to retrieve the gloves.

Sarah continued threading through campus until rays of sunlight began peeking over the mountains. With the return of the sun, she turned for home. The faint glimmers brought renewed warmth, but the sunrise remained below the crest of the mountains until she arrived at the door.

Sneaking inside, and up to her room, Sarah combed her fingers through her hair. Small crystals formed at the tips where sweat had gathered. Sarah tossed her clothes to the ground and jumped into the awaiting shower. The burst of hot water stung her nose and toes until the shivers relaxed away.

Basking in the now-fogged bathroom, Sarah began to think about the dream from the night before. Fewer and fewer details of the images remained. *Who was the guy and girl?* Only three blank outlines withstood her memory. *I hate those dreams. Why can't I remember the ones I want and forget the dreadful others?*

Giving up on recollecting any further specifics, Sarah released the shower stopper and gathered her towel. Dried and warm, she realized another hour remained before she was to arrive at the doctor's office. Going back to bed was appealing, and even if it were for a few minutes, she snuggled back among the still tepid sheets.

Sitting in various waiting rooms now felt customary. Between visiting Emily and her own appointments, the lobbies and examination rooms now served as a time to relax. Pulling a filer from her purse, Sarah rounded the edges of her nails until a knock proceeded from the door. A new physician peered through the opening before allowing himself to fully enter the room.

"Sarah Mills?"

"Hi, doctor . . ."

"Doctor Clay. I'm covering for your primary physician today. His wife had a baby last night, so he will be out a few days."

Sarah leaned back into her chair. *A baby, of course.*

"His notes state that you were coming in for a release. Your ferritin levels from our last test look normal. Are you feeling better? Is your period regular now?"

"I am. I just went for a run this morning and felt great. As for my period, it was a little behind, but everything feels normal."

The doctor shook his head as he scribbled on the paper. "Given your blood levels, I don't see us holding you up any longer. I do advise if next month you have any irregularity that you let us know. The main thing he was worried about was your diet, but again, your weight is up, and your BMI is back to a normal range." He removed a notepad from his jacket pocket and scribbled directions and his name at the bottom. "Here you go. You can start practicing with your team. Just set up a final checkup, four to six weeks out." Sarah smiled as she leaned forward for the paper. "Do you have any questions for me or concerns?"

"I do have one question. Is it normal to experience a rush of hormones when you get your period back?"

"I would say, likely. Your body is adjusting and trying to settle to normal. Anytime there is trauma, the body must rebalance, and that happens in the hormone department too, like puberty. That will fade in time, or at least will return to what you would typically experience."

"Thanks, Doctor Clay."

"You're most certainly welcome. Come with me and I'll walk you to the nurse's station." Offering her hand, Sarah slid down from the examination table and followed beside him to the end of the hallway. Doctor Clay passed the chart through the window before saying goodbye and heading down another corridor.

"I have you down for a follow-up in six weeks. Is the same time and day alright with you, miss?"

"Yes, that'll work fine."

Sarah walked through the double doors to her car. Switching on the engine, she gathered her thoughts before shifting to drive. It had been a while since she last talked to Paul, and picking him up before Emily on the way to physical therapy would give her the chance.

As Sarah pulled into the drive, Paul awaited her at the door, walking outside as the car met the driveway. Sarah unbuckled and leapt from the driver's seat to the passenger door before he covered the distance from the house. He carried a cane, which looked odd for someone his age, but Sarah felt no intentions to tease him.

Only after they both buckled did she attempt a conversation. Paul started by thanking her, but she soon cut to the meat of her words. "Paul, I wanted you to know that I've already talked to Emily."

"About?"

"You know what I mean. I'm fine with you two dating. As a matter of fact, it's a good thing. You both are going through this together and, well, it probably makes it easier to bear."

Paul smiled. "Thanks for understanding, Sarah." A long pause persisted until Sarah backed the car into the street and switched to drive before he continued. "While we're on the subject, did you ever talk to Nigel?" Sarah could see him watching her face for a sign of discomfort, as her stomach felt a slight twinge from the question. However, coming from Paul, the accompanying thoughts shown through less bothersome.

"Yes . . . we talked. I don't want to go into detail, but I'm glad we did. Also, as you probably know, he was leaving, but apparently his plans changed. So now I'm not sure where that leaves us. However," she continued before he could interject, "I talked to Emily, and I think it's best to concentrate on track instead. We'll see each other at practice, but I don't want any other reasons to make things unsettled between us."

"I would agree, but whatever you do with whomever, be careful." The words soured in Sarah's stomach. She turned and looked him dead in the eye, but before she could defend herself, his smile left assurance that he meant no malice or judgment.

"I will, Paul . . . .. Last semester really changed me, but I'm trying to not make those mistakes again."

Paul sat gazing out the window until they arrived at Sarah and Emily's apartment. Upon stopping, Paul started to move from the front seat to the back; however, seeing Emily roll toward them, he paused. "Let me help with the wheelchair."

"I can handle it. I actually have a system down packed already," Sarah said proudly. With Emily settled inside, Sarah lugged the chair into the trunk, dusting her knees as she returned to the steering wheel.

"I brought the bag with your suit," said Emily.

"Oh, I had forgotten about that. Paul, did you bring any trunks?"

He tugged at his sweatpants. "I have them on underneath."

"Emm? Do you have yours on already?"

"Yes, this time I'm good," she laughed.

Bouncing against the locker room door, the two girls met a dense heat that overlaid the pool. Goosebumps that etched their legs were replaced with moisture that clung to their skin. Sarah wiped her brow in adjusting to the temperature change.

Across the pool, along the wall sat Paul, with his legs dangling inside the water. Before joining him, Sarah dipped her foot, gauging its tepidness. Much like the surrounding air, the water felt like a bath that had been setting for a short while. "I was a little worried. Swimming in January doesn't sound like the most appealing thing to do."

"What did you expect, an outside pool?" Paul laughed.

"No, of course not," replied Sarah. "But I don't even care for getting out of a hot shower in the wintertime." Paul cupped his hand and slid his arm down beside his leg, as Sarah continued. When she turned to address Emily, he flung his hand, throwing a spray over the two.

"Paul!" they screamed, but before Sarah could retaliate, he pushed himself off the wall and into the pool. Sarah slid in beside him, attempting to spray his already wet body. The splashing continued as Emily's voice called out over the noise; however, Sarah stopped as another voice struck her ears.

"Fancy seeing you again."

Sarah rubbed the water from her eyes, trying to make out the figure standing alongside Emily, but she already knew the voice. "Michael? What are you doing here?"

"I could ask you the same thing, but it looks like you're taking a swim. Remember, I'm a physical therapist. Although, I suppose I haven't seen you since I received an offer with the hospital's rehab center."

Sarah swam to the side, propping her hands on the wall before pulling herself to her knees, then to her feet. Grabbing a towel from Emily, she blotched her face before wrapping the cover around her body. "So, you're assigned to Emily and Paul?"

"Correct. They're actually the first patients I'll have to myself." By this point, Paul was attempting to climb out of the pool alone. Seeing him struggle, Sarah bent down, offering him a hand. "We do have the handicap chair lift on the side, if that helps," continued Michael.

"I've got it," insisted Paul.

"Now that both of you are out, let's move to the shallow therapy pool."

Michael unhooked the brakes on Emily's wheels, then led the group to the other side of the room. As Paul and Sarah watched, Michael hoisted Emily from her seat and placed her in the mechanical lift. Only once everyone had transitioned did Michael tug his white t-shirt from his shoulders and toss it to the nearby bench. Emily turned to Sarah as they huddled in the pool together.

"Michael? Is that—" Sarah nodded as to silence the conversation.

"Alright, everyone, my name is Michael Vaughn, I will be working with each of you over the next few months. Well, most of you," he continued, eyeing Sarah. "Sarah, you can be my assistant since you've decided to join us." Sarah nodded in agreement. "First thing we'll do is strengthen those legs. I have some walking exercises to see how stable you are. Since Emily needs the most support, I'll work with her, and Sarah will be with Paul." Michael slid his arm around Emily's waist as she latched onto his arm. Sarah mimicked his gesture, but as they walked, Paul's gaze fixated on Emily until Michael pulled away.

"Very good, you two. Now for guided steps from the front."

Sarah moved ahead of Paul, holding his hands as he stepped forward, consciously blocking his view of Emily. She smiled as he progressed across the pool, seeking to center his concentration on the drill and not Michael.

Traversing the concrete floor, they found themselves separated from the other two. Paul glanced over his shoulder to check on them, but Sarah reined his eyes as she tugged at his arms. "I'm over here," she said.

"I know. I'm just making sure he doesn't get handsy with Emm."

"Don't worry about him; it's just part of his job." The tension in Paul's shoulders faded as they continued.

"Why are you so nice to me?" he asked.

"Why wouldn't I be . . .? I mean I know what you're trying to say, but Paul, we were friends before, and I think we still will be."

He gave a slight smile. "You know, Emily is looking so much better than when she was lying in the hospital," he paused, thinking back on those tragic days. "You look great as well," he continued. "I know I shouldn't say this, but you look like you've put on a little weight. And I mean that in a good way; you look womanlier, if that makes sense."

Sarah laughed, "Womanlier, huh?"

"Okay, how about you wear that bathing suit well?"

"Ha, thanks, Paul. I know what you meant, so I'll take both as a compliment."

A timer placed along the side of Michael's gear began to sound. Sarah looked over as Michael placed Emily into the mechanical chair. "That's it for today. Go ahead and make your way back, Sarah," said Michael. Sarah moved with Paul toward the handicap arm, but he instead diverged to the adjacent wall. With a stiffened grunt, he pulled himself up.

As he sat between Emily and Michael, Sarah proceeded to hoist herself out of the water, sliding her skin over the concrete edge, while bringing her legs underneath her. As she moved to stand up, she could feel the others staring. Noticing the strap of her top had slid slightly down her shoulder, she held one hand to her breast while fixing the strap with the other.

Michael tossed her a towel from his own bag. Wiping her face, she draped the towel over her shoulders and adjusted the seam of her bathing suit bottoms. As she stood by Emily, Michael handed them each a list of stretches and exercises to work on in between sessions. "Sarah, make sure they follow these. The more they adhere to them, the faster their recovery time." He waited for no reply before gathering his belongings. "I have to head to another appointment, but I'll see you all at the next session," he said with a final glance at Sarah before turning to leave.

When the three were alone, Paul was the first to speak. "How do you know him?"

"We met at a race. He was really helpful when I was struggling to finish."

"Well, I really don't like him."

Enjoying his defense, Emily decided to fuel Paul's aggravation. "Don't worry. He only grabbed my butt once," she chimed, holding a straight face. But as Paul began to redden in the cheeks, she cast a glowing smile. "Come here." Paul cradled his head on her legs, as Emily leaned over, meeting his lips with a kiss. "Sorry, Sarah. I had to calm the boy down." Laughter carried throughout the room, and the jovialness continued through the ride home.

Entering the apartment, Sarah stopped to consider something as she led Emily to her area. "Um, Emm. You need to take a shower."

"You're right. This chlorine needs to go."

"Can you help me lug you up the stairs?"

"Yep, that part shouldn't be too bad, but I'll need your help showering."

"What do you mean?"

"If I stand while showering, I might slip and fall, and if I sit down, I won't be able to get up."

Sarah nodded. "Good point . . . I have an idea though." Coming around, Sarah helped Emily to the stairs. "We'll take it one step at a time." Each step was unsteady, but to Sarah's surprise, Emily's legs offered some assistance.

Reaching her bathroom door, Emily paused. "Now what?"

"I'm going in with you."

"Ha, ha. I guess my commando scare at the store didn't warn you off. But I don't know if seeing you naked is a fair trade."

"Oh Emily, you're forgetting about the beach. That's not what I had in mind though. We can bathe in our swimsuits."

"Okay, but I probably should shave my legs too. They were looking prickly at the pool."

"That's fine. You can sit down for that, then I'll get in to help you stand."

Sarah eased Emily's legs over the tub wall, then held her under arms as she squatted to the floor. Turning on the water, Sarah went to her room for a clean towel. Shortly following her return, Emily handed Sarah the razor as she inspected her smooth legs.

"Alright," Sarah said, getting inside and bending down behind her. "Try to lift as much as you can." Emily hugged her legs as she pivoted her weight forward, and together they stood without slipping. "Go ahead and pull the shower nozzle."

Sarah clung to Emily's midriff as the blast of water began to pummel their bodies. She could feel Emily's knees quiver under the pressure. "I've got you, Emm. Just let me know if you think you can't stand, and we'll sit down to rest." Emily hesitated for a moment, but as she leaned back into Sarah for a brace, she relaxed.

"Okay. We'll try it that way."

Emily clasped the bar of soap from the cubby and began lathering her body. After she ran the bar along her face and arms, she began sinking down into the tub.

"Let me soap up everything, then we can stand and wash off. But first help me back up."

Sarah did as she was told and pulled Emily to her feet. "This blasted suit is getting in the way." Emily reached around to unhook her top, then slid the straps from her shoulders, dropping the garment to the floor. Tugging at the bottoms with her hands, she pulled the elastic down her waist, then shimmied them the rest of the way to her feet. Kicking free and squatting back down, she exhaled, "Much better."

Emily continued by rubbing the soap over her chest and underarms. "Here, grab my back," she motioned, handing the bar to Sarah. With a thick lather, Sarah ran her hands along her back, forming a foam cover.

"You've got the rest?"

"Yeah," said Emily reaching for the bar. "Can you work on my hair since you're right there at it?" she laughed.

"Ha. I suppose so." Sarah took the shampoo from the rail and strung her hands through Emily's strands, careful not to form or pull any knots. As Sarah worked on massaging her scalp, Emily worked her hands underneath and along the insides of her legs.

"Alright, let's stand up and wash the grime off," said Emily. Working to grasp Emily's slippery skin, Sarah's arms held tight but constantly slid from her stomach to her chest. "Hang on. I'll wash off my stomach first."

With another attempt, Sarah kept her position without Emily sliding through. Turning around for her backside, Emily closed her eyes as she tilted her head into the stream. Sarah tried to not stare at her naked body, but something had caught her eye. Something peculiar resided on her right breast. Feeling awkward, she adverted her eyes and focused on her grip instead.

"Okay, I'm done." Emily rotated around and turned off the water handles. Sarah led her to sit on the side of the tub as she unwrapped two towels.

"I'll help you to your bed, then finish showering."

"That works. Just toss me some undies. I'll dress myself."

With Emily secured on her bed, Sarah returned to the shower. Dropping her wet suit to the ground, she stepped into the still steaming tub. Soaking in the heat, her mind pondered continuously on the mysterious mark until she turned the water off again.

Covering herself in a towel, Sarah dried off before returning to Emily's room.

"See, I told you I could dress myself," said Emily, proudly displaying her undies with a slight shake. Sarah laughed only momentarily as she regained her thoughts.

"Hey, Emm. What's that spot on your chest? It looks like a bruise." Emily examined her skin before staring up in confusion.

"I don't see anything."

"I mean I saw it in the shower, about halfway down on the right." Intrigued, Emily pulled her bra down and inspected her chest. As her gaze moved upward, Sarah saw Emily blush for the first time in her life.

CHAPTER 5:

Happy Birthday

It was only enough to quieten the girl's conversation, when Emily and Sarah noticed Paul and Michael talking. From their first therapy encounter, Sarah doubted there would ever be any pleasantries between them, but now laughter erupted from both. Exchanging looks of confusion, Sarah and Emily moved closer to hear the conversation. Just as they reached earshot, Michael pointed, triggering Paul to turn.

"There's my birthday girl," he said, leaning over to hug Emily.

"Thanks, babe. Lucky number twenty-two this year."

"I'll say."

Michael moved beside Sarah, handing her a floaty.

"What's this for?"

"I'm going to have them practice moving their legs with some easy kicking intervals. You'll be working with Emily. I'm going to assist Paul for the rest of the sessions. I'll be right back; go ahead and get settled."

Sarah waited until he disappeared into an office before casting her eyes back at Paul. "What were you two talking about?"

"I told him that Emily and I are dating, and I thought it would be more suiting for you girls to work together."

"Then why were you laughing?"

"He said he completely understood and that he would be less likely accused of touching me than if it were Emily. It was kind of a weird funny, so I laughed."

"Oh. As long as you got it straightened out," Sarah said, turning to Emily. "Did you decide what you want to do tonight?"

"I feel able enough to go out instead of staying at the apartment."

"The three of us, or should we invite Abby and Ralph?"

"What about the four of us?" motioned Emily as she looked toward the office door.

"I rather not, Emm."

"How come? You said he was a nice guy at the race."

Sarah shook her head insinuating for Emily to hush as Michael returned. She could see the proposition still pondering in Emily's eyes, but Emily abstained from overturning Sarah's decision.

"Miss Emily, let's get you to the other chair, and Paul, are you still comfortable getting in from the side?"

"So far so good."

"Emily, would you rather try the stairs today?"

"Yeah, I think I would. I'm tired of sitting."

"With that attitude, we'll have you running in no time. You'd be surprised how many patients doubt themselves, only to hinder their progress."

"That's definitely not Emm," Sarah mumbled.

Paul slid into the pool and worked his way to the steps. Standing at the bottom, he waited to greet Emily as the other two clung to her sides. As she descended the last step, Paul grabbed her in his arms. "Good girl." She smiled up at him with a glimmer of satisfaction.

Sarah pulled the floaty in front of Emily, helping to fasten it into a ring. "We'll go this way, and you two can start in the opposite direction," Emily directed. As they circumnavigated the pool, Sarah's eyes watched the other two as they worked together. She wondered what they were talking about.

Paul's determined grimace portrayed his will to get through the exercise just like any track workout. No more laughs emerged from their voices, but a more cumbersome feel resonated from their actions.

"Don't stare a hole in him, Sarah."

"I'm not. Or I guess I was, but I was trying to hear what they were talking about."

"I'll get it from Paul later. Right now, I need you to watch my legs. Am I doing it right?"

"I think so. I don't think it's supposed to be anything fast. Paul's moving quicker than he should because he doesn't like to look vulnerable," Sarah assured. "Try lifting your hips so your feet aren't underneath you. That's what Paul's doing."

Emily arched her back the best she could, causing the pace to increase. "If I had some more fat, I wouldn't have to try so hard for my waist to float."

"You and your skinny legs. It'll come back, Emm. I'm sure of it."

Emily adjusted within the float before arching her back once again to kick.

"So, Michael is a no for tonight?"

"Uh, Emm . . ." Sarah said, looking into Emily's questioning eyes. "Fine. If it makes you feel better. But I'm not the one who's going to invite him. You have to. I don't want to give the wrong impression."

"Oh yeah, goodness forbid you go out with somebody."

"You yourself said I should be concentrating on track."

"Yeah, but that was when we were talking about Nigel. You've already been there, done that, and got the t-shirt."

"Umm no, no. I've never 'done that,'" Sarah said, provoking a laugh between them.

"Let's take a break, Sarah. The float is starting to rub."

Emily pulled alongside the pool and the two watched as the guys waded closer. Both of their physiques gave a tingle to Sarah's body. Not that either was a model of muscle, but there was something about trimness that played with her mind.

"Are you already finished?" asked Paul, as he splashed beside them.

"No. We're taking a breather," Emily replied.

"How are you feeling, Paul?" asked Sarah.

"Not bad. Working these muscles again feels great but awkward since it's been a while."

Following two more laps, Michael ended their session by gathering everyone at the stairs. "You both are progressing well. Given how much effort you're putting in, what if I treated you all to dinner one night? It'd help us all get to know each other outside of the pool too." The eyes of Sarah and Paul fell to Emily, who returned with an immediate response.

"I don't think paying is necessary, but we are going to dinner tonight for my birthday. Why don't you join us instead?" Michael rocked his head back and forth, considering her response.

"Sure. How about we meet at your place?"

"Okay. Sarah can give you directions. Just be there at six." Emily motioned for Paul to hold on to her handles as she wheeled away. "I'll be in the locker room, Sarah."

Sarah discarded Emily's intentions while taking hold of the conversation. "We live in the apartments a few blocks from campus, Setter Street."

"I know where that is. I'll swing by and pick everyone up."

"I rather drive. I can get Emily's chair in the trunk pretty easily now."

"That's completely up to you. I'll just make sure I'm on time."

Michael bent down to gather his equipment as Sarah stood waiting for him to finish. He glanced up at her dripping hair then back to his bag. Clutching the straps in his hands, he paused as his eyes fell over Sarah's legs.

"Humm, rashy knees. We have a great cream that helps with irritation." Sarah unfolded the towel to examine them herself, running her fingers over the rough skin.

"Ah, I didn't realize they were so raw. Seems like the chlorine probably made them worse. But thanks, I have something I can use."

Taking to Sarah's lead, Michael followed her until they departed the arena. Sarah soon encountered Emily awaiting with an inquisitive grin. Tugging on her sweatshirt, Emily's muffled voice soon broke through the layers.

"Umm, Sarah. Please tell me I'm seeing things."

"What are you talking about?"

"Either you have a lose thread or your string is hanging out of your swimsuit." Sarah's face flushed as she widened her legs enough to skim her hand between them.

"Oh, Emm. It's a thread, but it doesn't appear that way," she gasped.

"I'm sure you're fine. I barely noticed and it's not like either of the guys saw."

"I was standing next to Michael when he was packing up. He was looking at my legs, but what if he got a close-up view."

"It's barely hanging out. Besides, guys are dense about female stuff; he probably thought it was part of your bottoms."

Sarah rolled her eyes in optimism. "If he thought it was a tampon string then that serves him right for staring," she said, tossing her towel to the side and pulling her clothes from the locker. "Let's stop by the dining hall before heading home. I could use some food."

A frozen chill settled over Beval as nightfall covered the city. The last rays of sunlight had long disappeared when a knock came at the door. On the other side stood Michael wearing a button-down shirt and denim jeans. With his hair combed and moussed, he appeared more as a stranger. Entering, he greeted Paul with a firm shake before looking around the apartment.

"Where's Sarah?"

"She's upstairs, she'll—" but before Paul could finish, Michael rounded the corner and proceeded to the next floor.

Sarah jumped as her door burst open. "Sheesh! You scared the daylights out of me."

"I found out we can get reservations in Melnic for tonight, but we'll have to leave soon."

"Melnic? That's an hour away. I think Emily was leaning toward Mexican."

"I'll ask her, but hurry downstairs," Michael said, leaving abruptly. *Glad I had my clothes on when he came barging in,* she thought. Taking some urgency, she left her hair pins lying on the bathroom counter and positioned her hair with a hair band instead.

Emily awaited at the door as Sarah descended the final steps. "We're going to Melnic."

"Aren't the places there kinda pricy?"

"Michael knows the owner, so we'll get a discount."

"Well then, I guess we better get going," Sarah said, reaching for Emily.

"I've got it," said Michael, taking hold and wheeling her through the door. With his help, everyone quickly settled inside, while he finished loading the chair.

"All set," he said, jumping into the passenger seat. "Do you know the way?"

"I can get us to the town, but you'll have to point out the restaurant."

The excitement formulated by the rush to make a seven o'clock reservation settled as Michael pointed to a rock house tucked away in a well-planned landscape. Outside, a line coiled from the entrance, along the walkway, and into the parking lot. The lengthy drive for dinner seemed questionable to start with, but seeing the drove of people waiting heightened Sarah's curiosity.

As they approached the end of the line, Michael motioned for them to stick close and follow behind. Sarah frowned as she passed the glaring eyes that followed them to the door. A short, heavyset girl whose face was drained of enthusiasm from the questioning customers peered up as they approached. "Hello, we're currently at an hour wait and no longer taking names—"

"Hi, I spoke to Jason earlier. He saved a seat for us under the name Mikey." Her eyes widened as she frantically searched her book for a note left from the owner, but her frantic state soon eased upon hearing another voice.

"Mikey! You made it."

"Jason. Nice to see you," he said, reaching out to exchange hugs. "These are my friends: Sarah, Paul, and the birthday girl, Emily."

"Nice to meet you all. I have a special table set aside. Follow me." Jason veered away from the chatty wing of the restaurant, down a tranquil hallway, and into a room with people dressed in suits and dresses.

Sarah tugged at Michael's arm. "I didn't realize there was a dress code," but he offered no response. Instead, Michael continued conversing with Jason until they arrived at an empty table.

"Let me get your chair," Jason said assuredly as Michael helped Emily to one of the wooden seats. "I'll have a waiter right over to take your orders. And Mikey, try not to take so long in between visits."

Sarah sat beside Michael, inspecting the glamour that poured through the dim light. A white tablecloth stretched over the wooden table, and black leather backed chairs adorned each sitting area. A man appeared with four menus, distributing them to each, while placing a drink list in the middle. "Can you bring a pitcher and four glasses?" Michael requested.

"I'll have one," replied Sarah, "but I'm driving, so the rest is between you three."

"Fair enough. As a sidenote, their seasoned chicken breast is delicious."

"Sounds good to me," said Sarah.

"Make that double," followed Emily, with both guys upping the total to four.

Michael excused himself as the waiter left their table. As he disappeared into the restroom, Emily addressed what Sarah was thinking. "Why do you suppose he insisted on coming here? I mean, I like it, but I was fine with our Mexican tradition."

"He's just trying to be flashy, Emm," interjected Paul.

"Yeah, but an hour away?"

"You saw. He knows the owner."

"Do I detect some jealousy, Paul?"

"No. Not at all. I don't need heaps of money to be with you, now do I?"

"Money, what's that?" Emily laughed.

Settling the conversation, the waiter reappeared as Michael returned. Throughout the dinner, Sarah stuck to her drink limit, as the others partook in enough to only draw a buzz. Long after the chicken was consumed and another round of drinks was brought, the jovialness of the night continued. Sarah felt like a mother to Emily and Paul, watching their playful exchanges. However, Michael's appearance failed to waver. His proper sense and poise only diminished with a laugh at Emily's jokes.

With the main course cleared, the waiter brought a small chocolate cake with a single lit candle poking from the top. Taking an exaggerated breath, Emily made a wish before leaning back in her chair. "I'm stuffed. Maybe we should get this to go."

"It's getting late too," inferred Sarah, checking her watch. Michael motioned for a box before sliding back his chair and pulling on his coat. "He hasn't brought the bill yet."

"It's taken care of." Sarah squinted her eyes, evoking a questioning look. "I told you I know the guy. He always hooks me up," Michael continued.

Without furthering the discussion, Sarah slid out her chair.

"Let me leave the tip at least," Paul persisted.

"No need."

Sarah could feel the uneasiness that flowed from Paul's stance on the situation. Whether he was being flashy or not, the gesture displayed control of the evening.

Upon reaching the car, Sarah patted the gas as she turned the ignition. With a few rotations, the motor's lively vibe echoed through their ears. Emily rubbed her hands, cupping them around her mouth, searching for warmth. Paul worked his hands around the back of hers, forcing his own body heat inside. Their tight faces blocked the view of Sarah's rearview, leaving her to use the side mirrors.

As Sarah shifted to drive, she positioned one hand on the wheel while nestling the other underneath her legs. She switched her hands as the cold grasp of the steering wheel frosted her fingers, until the heater began to roast the car.

Music from the radio accompanied the now stifling air until Emily leaned forward to lower the volume. "I told Paul you saw my hickey."

"Emm!" exclaimed Sarah, turning her head to confront Emily's tipsy condition.

"Don't worry, I didn't tell him how you noticed."

"Although, I think I could fill in the gaps myself," declared Paul. "It's just one of those things, Sarah. You do it once, and it doesn't seem so bad the next time." A lax in his reputation came as a slight shock. Even seeing them together at the party had felt like a one-time ordeal, but maybe Paul was seeing Emily in a deeper sense, one where he felt comfortable bending the rules. Or, maybe almost losing Emily left him wanting her more. She did not know the details, and although Emily would freely share them if she asked, she decided not to.

"Paul, just make sure you take care of my Emily." Locking eyes with him through the mirror, she continued, "and yourself." Her sobering words caught Paul's attention. Their long understanding about how they each planned to pursue relationships had changed, but the underlining desire to stay pure had not.

"Where's this hickey you all are talking about?" Michael interrupted, as he adjusted his seatbelt to get a better view of Emily's neck.

"Wouldn't you like to know?" Emily taunted by tugging at her shirt.

"Yeah, well, it isn't on your neck, so it's not hard to figure out," he said, returning to his seat.

Sarah looked toward Michael who appeared to ponder something differently as he gazed out the window. Returning her eyes to the mirror, Emily had pulled back the top few shirt buttons and was showing the lingering mark to Paul. Her ability to read lips was far from a well-developed skill, but as Emily covered herself up, she could see Paul mouth, "I'm sorry."

They had all changed since the last semester. Some aspects were for good, and the others, she was not so sure about. Was she wasting her time waiting for the right guy to have a physical relationship with? She still wanted to wait until marriage, but the decision proved difficult.

Although she could have someone if she desired, what bothered her most was how much she had grown without trying, but now found herself back at square one. Inside the burning craving to be with someone continued to flame, but that was about to change.

CHAPTER 6:

A Surprise

The sun brought an unseasonable warmth to the field, as a wind blowing down the homestretch created a tailwind. Although such a push would not make or break any race, while walking from the fence to the pole-vaulting pit, the breeze continually swept at the backs of runners staggering along the rubberized lanes.

Throwers and sprinters had claimed most of the mat by the time Sarah arrived. The fleeing hope of relaxing on the plush pillow became an afterthought as she parked Emily in the grass. Squatting down alongside her, Sarah braced against the oversized foam. She watched as Paul took a clipboard from Coach Cavlere and claimed a nearby chair.

"What are y'all doing today?" asked Emily.

"Four hundred repeats. What else?" Sarah laughed.

"Are you ready for speed intervals?"

"Coach wants me to find my base. He said to go out however I felt and adjust to a time I'm comfortable with. Then, we'll see how I'm feeling. Don't worry; he gave no indication that he'd go easy on me this season. I think we're both itching to see what my body can do."

"Emily! Sarah!" Abby's words carried from beneath her hoodie as she and Ralph stepped off the track. Ralph's hood grasped tightly around his face, and Abby's identity only shown through as her auburn hair fell along her face. "I'm so glad you are coming to the practices, Emm."

"Me too. I think seeing everyone will quicken my recovery."

"Sprinters give me two laps for your warm up. Distance group, you have a mile!" yelled Coach.

As the three took to the track, Emily unlocked her wheels before maneuvering closer to Paul.

"Do you want to write or call out splits?"

"I'll yell the times," Paul replied. "But I need another watch for the girls." Emily placed the pen on the clipboard, resting her arm on the paper to unhook the band around her wrist. "How do you suppose Sarah will do?" Paul asked, taking the watch.

"It's Sarah. She'll do what she always does."

With the last of the runners finishing their jog, the team transitioned to drills and stretches while Coach delivered instructions for the workout. Sarah focused on her calves as he finished his speech with a customary, "Stick to your pace."

The guys toed the line first, storming off in a roar of pent-up energy. "Ladies, you're next!" At the sound of his voice, Sarah tugged her sweats over her head and down her bare legs. Within seconds of stripping, she started her watch as they too blasted off from the white line.

The freedom of her legs begged for the intensity as the group charged into the curve. Pulling through to the one-hundred-meter mark, the girls settled into place along the back stretch. An unwelcoming wind blasted against their efforts, making every step feel stationary. Adjusting to the resistance, Sarah quickened her stride, inching alongside Abby, who was leading the pack. Together, they pushed through to the halfway mark.

Turning into the second bend, Sarah merged to the first lane just behind Abby, her eyes fixated on her friend until they emerged into the homestretch. Breaking from the other girls, Sarah alongside Abby kept pace until crossing the line. "Looking great, Sarah," Emily called.

"One-minute recovery!" yelled Coach.

Stepping from the track, Emily attempted to hand her a water bottle, but Sarah simply shook her head. Until now, Sarah had failed to see Nigel. His presence throughout the beginning of practice had gone unnoticed. Only when he threw his shirt to the ground and stepped onto the track did her eyes consider him. Jogging beside the mat, she noticed Emily's eyes watching Nigel. "What is it?"

"It's warmer than usual, but it's not that hot today."

Sarah turned in time to see Nigel and Ralph leading off the wave of guys. Facing Emily once more, she smiled with mischief. "It's about to be." Emily raised a brow, questioning her remark, but just then, Sarah raised her hands to her shoulders. Clasping at the neckline, she lifted her shirt over her head and tossed it to Emily.

"Ha. What was that for?"

"I'm about to make my intentions known."

Running to catch Abby for the start, Sarah barely settled before sprinting off. Hugging the curve, she hung with the lead group and adjusted to pace by the time they met the far side. Abby ran close ahead, but the entire lap, Sarah never lost more than a few steps in distance.

A fire rolled in Sarah's chest, leaving steam to billow from her sports bra as she jogged during her rest time. The change was apparent to not only Abby but the others as well. Even Coach's words of encouragement were laced with concern. However, the only person that did not mention the sudden change was Nigel. Sarah could feel him looking at her in passing glances, but she cared not what he thought or if his wavering eyes were focused on her. There were a lot of miles missing that she unwillingly gave up, but now it was her time to reclaim her spot on the team.

Following the first two repeats, Sarah continually clocked a consistent pace. Her legs sprung out along the rubber with each step feeling natural. Beads of sweat marked her face without a shirt to wipe them away. Going shirtless in her mind was a one-time occurrence, but setting the future pace would not be.

As the remainder of the girls dispelled from the track, the sprinters and throwers had long disappeared from the field. Aside from the distance runners, pole-vaulters were the only remaining group. Sarah situated herself in the grass beside Emily as she bent her knees to thread each leg into her warm-up pants. Pulling the elastic over her bare feet, Sarah watched as Jenna Grayson lifted her pole and gave an effortless vault. As her body lifted into the air, her feet rose over her head as her knees kicked her light frame upward, inching her pelvis over the bar. When her back approached the apex of the flight, Jenna arched her spine, allowing her body to clear the marker.

Just as her head tilted forward, the last of her hair grazed the bar as she fell to the pillow below. The partition showed no movement from her flawless vault. Happy with the effort, she smiled cheerfully upwards.

Seeing Jenna fly effortlessly caught the attention of others that still stood nearby. However, Sarah's attention only peaked well after the follow through. Bending over to retrieve her pole, Jenna moved back to the mat. No other vaulters stood waiting behind her, but as she climbed onto the edge, Sarah noticed someone lying on the far end. Only when their weight curved the cushion did Sarah see the outline of Nigel's face. Bracing his hands behind his head, he rolled to his side upon Jenna's presence. He had been resting there after finishing the workout, watching Jenna practice.

Initially, Sarah could only consider what she was seeing. Still staring, she moved her eyes to tying her shoelaces. Over the past few years, like with most of the field athletes, friendships had been kept to the level of encouraging teammates. With little time between sets, and no common ground between the two groups, there had been little reason or opportunity to get to know the vaulters or throwers. Even so, the lingering thought of what qualities Jenna possessed that she did not, toiled her mind, questioning whether she had indeed moved on from Nigel.

Accepting that Nigel was forming feelings for another girl, she considered something she knew about Jenna. As some guys on the team professed, Jenna was not only a pretty girl with a nice body, but she also refrained little from sharing it. If she and Nigel were sleeping together, there was nothing Sarah could do; however, at least she knew what she had that Jenna did not.

Emily leaned across the arm rest, close enough for her breath to graze Sarah's ear. "Nigel and Jenna, huh? Good riddance, right?"

"Yeah, I think so."

"Do you suppose they're sleeping together?" Hearing the question aloud sickened her stomach. Thinking of the two having sex was one thing, but someone else sharing the same impression felt surreal.

"I rather not think about it."

A sense of worth, from either being herself or not being Jenna, followed Sarah to the car. Her blurry reflection appeared in the window, casting her eyes over her body. *No, it's not that she's prettier than me. He knew he could get Jenna. Now I wish I hadn't walked past him in the dining hall.*

While comparing herself to Jenna on the ride home, Emily discussed the performance Sarah put forth at practice. "If you're in that kind of shape, imagine what the end of the season will be like." Sarah merely nodded at her words, not coherent to their meaning.

Self-doubt and prior thoughts of loathing began filling her body as Sarah ascended the stairs to her room. Emily, now comfortable on the couch, was fast asleep for a midafternoon nap. However, her words still carried through the stairwell. *Jenna and Nigel, huh?* Why did she care though? Jealousy was the obvious answer, but not the complete picture. Having grown so close to Nigel, seeing him with another girl meant something. She no longer held that place in his life. He had moved on with ease. In over a month's time a new girl had taken her place.

Sarah discarded her running clothes on top of the hamper. Looking down at her stomach, she pulled off her underwear, examining her imperfect body as a whole. *Am I that ugly? Had he seen something he didn't like that night?* A few tears streamed her cheeks, continuing down her face, and onto her chest. She knelt to the floor, offering her humbled body to the coolness of the rug. Trembles rumbled through her arms and legs as she began to pray. She had been broken like this before, yet now she leaned on to what had helped previously. Her prayer centered not on an answer but for someone, a husband, a man who would not let her feel broken or ashamed, lost or unwanted. She prayed for a family of her own, with children. She prayed for a true love.

Hinging back on her legs, Sarah wiped her face with her bare arm. Allowing another person to alter her feelings struck all too real this year, and she no longer wanted such bondage. Coming off last semester, those feelings of loss had faded, yet here again they raised a grimaced face. Was the suffering and agony only beginning again? Had she not experienced the heartaches of life enough?

She recalled Nigel touching her as she gazed down at him seeking comfort, giving her body to him in hopes for togetherness. A sudden lurch pulled Sarah to the floor. She rushed to the toilet, barely reaching the porcelain before vomit spilled from her lips. Dry heaves followed as her empty stomach felt sickened. If he saw her in this state, would he hold her hair? Would he comfort her in his arms once more?

Standing up on her shaking legs, Sarah braced against the sink, looking into the mirror. The hair she once cherished so deeply was still short of a familiar length. *He took not only my heart but also the love for my hair.* Sarah let out a moan of pain, disgust, and disbelief. She spit a lingering trail of vomit into the sink before cupping her hand under the water and gulping a few sips to rid her mouth of the bitterness.

Her bare skin formed a chill as she loosened her tense muscles. Reaching underneath the sink, Sarah pulled out a bottle of bubble therapy mix. Hanging a towel beside the tub, she leaned over to place the stopper and turn on the hot water.

The water had yet to rise as she dumped the solution and stepped into the tub. Sitting in the shallow pool, she reclined along the porcelain. Feeling her body soak in the warmth, Sarah raised her foot, shutting off the nozzle only as the cloud of soap reached the brim.

Today's Friday. With the reassuring thought that she could relax as long as she pleased, Sarah closed her eyes. *I wonder if they are already having sex.* Her mind continued to wonder. *Was she enjoying him more than the other guys she'd been with?* Sarah blinked to push the images from her mind, yet blasts of Jenna climbing over his body still scarred her conscience. *Was it love or lust?*

Forfeiting the promises of a relaxing bath, Sarah drained the tub and washed the suds from her skin. Her own nakedness had brought the onset of her troubles, but the cover of clothes fetched a peaceful mind. With shirt and jeans now fortifying her protection, Sarah headed downstairs to check on Emily. She had awakened to retrieve a notebook from her backpack and was working on homework. Hearing Sarah, she laid the paper and pen aside. However, before either could speak, a knock came from the front door. Puzzled, Sarah turned mid step to answer.

As she opened the door, she looked long into the eyes on the other side. "Michael? What are you doing here?"

"Oh good. You're already dressed. I came to see if you wanted to get dinner."

"Well, I . . . Hang on a minute," she said, shutting the door, then returning to the living room.

"Who was that?"

"It's Michael. He wants to go to dinner. I don't know what to tell him. How about you come with me?"

"I'm pretty tired. You go ahead. I need to catch up on homework anyways."

"Are you sure? I don't like leaving you alone. And what are you going to eat?"

"Don't worry about me. I'm a grown woman; I think I can survive."

Sarah laughed as she grabbed her jacket. "Ok, Emm, I'll see you in a little bit," she said before shutting the door.

"Sorry about that. Where are we going?"

"I was actually making a lasagna at my place and have way too much."

A welcoming aroma of baked cheese and pasta filled her nose as Sarah entered the house. Michael slid her coat off her shoulders, placing the garment on a nearby hook. The manicured foyer opened into a stunning living space with an adjoining kitchen. Sarah rubbed her hands along the top of the leather sofa and wool blanket that draped across.

"What would you like to drink?"

"Water's fine," she said, gazing around the room.

"Here you are." Handing her a glass, Michael ushered her to the table that sat apart from the kitchen. "It's almost ready if you want to have a seat."

Sarah watched as he pulled the sizzling pan from the oven and placed it on the stove eye. Collecting two plates from the cabinet, he slid a spatula around the sides and proceeded to cut slices from the pan. Only as he joined her at the table did Sarah settle into her seat.

Blowing across her fork to cool a piece, Sarah bit through the crust that formed into gooey cheese below. "This is really delicious. Do you cook all the time?"

"Not really. It's just me, so it depends on how late I work." Sarah looked from the table and around the room. They were alone. "Well, I say that, but there's Bessie."

Sarah set her fork on the table as she swallowed hard. "Who's Bessie?"

Michael tilted his head toward the far side of the room where a crate lay against the wall. "My dog. She's just a pup. I put her in the crate earlier. She tends to be very rowdy when she meets someone new."

"I'd like to meet her."

"Oh, of course. Once we finish dinner, I'll let her out."

Sarah lifted her fork once again, savoring the warmth and lusciousness of the meal. She knew she could likely stomach two more large slices but decided to stop even as Michael offered seconds.

"Are you sure? I really don't want to eat this all week, and rather it not go to waste," he questioned again, taking a bite over the counter. At his persistence, Sarah conceded to another helping. She carried her plate to the bar and held it out. "Here," he said, digging his fork into the pan. "We don't have to be formal," he joked.

Rather than a slice, the two continued for what felt like three more pieces bulging in her stomach. The immodest indulgence would have felt embarrassing if Michael had not dropped his utensil and poked his belly out in exaggeration. "Well, well, I do say I overdid it tonight."

"There's no way that's from the food. You're making your stomach bulge. But how?"

Michael laughed at Sarah's direct acknowledgment. "It's really easy, you just suck air into your belly. Try and see." Sarah inhaled a deep breath while pushing on her abdomen, but there was little change in her appearance. "No, no, no. You put all the air in your chest." He lifted her shirt over her navel and placed his hand on her stomach. "Concentrate on pulling the air into here." Sarah closed her eyes and breathed deeply, feeling her stomach begin to rise. "There it is. You've got it." She opened her eyes to see how her rounded form had taken shape.

"I can't see my toes," she croaked.

"I knew you could do it."

Sarah expelled the air, followed by a gasp. "I'll have to show Emm. She'll love this."

Sarah lowered the shirt over her stomach as Michael wandered toward the crate. Leaning down, he unhooked the latch, which in turn transformed the sessile puppy into a frenzy.

"Sarah, this is Bessie. Bessie, this is Sarah." Sarah reached out to take the dog in her arms.

"How cute! I have a similar breed at my parents'. Her name is Daisy." Bessie licked Sarah's face, then tickled the side of her neck. "I think she likes me."

"Well, she does have good taste," he joked.

"And just how would you know?"

"For starters, she did the same thing when I got her. And she tends to like the same people as I do," he said, causing Sarah to lower the puppy and look up at him. "I'll put her back in the cage. It's getting late; I better take you home."

Sarah glanced at her watch, questioning his gesture. It was only nine thirty, and a young night for a Friday. "Oh yeah, I suppose so. I don't like leaving Emily alone long either."

Michael placed his hand on the small of her back as they walked to the door. Lifting her coat from the rack, he held open the front while Sarah ran her arms through the sleeves. As she turned to face him, she pulled the jacket onto her shoulders. Michael proceeded to run his hand across the gape of her neck before pulling her hair from beneath the collar. A small pause lingered at the possibility of a kiss; however, neither of them merged from their post. To avoid feeling awkward, Sarah laughed and reached for the doorknob.

"What's so funny?"

"I was just thinking about the dog licking my neck. It gave me the same tickling feeling."

"Oh, you don't like to be tickled?"

"No, I didn't say that. I just meant—" but before she could finish, he ran his hands across her stomach just below her ribs. He latched his arms around her as his fingers gently flickered over her shirt. "Ha, stop! That tickles!" She squirmed, but the harder she resisted, the more he urged her body to convulse in laughter. Sarah sunk to the floor, trying to conceal her vulnerable spots. "For real though, you're going to make me—" she gasped.

Michael loosened his grip, allowing Sarah to catch her breath. "You enjoyed it with Bessie, so I thought I'd try."

"Bessie's an innocent puppy. You were just trying to make me laugh until my sides ached," Sarah joked.

"Fair enough. Here," said Michael extending a hand to help Sarah to her feet. "Next time, I'll hold Bessie and let her do the tickling for me."

"What about you?" Sarah questioned, trying to attack his sides in return.

"It's no good. I'm not ticklish." He raised his arms allowing Sarah many attempts, but seeing her efforts were useless, she conceded.

"Alright, I give up. We better get going so I can check on Emily."

Sarah bid Michael good night before shutting the car door. No other playfulness or possible farewell kiss stemmed after they left his house. Returning to the cool air, Sarah snugged her jacket closer as Michael steered his lights away and drove off. She fumbled with the keys before cracking the door open. Likely that Emily was asleep, she tried not to create any loud noises. Creeping through the door, she heard a voice from the living room. Announcing her presence, Sarah pushed the door closed with a purposeful slam.

"Sarah, is that you?" came Emily's voice.

"Yeah, it's just me. I take it you're still awake."

"Yep. Hey, come here." Sarah followed Emily's voice as she felt for the light switch. Reaching the edge of the couch, she found the overhead light as she lifted the curtain.

"Oh, Paul. I didn't realize you were here." Paul and Emily sat nestled together on the side of Emily's bed, anticipating her arrival. Paul looked at Sarah and then to Emily as if waiting for one to say something. Finally, with a soft whisper, he murmured to Emily. With her hands placed in her lap, Emily turned from Paul and finally looked up into Sarah's eyes.

"There's something we want to tell you."

CHAPTER 7:

Just a Dream of Possibilities

Sarah's stare shifted between Emily and Paul. Her heartbeat quickened in anticipation of the words to follow. A million life-altering, frightening possibilities flashed before her eyes. Only when a smile drew across Emily's face did she realize the news had a benevolent nature. Emily's hands unfolded from her lap and a princess-cut diamond sparkled from the ring around her finger. "We're getting married!" Emily announced. Excitement blossomed upon Emily's face, as her eyes filled with joyful tears.

Sarah found her voice searching for words to deliver her own excitement. "Oh, Emily. I'm . . . so happy for you two!" A sole suppressed tear gleamed her eye as Sarah leaned in to hug Emily. "And, Paul, I didn't know you were planning on proposing. This ring is beautiful," she continued, pulling Emily's hand from her lap to gain a closer look.

"I know. It happened so fast. After the accident, I realized I didn't want to waste my life waiting and possibly losing someone I love." He looked to Sarah, and she nodded, offering the approval she knew he hoped for. "I just bought the ring, planning to see what you thought, but I couldn't help myself."

"Well, you did a good job." On the cusp of a sob, Sarah continued, "When are you thinking the big day will be?"

"Most likely this summer. We'll be out of school, and I intend to walk down the aisle, without help," Emily said. Her eyes blinked with determination as she detested the wheelchair beside her bed. Returning her attention to Sarah, she continued, "Oh, and will you be my maid of honor?"

"Emm, I'd be flattered! It'll be so much fun planning and throwing a shower."

"Thanks, Sarah. I'm going to really rely on you as we coordinate everything." Emily scooted away from Paul on the bed and patted the mattress for Sarah to take a seat. As she squeezed between them, Emily leaned her head on Sarah's shoulder and wrapped her arms around her.

"I love you two very much," Sarah said.

"We love you too, Sarah," Paul whispered.

After a moment of enjoying the warmth between them, Sarah rose to her feet. "I'm sure you two have plenty to discuss, so I'll head to bed," she said, offering a yawn. "Good night, Emily. Night, Paul."

"Good night, Sarah," they echoed.

Pushing the door closed to her bedroom, she could still hear their soft voices below with a few giggles from Emily. *Two weddings in less than a six-month span.* She had always heard life travels fast, but at this rate, she wasn't sure if she could handle the ride. Perhaps Wesley's wedding was a bad idea. For whatever reason he decided to invite her, she saw no obligation to go. More importantly, it was her that would have to endure two previous loves promise their futures to other women, while she watched unaccompanied.

Sarah pulled her toothbrush from the drawer and massaged her gums as she closed her eyes. When she finished and spit the paste from her mouth, she took a hard look at herself in the mirror. She was happy for Emily and Paul. As far as that went, the same stood for Wesley. There was no reason to pity herself. Instead, she bent to her knees and braced her head on the sink in prayer. *Dear God, please send me the right man. Let love guide us together for your purpose.*

Sarah's murmurs slowed to a hush before she found herself curled on the floor. Switching off the bathroom lights, she wandered to her bed in the blanket of darkness. Her head recessed into the pillow as she gazed through the shadows toward the ceiling. She rested her hand along the empty bedside, caressing the sheets that remained cold. One day, her hand would meet the warmth of another, and the bitter cold would be gone.

She retreated the lone hand before tugging the covers closer. An unsuspecting smile crept across her face. Sarah turned to her stomach and sprawled her arms and legs as far apart as she could. *If I must sleep alone, then I might as well take up the whole bed.*

The alarm's beckon did not sound an awakening call the next morning. Pulling the covers over her head, Sarah refused to leave the sweltering layers to reach the shower or even her robe. Only a rumbling stomach disagreed with her choice to stay in bed. Giving in to breakfast over warmth, she slid from the covers, jetting to the bathroom for her robe. Wrapping the threads around, she snugged the sash against her waist.

Creeping down the stairs, the floor creaked as she hesitated upon noticing Emily's lamp was off. She continued, tiptoeing around the corner, only to stop suddenly in fright of Paul's presence.

"Paul!" she gasped. He waved his hands, but she was already clasping her mouth.

"Emily's still asleep."

"Sorry. You scared me though. I didn't realize you'd be here—"

"I wasn't planning to, but I ended up staying the night. I hope that's alright."

"Oh, the night; yeah, understandable," she wavered. Not considering he stayed the entire night, she now questioned what her original thoughts were.

"Don't worry. It's not an everyday thing."

Sarah reached for the refrigerator handle and pulled out the milk. "Would you like some cereal?"

"No thanks, I helped myself to some water though."

"Here," she said, pulling a second bowl from the cupboard. "Emily likes to sleep in late, so if you plan on waiting for her to get up, you might as well have breakfast. What kind would you like?"

"Thanks, Sarah. Hmmm . . . Surprise me."

"We're out of the soggy dog food flavor," she countered, only to pour her cereal into his bowl.

"Dang. I was hoping for an upset stomach."

Sarah snickered as she placed the spoon on the table and sat down beside him. "How long have you been awake?"

"Maybe thirty minutes. I was going to head home and do some homework, but I didn't want to leave without telling her goodbye."

"You really love her, don't you?"

"I do. After the accident, when she recovered, I knew I wanted to be with her the rest of my life." He paused from stirring his cereal and looked to Sarah. "I don't mean to belittle anything we shared." Sarah gulped the milk before placing another bite in her mouth, delaying her response.

"Paul, I think we liked each other, but if we're being honest, it wasn't love like you have for Emily, and I'm fine with that. We just need to stop rehashing the subject like I'm an abandoned puppy, or that you feel bad for only marrying one of us and not both."

"I'm sorry. You're right. So should we forget any feelings we had?"

"If that helps you, then sure."

"Okay, but I have one last question, then I'll drop it."

"Alright."

"If we had dated, do you think it would be us getting married?"

Sarah's attention was abruptly withdrawn from her bowl. "Paul, if you had asked me that before you and Emily, I would have said yes. Now though, I'd say no. Too much has happened in my life, and I think you know that." She returned to her spoon, but before taking another bite, she looked to Paul for assurance. "Paul, for Emily's sake, tell me you're not in love with me." She looked to read his eyes, but neither his expression nor words brought true clarity.

"No, I'm not. At least I don't love you like that anyways."

"Okay, good. Then that settles that, right?"

"Yeah. So now we can continue as normal friends?"

"Of course."

Paul leaned over to hug Sarah. Meeting him with her spoon still in hand, she dropped the utensil and reciprocated the embrace. As their chests bore together, she could feel the beats of their hearts echoing one another.

Sarah was the first to pull away, leaving the conversation to sit in silence as they finished their breakfast.

Slurping the remaining milk from their bowls, Sarah gathered their dishes and placed them in the sink. As she returned with a banana for each of them, a sleepy-eyed Emily rounded the kitchen corner. Her ruffled hair gathered along the sides of her head, and a baggy shirt cascaded down her chest and halfway to her knees. The wheelchair bumped against the table as she joined them.

"Want me to fix you something?" asked Sarah.

"Do we have any toast and jelly?"

"Yeah, I'll drop two slices in the toaster," Sarah said as she headed to the cabinet.

"Did you sleep okay, Paul?"

"Yeah, it took me a while to fall asleep after you did, but then I was out . . . You must've since you're the last one up."

"Emily isn't a morning person," called Sarah over her shoulder.

"I'm not. If not for Sarah, I'd never make morning practices," she laughed.

"I hate to eat and run, but I've got a mountain of homework." Paul gave Emily a kiss on the lips and bid Sarah goodbye before letting himself out the front door. As they heard him drive away, Sarah placed a plate in front of Emily before settling across the table with her banana.

A silence persisted until Emily finished spreading her jelly. "I should've told you Paul was staying over, but we didn't plan on it until you had gone to bed."

"That's alright. He scared me this morning when I came downstairs and saw him at the table," she laughed.

"He was just sitting here? Did he say anything?"

"No, he had a glass of water and wanted to wait until you got up before leaving."

Emily toyed with her toast, inattentive to Sarah's words. "Emm, did you hear me? He only stuck around so that you didn't wake up alone."

"Oh yeah," she smiled. "That was sweet of him."

"What's going on? You're awfully quiet."

"I'm just thinking about Paul and the wedding."

Sarah paused, pondering her own silent thoughts before allowing herself to deepen the conversation. "Emm, I've been meaning to ask you."

"About the wedding?"

"No, not at all. I mean when you were in the coma. What was it like? Did you have any dreams?"

Emily looked up and adjusted her focus to Sarah. "Dreams. Yeah. I had lots of those. I don't remember them all though. Like any other dream, losing consciousness at the wreck was much like falling asleep, I can't tell you any details, but I know it happened."

"Could you tell we were around you, or that you were still alive?"

"I felt you crawl in the bed. I wanted to tell you I loved you too. I wanted to tell you not to go; that I was still there."

"You knew they were going to take you off—"

"I knew. So much so, I tried to scream. I pleaded from inside begging the doctors, then for my parents to not listen to them," she mourned.

"Were you scared of dying?"

"No."

"What was it then?"

Emily swallowed hard, "I . . . I . . . I saw something. I saw a lot of things, but when I first regained some awareness, or started dreaming, I was floating. My body was rising to what I could only imagine was heaven. Initially, there were no thoughts of returning. Happiness filled my soul, and I was no longer part of this world as far as I'm concerned. But then it happened. I started to fall. At first, I couldn't tell what was happening, then I looked down and saw Paul and he was dead. In a blink of an eye, I found myself rejoined with my body, but unable to move or speak. I could hear everything and feel each movement. I knew if the only thing I ever did was wake up, I had to do it."

Sarah batted her eyes, "You didn't tell your parents or Paul, did you?"

"No. I wanted to, and still do, but there's something else. I saw a mother coddling a baby and a man walking toward them. I considered the couple was Paul and me, but I really couldn't tell. All I knew was, if I didn't come back, they'd all die."

"So why are you bottling this up?"

"When Paul asked me to marry him, I knew I wanted to, given everything we've been through, so I immediately said yes. I wanted nothing more than to be with him while I was in the coma. However, last night all of this came rushing back, along with something else. Something I believed I fabricated in my head, and not a dream." Emily reached for Sarah's hand. "In the dream with the couple and the child, the child was covered in blood."

"Okay—"

"Sarah, now . . . I think the woman was you."

"Me?"

"I don't know, it's all so much. I just thought I should tell you, and somehow, I need to tell Paul."

"Emm, I too recently had a dream about a couple with a baby. Just like you described, but no blood. I couldn't tell who they were, but then I learned my doctor's wife just gave birth."

"So, you don't think it was you?"

"I didn't after that."

"But still, the vision with Paul, then you, and me having to return to my body. It has to mean something."

"What do you think it means?"

"It means I couldn't die!" she sobbed. "It means I had to live, for you, for Paul."

Sarah jumped from her chair, wrapping her arms around Emily. "I'm sorry, Emm. I didn't mean it like that."

"I know. I know," she managed, choking back tears. "I love you both, and I don't want something bad to happen. That's why I want to get married. I've almost lost him once."

"Tell him how you feel. Let him know. I don't think you have anything to lose. Have you seen the ring on your finger?" Sarah teased.

Emily succumbed to a laugh that accompanied her slowing tears. "Ha . . . He did good, didn't he?"

"He did great by asking you to be his wife; the ring is a nice touch."

"I'll tell him."

"Do you want me to be there with you?"

"No. That's alright. If he's going to spend the rest of his life with me, he'll understand."

"Emily? Do you suppose you and Paul would've ended up together, if not for the wreck?"

"I'd like to think so. He tends to make me a softer person, and the wreck changed everything."

"So, what made you two get together the night of the party?"

"Well, for one, we had been drinking, but two . . . You know how when it's late at night and you want something sweet to eat, thinking it will make you feel better?"

"Yeah . . . Was Paul your candy?"

"I think we were each other's candy in a sense. The thing is, when we started kissing, it didn't feel physical. It felt more like a connection."

"But you don't remember Paul following you in there?"

Emily turned her head with a questionable look. "No, I was alone initially, feeling sick. I forgot to lock the door, and a minute later, Paul came stumbling in. Then, you know the rest. I'm not sure if he followed me or came in by chance."

CHAPTER 8:

Waiting on Chance

The tepidness of the pool had vanished, allowing a frigidness to take its place. Sarah pulled her toe from the water, refusing to jump in. She snugged the towel closer as she looked for Michael.

"I wonder where he is," said Emily. "Usually he's on time."

Turning from the therapy pool, Sarah noticed the man who was swimming laps. She stepped in front of his lane, eyeing each stroke. As he flipped around, she barely caught a glimpse of his face, leaving him unrecognizable. Only as the man stopped, lifted his goggles, and tugged off his swim cap, did she realize it was Michael.

"What are you doing?"

"The heaters aren't working, so I figured we could improvise."

"What do you mean?"

"Swim laps instead. It feels great once you get started."

"I think I'll pass."

"Me too," echoed Emily.

"Hey, wait a second. Don't leave," Michael called as he hoisted himself out of the pool. "It'll still help. Your arms will do most of the work but adding a kick will give you a feel for your legs."

Emily hesitated, trying to determine if his claim was valid. "I'm concerned with being able to stand and walk on my own, not swim."

"I tell you what, if you can do laps while using your legs, I guarantee you'll have the strength for both. And I know it's cold. You have to trust me though. Just dive in and start swimming. By the time you finish the first lap, you won't even consider the temperature."

"What do you say, Sarah?"

"If you think it will help, I'll join you."

"Okay, but you have to go first."

Sarah stood over the edge of the pool, judging the water below. "I'm a horrible diver, so I'll jump feet first." Dropping her towel to the floor, Sarah pinched her nose with one hand, and covered her mouth with another. With one last breath, she jumped. The crashing water engulfed her ears as the cold pierced her skin. The darkness of her eyelids and a shocking chill left her unsure of how deep she sank. Only as her feet reached the bottom did fear course through her body, realizing the need to breathe. Springing from the floor, she waved her hands, forcing her way to the surface.

A rush of air filled her lungs. Still gasping, Sarah pulled her arms closer as she noticed her displaced swim top. Fumbling her hands to hide her bare skin, her topless predicament brought additional fear. Struggling to stay afloat and seek cover, she found neither and began sinking once again. As her head disappeared underneath, she inhaled a liquid breath. Still fighting the water's grasp, two arms latched around her stomach and dragged her to the surface. Sarah coughed, excelling the water from her mouth. Braced against the chest of her rescuer, she soon felt concrete beneath as she was pulled from the water.

"Sarah? Are you alright?"

She opened her eyes to a circle of concerned faces.

"Pull her top down," Emily persisted.

"I'm fine, I just . . . lost my top."

Michael flipped the cups back over her breast before handing her the towel.

"Lost your top?" he chuckled. "I see that, but it looked like you were drowning."

"I was fine until the panic of being disoriented kicked in, then I noticed my top."

"Have you never swum before?"

Sarah's ghastly face found color as embarrassment stroked her cheeks. "Yes. I have. But like I said, I got disoriented, and I couldn't see anything."

"I should've brought goggles for you all. I'll go get them—that is, if you want to try again."

She slanted her eyes at the commentary.

"Hang on."

He rushed to the office, returning shortly with three pairs of goggles.

"Don't psych yourself out."

Sarah wrapped the band around her head and positioned the nosepiece. With a few more breaths, she bent over the pool, this time hesitantly diving in. The rush of water swirled past while the cascading current rung in her ears. Her body slowly rose toward the surface as she began kicking. Figuring her technique likely appeared amateurish, she concentrated only on moving forward. Determined to hit the wall on the other side, she raised her head above the surface, inhaling only air this time. Her momentum momentarily ceased until she lowered her head and continued propelling forward. Over the splashing of her arms, she could hear shouts, but they came as meaningless roars until her strokes came even with the wall.

"Good job, Sarah! Can you make it back?"

Their words danced in her head, as if she was breaking away during the last stretch of a race. Her heart fluttered while her lungs remained heavy. Sarah clasped to the edge as she worked to control her breathing. Inhaling a final time, she pushed off the wall. With each stroke, the required effort increased. Her body demanded more oxygen, causing Sarah to stop every few strokes. By the time she reached the other side, she exhaustedly broke into a doggy paddle.

The end came just as she extinguished her will to keep swimming. Closing her eyes, Sarah felt a hand meet hers. "Need help?"

"Yeah, please," she gasped.

"What do you think? Quite the workout, huh?"

"Swimming isn't like running at all," she laughed. "Come on, Emm. It's your turn."

"Let me try in the shallow pool, in case I need to stand," she teased.

Within the move across the floor, Sarah felt her body's built-up heat begin to dissipate. Quickly she jumped into the therapy pool as Michael helped Emily.

"Come on, Paul. I want to see what you've got," challenged Sarah.

Leaving Paul to start alone, she pushed off the wall. Determined and focused, Sarah worked to relax her breathing. The effort however still proved more than her lungs could handle. There was humility in finding a new limitation. Heavy breaths were something she only found familiar while kicking through the finish line, but even that felt different. Sarah waded in the pool, lifting her chest above the surface. Feigning to appear less winded, she anchored her hands on her hips as she called out. "You and Emily have to at least try."

Both Paul and Emily lowered their goggles before dipping their bodies beneath the surface. She watched as the two crawled with their arms, slowly kicking their legs. Three-year-old children likely had better odds of staying afloat, but before they reached halfway, Michael stopped them.

"Try this. Bow your arms; it'll catch more water," Michael said, demonstrating from the side. "Give it another go, keep your head down, and come up on your side to breathe."

Michael swam to meet them as they sought another try. Sarah watched Michael assist with their form, making changes of her own. Aside from the awkward sights of true novices, each eventually formed a rhythm to pull themselves along.

Working across the water, Sarah lapped the others with two rounds to their one. Each time she passed, her mouth would open for a breath, yet as she submerged under, she could taste the cologne Paul wore. She also noticed an odor that she recognized as Emily. But there was a third as well. And although she knew it as Michael, she had never noticed his scent. Whether he always emitted the alluring smell, or if it was new, she failed to recall, but after it engulfed her scents, the aroma lingered in her mind.

"Sarah. Sarah!" She stopped, perking her ears to where the voice was coming from. "Sarah. Your legs and bottom are angling below the water. Focus on keeping your whole-body level with the surface."

"How can I do that?"

"Usually, it happens when your leg muscles are tense. If you can relax a bit, that should do the trick." She nodded before taking off once more. He was right. The tension in her legs failed to cross her mind as she powered most of the effort from her arms. Pausing, she lay flat in the water, but this time, she let go of the stiffness found in her legs. Each limb slowly rose in response. Then, slowly she initiated a sustainable kick.

The waters calmed as they stepped out of the pool. No more than eight laps each, and a burn had settled into their arms. Sarah patted her face dry as water dripped from her suit. Lacing her finger underneath the seam of her bottoms, she adjusted the bikini before wrapping the towel around her.

"Emily. I think you're ready for more walking and spending less time in your chair," Michael urged. "When you and Sarah are at home, focus on doing the simple things. For example, going to the kitchen or the bathroom with minimal assistance. You can use a walker if you like, but my main concern is spending more time with weight on your feet."

"Can I go to the locker room without it?"

"I wouldn't today since we got the floor pretty wet. Maybe next time. I have to run now. Keep up the good work." Michael turned and headed for the locker room, leaving the three behind.

"Who knew we were getting swimming lessons today?" asked Paul. "Although, I'll admit it was nice letting my legs put in some work." He paused, looking to Sarah. "Don't you have a speed work-out today?"

"Yeah, I do, but my legs feel fine. And even though I looked foolish, I kinda like it."

"If it'll help me, then I'm on board," replied Emily before changing the subject. "Oh, Sarah, can you stop by the science building when we leave? I'm behind on my labs, so I need you to drop me off."

"You don't want to eat lunch first?"

"I brought some snacks to pacify me, but usually there are less people during lunch, which is easier for me to navigate."

"Oh, alright. Paul, what about you?" He pointed with his expression toward Emily.

"I'll make sure she gets settled. We'll meet later for practice."

Sarah and Emily veered to the women's changing room as Paul split to the men's. Opening her locker, Sarah sat alongside Emily who was half dressed before Sarah could fish her own sweats from the bottom of her bag.

Tugging her hoodie over her head, Sarah pulled her hair through and bent at her waist, flipping the strands behind her. Wrapping the towel around her hair, she pressed out the remaining water then twisted the ends to form a bun. "How do I look?" she teased.

"Like Cleopatra, of course."

Their laughter quietened as the door to the main lobby opened. Following the click of heels, a tall blonde with a noticeable chest that showed through her braless shirt rounded the corner. "Hi," offered Sarah. The lady returned with a polite smile but said nothing. Sarah's eyes followed her to the next bench. Without consideration, the blonde removed her shirt and pants while taking her underwear with them. The thought of stripping in front of strangers felt odd but seeing someone else do so developed a new awkwardness. Leaving the woman to change, Sarah closed her locker and quickly wheeled Emily to the door.

"Do you know that girl?" asked Emily.

"I've never seen her in my life. Why?"

"You acted like you did."

"Oh, I just thought I'd say hello, and then she caught me by surprise."

Losing interest in the girl, Emily returned to her main thought, "Did you ask Michael about the wedding?"

"No. Not yet."

"What are you waiting on?"

"We've only seen each other once. Even that was only dinner at his place, so I don't count it as a date."

Emily settled into the car as Sarah loaded the chair. Paul's face appeared at the door moments later as they concluded their conversation. Sarah placed her hands on the wheel, intending on heading toward school as soon as Paul was buckled. However, she knew Emily was right. Taking your girlfriend to a wedding felt desperate, and besides, she needed a date for Emily's wedding too.

Sarah pulled the gear shift into reverse, but her foot remained on the brake. With one final thought, she shoved the handle into park and jumped out of the car.

"Where are you going?" asked Paul. But Sarah did not give a reply as Emily was already explaining before the car door even closed.

A breeze met Sarah's damp hair as she scurried to the entrance and pulled the door open against the wind. Michael's office sat just to the side of the pool, leaving her to venture down the hall, past the locker rooms. As she approached the training room, Sarah heard laughter emerging from inside. She slowed as she reached the doorframe to peer inside. At first, she noticed the blonde that displayed quite a show to her and Emily, but only when she realized the girl was not alone did Sarah halt mid step. Dressed in scrubs with his wet hair combed sat Michael. His chair edged the table on which the blonde was seated. Her legs lay stretched out as his hands ran up her calf, past her knee, and rested on her upper thigh. Before he could slide his hand further, Sarah coughed to announce her presence.

Turning from the girl, Michael's smile never faded as he greeted Sarah. "Hey, Sarah. Did you forget something?"

"Umm, no. Not exactly. Can I talk to you in the hall for a second?"

"Sure. Isabel, I'll be right back." He stood from his stool and followed Sarah outside, closing the door behind them. "What's up?" Sarah focused to regather her thoughts, but in good faith, she could not continue without clearing her mind from what she had seen.

"Who is Isabel?"

"She's a new patient of mine. Started coming right after Emily. The poor girl injured her knee. I'm having to massage all the muscles above, below, and around to prevent any further damage." Settling his eyes on Sarah, his smile faded. "Was that what you came to ask me?"

"Oh no. I bumped into her when we were changing, so just curious. Actually, I was wondering, that is, I have to attend a wedding and wanted to see if you would go. Emily was going to accompany me, but I thought I might ask you."

"I like a good wedding. Is it anyone I might know?"

"No, it's a friend from home. I hate not to go but—"

"Yeah. You can count me in. We'll talk details later but let me get back to Isabel." He leaned over to kiss her forehead before rejoining the blonde. She waited to listen as they began talking, but his words were muffled through the wooden barrier.

Without any security from eavesdropping, Sarah peeled her ear from the door. This was his job, and even though his hands were running across another girl's smooth legs, she had no reason to doubt him otherwise. More importantly, they were not a couple; however, they were set for another date. The thought appeased her unrest as she walked back to the car.

Emily wasted no time once the door opened. "So . . . What did he say?"

"He acted glad to."

"Oh great! But you don't look so happy."

"It's nothing really, but the blonde from the locker room is apparently one of his patients."

"Yeah . . . I'm sure he has lots of female patients. What's your point?"

"You saw her."

"I did, but—" Emily turned and faced Paul. "Do guys want to sleep with every girl that walks by them?" He raised his brow and glanced at Sarah's face through the mirror.

"Thanks, Emily . . ." he sighed, "We're not animals, but sure, we think a lot of things, but that doesn't mean we'll act on it. I'd say with any guy there's that chance, but that's why you get to know them first."

Sarah relaxed, realizing the overreaction. Buckling her seat belt, they headed to campus. Paul and Emily continued to talk as Sarah considered that perhaps her prayers would be answered sooner than later. Michael could be the guy she had hoped for all along, and now the pieces were starting to fall in place. A smile formed on her lips as she awaited the traffic light to change.

"Sarah? Did you hear me?"

"Sorry, Emm. I was . . . Never mind. What did you say?"

"Where's the wedding going to be?"

"They decided on having it at his church, so I'll go home that weekend."

"That sounds good and all, but what about Michael?"

"What about him?"

"You invited him to the wedding, remember? He will either have to stay at your parents' with you, or you two can get a hotel, but either way, it looks like you'll be spending the night together."

CHAPTER 9:

Stay with Me

Rain droplets blurred the windshield as the wind rocked the car. Pulling into a parking space outside the dining hall, Sarah ran to the awning, realizing opening an umbrella would prove useless. Pulling her hood from her head, she reached to open the door as a group of girls bustled outside. One caught the side of her shoulder but showed no remorse as they hurriedly dispersed in anticipation of the rain.

Inside, a lunch crowd slowly formed around the buffet and hot lines. Sarah fixed a salad before finding chicken strips sizzling under a heat lamp. Placing the tongs back on the stand, she turned at the sound of a soft voice.

"Hey, Sarah."

"Abby! What are you doing here? I usually don't see you during the day unless you're studying."

"I know, but I have some good news. This semester I started a new job with the school. The hours are much better and with the money I put away last fall, I won't have to work as much."

"That's great. So, shall we get a table?"

"Yeah, pick out a table while I get my drink."

As Abby made her way across the room, Sarah watched as she weaved through the crowd, as to join her moments later.

"Have you been coming in about this time every day?"

"Pretty much. Usually, I'm in the back by myself. Ralph can't meet me, so it's been lonely," she laughed.

"How are things going between you two?"

"I've been trying to slow things down with him."

"Are you thinking about breaking it off?"

"Oh no. Not like that. You remember what I told you and Emily before?"

"Yeah, so physically?"

"I mean I love him and being together, but I want to keep things in perspective." Abby's eyes deviated from Sarah to solely on her plate.

"Sorry, we don't have to talk about Ralph."

"Actually, there's something I wanted to talk to you about."

"What is it?"

Lowering her voice just above a whisper, Abby struggled with how to convey what she wanted to know. "The other day, Ralph started to run his hand up my leg, but he kept going. At first, I was nervous, but then those feelings turned into something I've never felt."

"What do you mean?"

"Just as I was getting comfortable with the idea, he pulled his hand away. However, in the same motion, he slid it beneath my jeans and into my underwear."

"Did you stop him?"

"That's the thing. I didn't want him to stop."

"So, what happened?"

"The way we were situated, was kinda odd, so he loosened my jeans and slid them down to my thighs. The next thing I knew he was inside me."

Sarah leaned back, puzzling at what Abby was trying to tell or ask her. "Did Ralph do something stupid?"

"No, he didn't. But I did. I'd never done that with anyone, so I wasn't sure what to do. The initial uncomfortable part passed when I started to relax. I think we were doing fine just enjoying the intimacy. However, just as I felt fine with everything that was going on, I looked down and noticed blood on his fingers. At first, I thought I had somehow started my period early, so I stopped him immediately. It was really embarrassing, and I could have handled it better. Honestly, I freaked out. I pushed him off me and ran to the bathroom. He started to follow, but I yelled at him to go home."

"You yelled at him? I would think you were too quiet to muster that kind of response."

"Sarah, I don't know where it came from. That's not like me at all. By the time I returned from the bathroom, he was gone."

"Have you talked to him since?"

"I'm afraid to, so I've been avoiding him. Not only am I embarrassed for how I acted, but I can't even explain to him what happened."

"Abby. It's alright. If Ralph was willing to take the relationship that far, he should know that means a whole other level of female issues to deal with," she laughed.

"You think?"

"I mean he started to follow you to the bathroom, didn't he? I doubt he would have ventured to check on you if he didn't care."

"Maybe. But what if we do it again and I freak out on him a second time?"

"I don't think you will. Once you've been in a vulnerable spot with someone, and they help see you through it, the situation will just make you closer."

"I hope so. Not just for him, but for me. Really, I just want to be the perfect girl for Ralph."

"That's great, but don't forget to be yourself. If he doesn't like you for you then he will never be pleased to have such an amazing girlfriend. Look, if you want, I can talk to him. I know Ralph well enough to discuss something like this."

"That's alright, Sarah. I really appreciate it, but it would be better coming from me. Thank you for talking. Just having a friend to listen and get advice from makes a big difference."

"Anytime, Abby." Sliding back from the table, Abby stood with her tray. "Where are you going?"

"To find Ralph."

"You can finish your lunch first. He can wait fifteen more minutes," she directed. Abby smiled and sat back across from Sarah. "I will say one thing you should consider: Are you going to want to have sex with him?"

"Honestly, I'm not real sure."

"If he is moving the physical part of the relationship along then that would be the next step."

"Yeah, I know. He's already mentioned it. He asked if I was on birth control, or if I thought about getting on it."

"What did you say?"

"I'm not, but I'll think about it. I really didn't know how to respond."

"Do you think he was asking in a way to show he was ready to, or was he digging to see if you were already on the pill and looking to move the relationship along?"

"Humm, now that you say it that way, I didn't consider the other possibility. When I told him no, he settled down for the most part. At least, he didn't mention it anymore."

"What do you want, Abby?"

She exhaled deeply, looking down at her thumbs. "I'm just afraid. What if I regret it? What if he thinks I'm a whore for being willing? What if we break up after I lose my virginity to him?"

"Abby," Sarah said, clasping her hands. "Clearly, you're thinking about this to the point that you're not ready. And, you can always tell him no. No rule says you must have sex if you're dating. Honestly, I think you would be happier if you waited."

"But what if he leaves me to find a girl that will?"

"He could, but sex won't be the last decision you make as a couple. If he leaves you over that, he'll leave you over anything else that hinders the relationship."

"Do you think I've already messed up by letting things escalate this far?"

"It probably gave him the wrong impression of what you were comfortable with. Like I said, just tell him what you want and set the boundaries. Most guys need some direction."

"Is that what you usually do in this situation? I mean, have you dealt with this before?"

Sarah sighed knowing the truth, yet considering, it would benefit Abby more than for her to pass off the experience. "Not exactly, but similarly. I've let myself get comfortable with a guy too soon, when in reality I just wanted someone that cared about me. I still struggle with finding the right way, but I just know it would have been better if I had taken things slower, whether I wanted to be more intimate or not . . . How does Ralph treat you though?"

"He's been amazing. I doubt he tells anyone, but he waits on me whenever I come home late from work. And don't get me wrong, you've seen me after an argument, but we always make up. I think that's what makes it so hard to slow down, because of how much we love each other."

"Speaking of Ralph, here he comes now," Sarah interrupted.

"Hey, Sarah," he smiled before looking to address Abby. "Hey, Abby. Do you have a minute?"

"Here. You can take my spot. I need to head to class anyways. See you later, Abby?" she questioned for assurance that it was alright for her to leave.

"Yeah. Oh, and if you like, I can swing by to pick you and Emily up for practice."

"That sounds good to me. Ralph, can you get Paul today?"

"Paul, yeah sure," he responded, still focusing on Abby.

Not that Sarah worried to leave Abby with Ralph, but she was curious as to what Abby would say. Walking away from the table, Sarah rounded the section of booths and sat on the other side of the partition. Sipping on her water she listened as Ralph talked.

"Is everything okay? I'm not sure what happened the other night. Just as I thought we were going good, you . . . you . . ."

"Freaked out. I know, and I'm sorry. Some of this is new to me and I got embarrassed."

"Embarrassed? Why?"

"I rather not say."

Ralph scratched his head, revisiting that night. "You've got me, Abby. But how are we supposed to do things like that if I can't tell how you feel?"

"You're right, and I won't do it again. I promise."

"It's not like I'm mad, just really confused. What if we were having sex, and you weren't able to just get up and run off?"

"Ralph, I don't think we should have sex." Abby said, just barely over a whisper. Ralph remained silent before Abby continued. "It's nothing to do with us, but you're right, what if we were, and I couldn't handle it. Clearly, I'm not ready to go that far." Ralph remained silent as she waited. "Say something . . . Please, Ralph."

"What am I supposed to say? My girlfriend just told me she doesn't want to have sex, and I wasn't even asking."

"Not ever. Just right now. Who knows, I could be ready after a few more months."

"Do you think you will?" he questioned, but no reply left Abby's lips. "I guess not."

"What do you want from me?" Abby choked.

"Abby, you're painting me out as someone who just wants to get lucky. I want to do like everyone else and date, have a fun relationship, and experience things together. Sex just happens to be one of them. If you aren't ready, then there's no use in trying to convince you." Ralph gave a heavy sigh, as Sarah moved to the edge of her seat, debating if she should come to Abby's rescue. "How about this? We'll forget about sex; instead, what if we pick up where we left off? We won't go any further, until you say so."

"You aren't going to find another girl to hook up with, are you?"

"Seriously? No. Just try not to leave me in the dark again. That stuff messes with a guy's head."

"Okay, I promise."

Realizing she was still eavesdropping, Sarah snuck away from the booth before they were able to spot her. Walking outside, she couldn't help but smile. Although Abby had not stuck completely to her guns, she was starting to speak up for herself. Even though she herself still struggled in the relationship department, seeing two people come to an agreement brought Sarah hope.

Abby's face shown through the doorway as Sarah led Emily to the car. Unsure if she was comfortable discussing their earlier conversation in front of Emily, she greeted her accordingly. "Ralph's still getting Paul, right?"

"Yep. I just came from there, and Ralph left the same time I did. And Sarah, thanks again for earlier."

"You're welcome. Everything went well and you feel better about the situation?"

"I do. Much better."

Unaccustomed to being excluded from a conversation, Emily quickly affirmed the need for the complete story. Abby filled in the missing details and recounted the conversation as she drove to the track. Sarah nodded intently as Abby's story remained true to what she overheard.

"Good for you, Abby," said Emily. "You give them an inch, and they will take a mile if you don't watch them."

"Is that how you got your hickey?" Sarah interrupted.

"We're engaged—"

"I remember that mark being before he proposed."

"Okay, you win, but he wasn't going too far without a ring. Speaking of which, Abby, Sarah is going to be my maid of honor, but I would love it if you would be a bridesmaid."

"Emily, I'd be honored! When are you having the wedding?"

"We're planning for this summer. Sometime soon after graduation."

Abby turned onto the road beside the track that led to the parking lot. As the car stopped, Emily waited inside as the others came around to her door. Each took hold of Emily's sides, bracing incase her strength faltered. Slow but steady, Emily walked to the fence before grabbing hold of the rail. Sarah remained on her left as they started the trek to the pit.

Easing the weight on her shoulders, Sarah shifted her concentration from Emily. Lifting her eyes, Sarah noticed the team starting their warm-up. At first, the sight of Nigel bore little concern for her, but as the group spaced out, his distance with Jenna remained the same. Upon their entering the curve, Sarah could hear their voices amongst any other distractions.

"Are you coming back over tonight?" Jenna asked.

"I can," Nigel said suavely.

Her heart sank and fear coursed her body. Questions with answers of further discontent rose in her head. Neither Nigel nor Jenna drifted their eyes in her direction, nor did their voices carry unusually loud. The conversation was true, sincere, and not meant to bash her presence. Losing Nigel brought heartaches she had overcame, but the confirmation of his new relationship struck with a blunt force.

"Did you hear that?" Emily sputtered. Sarah refused to admit the obvious, but her slight nod left no question to the fact that denial was of no use. "I bet they're already sleeping together. He probably—"

"Emm, please don't. I rather not think about it."

"Sorry. I guess we were right about them being a couple. But the good news is you've moved on too. Maybe you should get Mr. Physical Therapist to come watch you race. Then you can snuggle up with Michael in front of Nigel. Give him a taste of his own medicine."

"That's not a bad idea, at least inviting Michael to a race. He runs, so he'd probably enjoy it."

"I still think you should rub it in Nigel's face."

"That might make me feel better," Sarah laughed, "but I don't really want him back."

"You just don't want him to be happy, or happier than you, right?"

"Ha! Exactly, Emm. You know me so well."

Sarah lowered her voice as they made a second pass around the track, listening intently. "Try to be quieter this time. I don't want to wake up my roommates."

Sarah's heart fell, heavy with confrontation. All lingering doubts of their relationship's details vanished, and a crushed conscience took their place.

"Sarah, I wish you hadn't heard that."

"Me too. But I did." Sarah wiped her cheek with her finger before dispelling a deep breath. "If he wants to screw her then by all means."

As Emily reached the bleachers, Sarah took off to warm up with Abby. Her thoughts remained fixed on Nigel and Jenna's conversation, but she forced the pain through her muscles and out her legs. The desire to release all her energy hung in the balance as she maintained control of her emotions throughout the mile.

Going through the stretches, her heart pounded as the intensity of her emotions pulsated her blood. "Are you okay, Sarah?" Abby whispered.

Again, Sarah nodded. "Abby, I want you to stay with me on these two-hundreds."

"Of course, we're in the same pace group."

"That's going to change, just stay with me."

After the guys took to the track, Sarah and Abby paired together on the line. To the sound of her watch, they launched forward, digging into the track. They took the curve, not settling into pace by the time they reached the other side. Instead, Sarah increased the speed. Her eyes narrowed as they approached the two-hundred mark. Seeing the guys waiting to start their next repeat, she closed her eyes to drown out any sight of Nigel.

Abby broke stride just behind Sarah, placing her hands on her rib cage to aid in breathing. Once Nigel and Ralph left, Abby muttered, "You weren't kidding. I'm sure you're upset, but don't kill yourself."

"Just stay with me, Abby," she whispered as a half plea.

"Alright, I've got you."

Sarah took off again with the same fierceness. The pain drove her, convulsing her to strive harder. Each step landed and pushed with such agility; her body streamed down the front stretch. This time upon their arrival, she kept her eyes open. Seeing Nigel was fuel, and there were still laps upon laps to go.

Sarah avoided looking winded and exhausted, not giving any sign of weakness to Nigel. Her will to push through centered on her feelings but was anchored by Abby's presence. As she rested in between turns, she kept her posture straight, even though the urge to double over at the waist persisted. Even the lurch of vomit crept into her mouth, but failing to spit it out, she swallowed the bile instead.

Coach merely watched as Sarah ground around the track, his voice never ringing her ears, cautioning her to slow down or relax. Perhaps he knew what was going on, or maybe he knew her well enough to not interfere. Either way, stopping was not the answer.

CHAPTER 10:

The Past in Truth

A cold breeze howled outside the window. Seconds later, an alarming explosion sounded through the windowpane and into Sarah's room. The light that usually radiated from her nightstand clock was now dark and void. Taking hold of her watch, the time indicated what she feared for a Saturday morning. Only five o'clock, and with no power and a heart rate fast enough to win a race, going back to sleep felt useless.

The thought she had tussled with over the past few days ran back through her mind. Staying here with no power or heat no longer seemed an option. Having considered going home this weekend, Sarah threw back her covers and began fumbling across the room and down the desolate stairs.

To her surprise, the sound of Emily's snore was replaced with her voice. Unlike her sleep talks, they sounded directly at her. "Is that you?"

"Yeah. It's me. Did that loud noise wake you up too? Usually, you sleep through the worst of storms."

"No. I've been awake for about an hour. I was having a hard time sleeping, so I tried reading a book, but then the power went out. Scared the breath out of me. What are you doing?"

"I'm going home for the weekend. I need a break from everything, and who knows when the power will come on."

"Oh, alright then. Are you leaving now?" Emily said softly.

"Yeah. I can't sleep, so I figured I would," Sarah said, turning for the door.

"Have fun, Sar."

She paused, then looked back to Emily. "You're coming with me," she laughed, and although Sarah couldn't see, she felt the smile that brightened Emily's face.

"I would need to pack some clothes first, and I don't want to impede on your family time."

"Emm. You are family. I'll start the car, then come get you. As for clothes, don't worry about it. You can wear anything of mine that you want."

"What about your parents, and where would I sleep?"

"My parents would love to see that you're getting better. Also, since when have you worried about where you'll sleep? My bed is big enough for us both."

"I'll be right back." Sarah grabbed her jacket and rushed into the cold darkness, slamming the door behind her. Running her key into the car door lock, Sarah yanked on the latch, making several tugs against the frozen precipitation. A night owl hooted in the distance, making a mockery at her dismay, until she finally broke through the ice and jumped inside. Patting the gas, the engine clicked repeatedly until finally firing to life. Sarah knotted her sleeve inside her fist, then ran her arm across the window to dispel the fog. Peering out, she could see the source of her morning chaos. The transformer on the power pole connected to their apartment had blown and now lay dangling above.

She fingered the console, adjusting the thermostat before jutting outside. Dashing through the door, Sarah kicked off her shoes while blindly running toward Emily. As she reached the bed, Sarah dove onto the mattress, pulling the covers up and around them.

"Emm, it's freezing."

Emily's heated body latched around Sarah, attempting to calm her shivers. Resting her head along the pillow, Sarah could feel Emily's breath upon her face as she inhaled her warmth. Despite their closeness, the outline of Emily's body was lost in the darkness.

Almost settling into a comfort to which she could return to sleep, Sarah lifted her head. "Have you been drinking coffee? And your pillow feels damp."

"Oh, sorry. I said I couldn't sleep, so I figured I'd wake myself up with coffee. I must have spilled some on the pillow when the power went out."

"You made coffee at four in the morning?" she laughed.

"Actually, it finished perking just before the power shut off."

Sarah lifted her arm and felt her way to the bedside table. Her hand paused over a steaming cup. Looping her fingers through the handle, she pulled the rim to her lips and took a sip. She enjoyed the burn running down her throat, revitalizing her insides from the morning chill.

"That feels better. Are you ready to get going?"

"I'm ready when you are."

Emily steadied herself to the side of the bed as Sarah assisted in tying her shoes. Once on her feet, Emily remained stable, even as Sarah turned away for a few seconds to retrieve their coats.

"Should we bring your chair?"

Emily looked back across the room, imagining where she last left it. "No. Michael said I needed to get on my feet. I rather leave it."

"If you insist. I don't imagine us doing much walking anyways."

A new welcome sign marked with green letters and a white backdrop greeted them as they entered Sarah's hometown. In the distance, the sun's rays began to shine over the trees and the winter morning drifted away, allowing a new brightness to fill the day as they rolled to a stop at a lone traffic light.

Following the signal, Sarah turned on Main Street, pointing out places as they passed. "The old brick building along that side road is my elementary school. And that over there is—" she paused as they slowed in front of a steeple faced church.

"That's what, Sarah? Why did you stop?"

"The church."

"Whose? Yours?"

"No. No, it's Wesley's. I haven't been inside since we dated. Seeing it feels surreal."

"Didn't you say the wedding would be here?"

"Yeah. Honestly, I'm not sure how I feel about going anymore. Michael said he would come, but will that be any better?"

"I know what you need," Emily said, unbuckling her seatbelt.

"Where are you going?"

"We . . . are going inside. If you go in now, that'll help get rid of any residing emotions before the wedding. The last thing you want is to have an awkward breakdown, at an ex's wedding, with some other guy."

"That's not a terrible idea. However, it's Saturday morning. I doubt the doors are open."

"Only one way to find out."

Sarah parked and rushed around to Emily's door, as she was already halfway to her feet. "What if someone sees us and calls the police?"

"Oh, I can see the headlines now. *Two young, innocent-look-ing women, one handicapped, were arrested for wanting to go inside a church.*"

Sarah knew if Emily had the strength, she would have dragged her inside regardless. Instead of resisting, and hoping the idea would work, she complied as Emily anchored herself to the handrail.

Emily reached out and jostled the knob, but to Sarah's surprise, the door opened. Sticking their heads inside, Sarah broke the silence, "Anybody here—" Emily cupped her hand over Sarah's mouth.

"Quiet. We don't want anyone to know we're here. Just walk around and envision what the wedding will look like, then try to focus on keeping any tears to yourself."

"Okay. Should I walk down the aisle to the front, or sit in the back?"

"Well, you aren't the bride . . . so let's just sit down for a minute."

Sarah led the way to the back bench and slid in, allowing Emily to take the edge. "Please tell me this isn't where you used to sit with Wesley."

"No, we always sat toward the front," Sarah recalled, pointing to the exact spot.

"Maybe this wasn't the best idea."

"Just give me a few minutes to process. Like you said, I rather get out the emotions now and not have issues at the wedding."

Sarah sat pondering her past, letting the emotions come and go freely. Being here again felt more like a dream than anything. Everything remained exactly as it was before, yet nothing around her seemed real anymore. Maybe the past was just that, and there was no place for it in the present.

A closing door echoed from within the church. Sarah jolted her head into Emily's lap, attempting to conceal her whole body. Unable to move, Emily lowered her body onto Sarah, hiding herself below the back of the bench. Footsteps echoed down the aisle and carried closer and closer until finally stopping.

"Can I help you?"

Emily lifted her face and wiped her eyes with one hand. "No thanks, we're just praying." The man displayed a confused look as Sarah kept her head buried.

Studying the two girls, he leaned over the bench for a closer look. "Sarah, is that you?" She grimaced at the sound of her name, but slowly retreated from Emily's protection.

"Hey . . . Wesley. Fancy seeing you here."

"Ha. I would say the same, but this is my church you know. I like to come in on Saturdays before services, make sure the heat is on and no pipes are leaking," he said, looking about the building.

"I mean, I thought you moved?"

"You're right; I did. But Haley and I began discussing how it'd be better if we started our life together in a small town. Next thing I knew, we found a place here."

Sarah nodded along to his explanation until the questioning returned to her.

"So, did you come to actually pray?"

Sarah searched for an explanation, but Emily proved to be a few steps ahead.

"Actually, I wanted to stop by and see where the wedding would be. Then, we got scared when we heard you," she laughed.

"Oh, I see. Well, make yourselves at home. Are you Sarah's plus one?"

Sarah knew this question rested on her. There was no need to lie. Even after all these years, she knew better than to consider lying to someone that knew her better than most anyone.

"Originally yes, but actually a guy I've been dating is coming now."

"Oh good, you've met Haley already, so it'll be nice to meet . . ."

"Michael."

"Hey, since you and Michael will be traveling, why don't you attend the dress rehearsal dinner?"

"Oh, I don't know. That's usually for the family and wedding party."

"You would actually be doing Haley and me a favor."

"A favor?"

"My aunt and uncle RSVP'd for themselves and two kids, but I received word she is having surgery that week, so they thought it best not to come. We've already paid the caterer, and I told Haley I'd take care of it. However, we've already invited all our close friends, which leaves me in a bind."

"And, you'll have to excuse me for being rude. I'm Wesley, what's your name?" he said, extending a hand to Emily.

"Emily Ellis. It's nice to meet you. Sarah has told me about you." Sarah managed a nudge into Emily's side, unnoticed by Wesley.

"Only good things I hope," he smiled at Sarah.

"Of course," she teased.

"Well, Emily, now that we've officially met, can you make it to the rehearsal dinner, and possibly bring a date?"

"Certainly, I'll bring my fiancé, Paul."

"Ah, then congratulations are in order for you as well."

"Thanks. Perhaps you and Haley can attend. I'll get your address from Sarah."

"That sounds great. Speaking of Haley, I told her I would meet for breakfast, so I must get going." He paused before leaving, adding, "Do you two need to stay here longer? I just ask because I'll need to lock the doors, but I don't mind swinging by later if I need to."

"We appreciate it, but we're on our way to my parents."

The two followed Wesley down the aisle and out the front. He gave each of them a hug before locking the door and heading to his truck. As he disappeared into the cab, Sarah cut to Emily, who was walking unaccompanied to the car.

"Umm . . . what are you doing?"

"I'm walking. I think I'm progressing quite well. Don't you?"

"I mean with Wesley. We don't have any business at the rehearsal."

"Sarah, you overthink way too much. You should be thanking me now."

"Thanking you?"

"Yeah. I just saved your rear in two ways. One, by suggesting that I was the one who wanted to see the church."

"Thanks, even though it was your idea. But what was the second?"

"Now I'll be at the wedding with you, which will take some of the pressure off spending the night with Michael."

"Was that your plan the whole time?"

Emily shrugged her shoulders. "I guess it doesn't matter either way," she laughed.

"I guess not."

"By the way, he is really cute. Why did you two break up in the first place?"

Sarah pondered the question before trying to give an answer. "You know, I'm not really sure. When he left for college, I remember the distance was a heavy strain for us both. The entire summer beforehand was nothing short of perfect. I loved him, and he loved me. I remember thinking that we might even get married. He was a great guy, but not long after Christmas break, we started arguing about something. That broke my heart more than anything. I knew I wanted to spend the rest of my life with him. However, when we were together, our conversations went from loving to lashing out. Once we broke things off for about three months; I didn't speak to or see him. It felt like the hardest time ever in my life. Every night I cried myself to sleep. I envisioned him dating a college girl who would surely convince him to sleep with her."

"What happened after three months?"

"One Friday after getting home from school, he was waiting at my house. Seeing him, I felt elated, but still extremely hurt. When I got out of the car, all I could do was fall into his arms. I'd never stopped loving him, so I agreed to give the relationship another chance. The rest of the semester was tough, but we made it to summer. At that point, we began talking about marriage. I never told my parents, but we looked at rings and I picked one out. I'm fairly certain he went to Dad to ask for my hand, but neither of them said anything to me about it."

"Wait, were you engaged?"

"I guess you might as well know. We didn't tell anyone, but yes. Wesley asked me to marry him the night before he left for school. I told him I loved him, and I would be his wife. We planned on making the announcement at Thanksgiving, so we could share the news with our families. Then, the wedding would take place the following summer after I graduated. To be fair, I kept the ring tucked away, so my parents wouldn't find out before his. Every night, I would take it out of the box, and wear it to sleep. I couldn't wait to be Mrs. Wesley Parker."

"You've never told anyone?"

"No. Never. Later that semester, the distance again drove us apart. When Thanksgiving rolled around, Wesley and I talked and decided to not tell everyone else. I was heartbroken but knew we couldn't go on like we were. That night I cried in his arms. Seeing me devastated left him in tears as well. We didn't want to end it, but we needed a break, and we rather not keep hurting one another. So, when he left to go back to school, we said our goodbyes and parted ways. The last thing we talked about was agreeing not to mention the engagement. We thought doing so would only make matters worse. We wanted to stay friends and try to move on with our lives. However, after that night, I probably didn't speak to him again until this past Christmas."

"Sarah, I didn't realize y'all were so . . . so—"

"It's alright, Emm. No one does."

"Is his invitation to the wedding a peace offering? Or what?"

"I don't know, but I was afraid to say no. If we're ever going to be friends then it has to start with his new life."

"Are you that concerned with remaining friends?"

"You met him. He's a hard person to hate. And I don't have room for real hate in my heart."

"Even for Nigel?" Emily joked.

"Easy, Emm. But I don't hate Nigel. He just knows how to upset me, or rather I still need to find peace with him." Sarah looked to Emily, who was still considering an idea on the tip of her tongue. "What . . . What is it, Emm?"

"Can I ask what you did with the ring?"

"Wesley's ring?"

"No Nigel's . . . Yes, you conveniently skipped over that part."

"Umm . . . I'd rather not say."

"Sarah, you didn't!"

"It's not like that. I offered to give it back to him on Thanksgiving Day. I told him I would always love him, but the ring no longer belonged to me. When I pulled the box out of my coat jacket to hand to him, he just stood there. I told him to take it, and not cause a scene. Then, he did something I will never forget. He took the ring out of the box, slid it onto my finger and asked, if you love me, will you still marry me whenever we can finally be together?"

Emily's mouth dropped, holding as she waited for Sarah to continue.

"Don't stop, what did you say?"

"I said no."

"No?"

"I said no . . . If you want to marry me then we do it now, tonight. He took a moment to think it over, but eventually he said yes. He gave me the most loving kiss I've ever had and grabbed my hand as we drove off in his truck. He decided to head to his preacher's house, but we didn't take a moment to plan anything else. I had on jeans and a jacket, and him pretty much the same. The whole drive, we were excited. Wesley even said he'd rent a nice hotel room, so we'd be together that night."

"Are you saying that you went through with the wedding?"

CHAPTER 11:

The Ring

Matty ran from the kitchen to greet them upon hearing Sarah's voice. For whatever reason, he latched on to Emily's waist first before turning his attention to Sarah. "I see who you're more excited to have home than me," Sarah joked.

"Haven't you noticed though? She's standing!"

"She is much better. I can't argue with you there."

"Sarah!" called her mom. "I wasn't expecting you home for the weekend. It's so nice to see you. And Emily, you are looking amazing. What made you decide to come home?"

"For starters, we lost power this morning, but I'd been considering making a trip soon, so the timing worked out best for today."

"Make yourselves at home. I was about to start breakfast. How do pancakes sound?"

"I would love some," said Emily.

"I'll second that," Sarah followed.

"I third it," Matty persisted.

"Matty, you don't have to third a motion."

"If I didn't, then how would Mom know to include me?"

"Honey, I always know to account for you. You girls can relax upstairs or on the couch if you like. Your father went to town but should be back in an hour or so."

Emily followed Sarah to the stairs, determined that she could walk on her own. Even as they ascended, Emily worked her way carefully from the bottom to the top as Sarah stood anxiously behind her. Despite the exertion required, Emily looked pleased as she cleared the last step.

"I told you I could do it. I'm bound and determined to stay out of that chair."

"I'm proud of you, Emm. Now can I interest you in lying down?"

"That's probably a good idea," she laughed. "I said I could do it. That didn't mean I wouldn't have to rest afterward."

Emily continued to the edge of Sarah's bed before plopping hard onto the mattress. Sarah took a seat beside her, bracing her arm behind Emily. "Do you think you could actually take a nap?"

"No, I'm wide awake, but I should probably rest my legs."

The door creaked open and a curious Matty slid his head through the opening. "Can I come in?"

"Sure, Matty. We're just talking about girl stuff," Sarah said in an effort to deter him.

"Yuck, what if we change the subject?"

"I guess. What are you wanting to talk about?"

"Emily, can I sit beside you?"

"Sure, what's up?"

Matty climbed on the bed beside Emily and laid his head in her lap.

"Matty, I don't think she meant that she would hold you."

"He's alright," said Emily as she stroked his hair. "I don't have siblings, so I get it."

Matty lay in silence for a few minutes before revisiting a conversation that likely floated through his head since their arrival.

"Where are your parents? How come you don't have a brother or sister?"

Emily looked to Sarah whose appalled face only lightened when Emily met her with a smile. "My parents are at their house. Sarah invited me to visit this weekend. As for siblings, I'm the only child because they only wanted one kid, or I probably proved to be too much of a handful for them to handle another."

"Matty, are you sure you don't want to help Mom?"

"Not really, but I guess I can," Matty said, lifting his head slowly from Emily. He bounced from the room, leaving the door open. Sarah lifted from the bed and went quietly to shut and lock the door behind him.

"I'm sorry. I don't know what got into him."

"It's alright. He just wanted to be held," said Emily, reclining onto Sarah's pillows.

"Does Paul ever just hold you in his arms?"

"He does. And the best part is, I don't have to make him. He usually does it on his own."

Sarah climbed on the bed beside Emily and closed her eyes. She imagined being held by a guy once again, not cuddling after fooling around, but concluding a long day by wrapping up in someone's arms.

Emily continued to talk about her relationship and Paul's gentleness, as Sarah's eyelids flickered heavily. Exhausted, both girls fell asleep from the adventurous morning.

Only moments later, a rapid knock emitted from the door, causing the girls to startle awake. "Sarah, Sarah, Sarah! Dad's home, and breakfast is ready. Are you going to let me in?"

"Coming, Matty," Sarah said answering his unceasing call.

She waited for Emily to reach the door before she attempted to help. Going up the stairs was likely harder for her, but Sarah feared going down more, on the off chance that Emily could fall.

"Good morning, you two," said Cliff. "Emily, it's nice to see you on your feet. And, we're glad to have you this weekend."

"Thank you so much. I appreciate you having me."

Cliff set the plates on the table and waited for Megan and the others to join before passing around the stack of pancakes. As he lifted the spatula for Sarah, he continued his conversation.

"I ran into Wesley's mom this morning. She mentioned you're going to his wedding," he said with an inquisitive look.

"Yeah, I was a little unsure if I should go, but seeing he thought well enough to invite me, I figured why not."

"I suppose. Are you going alone or taking a date?"

"Right now, it's shaping up to be a group thing. Caroline and Bryant will be there, and now Emily is going."

To Sarah's relief, Cliff made no further inquiries. Unsure if she should mention Michael, she thought it was best to wait. Their relationship was still new, and if Michael decided last minute not to go, there was no reason to mention him.

Throughout the remainder of breakfast, Emily remained unusually quiet. However, Sarah already knew why. Neither one contributed to the breakfast talk, but fortunately, Matty covered the speaking part for all three of them.

Once the last of the pancakes were finished, Sarah helped with cleaning the dishes, while Matty entertained Emily. For some reason, Emily appeared to enjoy his childish conversations; but his antics were cut short when Sarah pulled Emily away. Implying Emily needed to rest, Sarah hoped Matty would take the hint to not follow them upstairs.

Sarah listened with her ear to the door as Emily made herself comfortable on the bed. "I think we are fine," said Emily.

"I'm just making sure." Sarah locked the handle and bounced over beside Emily. "Okay, where were we?"

"You were saying you drove to the preacher's house, then someone you knew from high school spotted us outside the church and cut you off."

"Right. The whole drive we continued to make plans, decided how we would break the news to our parents, and what our new lives would look like. When we stopped in front of the house, we both froze. Eloping started to feel like a bad idea. I was seventeen still, and we were unsure if we could legally get married."

"So, you stopped because you were nervous about being seventeen?"

"Not exactly. Wesley started saying he'd rather get married with our families present. Which I thought so too, but I wanted to marry him then and there. However, the more he talked, the less I wanted to go through with it myself. We ended up not getting out of the car, and he drove us to a hotel."

"Why did you go there?"

"We were both pretty emotional at the time and going home seemed like it would cause more questions. Inside, we sat on the bed and talked for a few hours. At one point, I looked him in the eyes and said, 'If we had gone through with our vows, we'd be losing our virginities right now.' I don't know why I said such a thing. I think it was because I'd imagined how magical that night would be, and to be sitting on that bed and not fulfilling a marriage I'd hoped for felt surreal. Nonetheless, I said it, but it was what he said afterward that changed everything. He said, 'I've imagined us having sex and how great it would be, but it was always when we were older.'"

"What's that supposed to mean?"

"I asked him the same thing. The casualness in his voice was upsetting. He assured me nothing bad was meant, just that he felt like we were still kids. We sat in silence for a while, until he eventually asked if he should take me home. I shook my head yes and we left."

"After that night, we decided to call it quits for good. He went back to college, and I finished out my senior year. I don't know if he ever came home the following summer. I didn't tell Caroline what happened either. We agreed not to tell our family or friends and hoped everyone would assume we'd broken up. Fast forward to this past month, I've seen him twice now."

"Sarah, you never told me what happened to the ring."

Sarah looked down at her finger, twisting an imaginary ring where the engagement piece once resided. "On the way home, I looped it around my finger the entire ride. I knew once I took it off, that was the end of our relationship, and the last time I'd wear it. You know when you realize something's happening for the last time? Your stomach sinks and you can only anticipate the passing of time. When we pulled into the driveway, he leaned over and gave me a kiss. Our lips touched with such passion, I almost cried when we finally pulled apart. As I reached for the door, I slid the ring over my finger and clasped our hands together. I fixed my eyes toward the floor, afraid of what I'd do if I ever looked through his eyes and into his soul. As I pulled my hand away, he grabbed my arm. 'Keep it,' he said. 'I gave it to you.' I finally raised my glossy eyes to meet his. It took every bit of control not to burst into tears.

'What would I do with it? I can't wear it.'

'Lock it away. Seal it inside your heart. Keep it forever to remember me by.'

'To remember you by? How could I ever forget you?'

'Keep it to know I love you and there's a piece of my heart that will always belong to you.'

After that, I gave him a kiss on the cheek and got out of the truck. And that was the end of us."

"And the ring?" Emily persisted. "Where is it now?"

Sarah slid to the edge of the bed and walked to her chest of drawers. Rummaging through rolls of socks, tucked in the rear, resided a velvet black box. Shoving the socks back in place, she clasped the small case in between her hands, as if cradling an egg she wished not to break.

"Open it. I need to see."

Hinging the top back, a three-diamond piece arrangement sparkled from within. Sarah's fingers gently guided the ring from its slot, laying the sentiment flat in her palm.

"You still have it after all this time?"

"Yeah. I couldn't bring myself to sell it. So instead, I buried it where only I'd know."

"Do you ever wear it?"

"Emily!"

"I'm just asking."

"This is the first time I've taken it out in years. The following few months, I wore it at night. Having done so for so long, I'd gotten to the point I couldn't sleep without it. Then one day, the thought that we'd get back together seemed childish to believe. After that, I never wore it again."

"Put it on, Sarah."

"No. That's weird and probably sinful in some way."

"Then, why do you still have it? Why would you hang on to something that long if not on some level you still believed?"

"I'll return it to Wesley. He can sell it and spend the money on his wife."

"No, no, no. Are you crazy? He can't know you held on to it all these years."

"And why not?"

"He'll think you're crazy for one. And if Haley sees it, she'll flip."

"You're right. So, what do I do?"

"Do you still love him?"

Sarah twirled the ring between her fingers, considering the question.

"Time's up. You're taking way too long to think."

"I don't not love him. We were our first loves. Doesn't that always last?"

"Maybe in fairytales, but it's time to get rid of it. I mean can you imagine if Michael knew about this. He would run away so fast, you'd never see him again."

"Okay. We can go tomorrow and sell it. You're right, he's getting married, I've moved on, so there's no reason to keep the ring. But Emily, you must promise you won't mention this to anyone. I swore I would never tell."

"I kind of pried it out of you with a million questions. Speaking of, I need to know, do you have anything else around here that's his? Pictures, shirts, letters—"

Sarah clinched her cheeks and eyes together at the interrogation. "I kept all his letters. But honestly, I had forgotten about those."

"Where are they?"

"Stashed away in my closet. I think with a bunch of high school sentiments."

"Go get them."

"Why do I need those?"

Emily responded by pointing to the closet door. Sarah grudgingly did as she instructed, returning minutes later with an overstuffed box. Opening the flaps revealed pictures, knickknacks, and memories collected from the four years. Most of which were of cross country or friends, but laced together with a rubber band was a stack of letters.

"Here they are," she said handing them to Emily. "Let me guess, you think we should burn them."

"Oh no. I'm not that heartless. I have something better in mind."

Sarah rolled her eyes, "Okay, Emily. What is it then?"

"You're going to read them . . . all of them . . . to me."

"Read them all to you?"

"Don't argue. You'll either realize why you broke up and see it was dumb to keep the ring, or you'll know the whole breakup was a mistake."

"What good does that do at this point?"

"For me, I'm just nosy and want to see what went on. But for you, it'll give you closure. Just try and see." Emily handed her the top five letters and laid the others on the bed between them.

Sarah unfolded the first one and began to read aloud.

The weeks we spend apart have filled my life with darkness and sorrow. Each night I lay down to the thoughts of where you are, and what you're doing. It pains me to think you are anywhere but by my side. I know it's not fair to you to think that, but my heart hardens to bitterness and only softens in your presence.

In our last letters, you said Caroline invited you to a spend the night party; I almost drove down there myself to see who you were with. I had hoped you wouldn't go, but since there were only girls there, I felt better about the situation.

I assure you that I have only been out with the guys on our team. Some of their girlfriends tag along from time to time, but there's no need to worry. Honestly, the part to fret about is how it sickens me to see them together, wishing you could join us. I enclosed a copy of our game schedule. I thought perhaps you might come visit and watch. If you come early in the morning, we would have the day together, then after the game, you can make it home at a reasonable time. Let me know what you think.

Love,

Wesley

"Sounds like you were already having a tough time when he wrote this."

"We were, but I went to a game. And all his friends were super excited to see me, saying they wanted me to visit more often. It also helped to meet some of their girlfriends. After that day, I didn't worry as much, but the tension between us just found another issue to tug at."

"Why else were you fighting?"

"This was their fall season before Thanksgiving, so announcing the engagement was still our plan. However, I told him that I wanted to wear the ring at the game, but he said no. I guess it worked out since Mom went with me, but the way he handled it hurt. I felt like he was ashamed of us. Looking back, I know better, and he just wanted to make it official with our families first, but why not enjoy the secret between us, so I thought."

"Sarah, this all sounds weird to me."

"What do you mean?"

"Wesley inviting you to the wedding, you keeping the ring and letters; I don't think either of you have moved on."

"I promise I have."

"Prove it then."

Sarah clasped the ring in her right hand and went to the window and slid the glass open. Closing her eyes and taking a deep breath, she threw the ring into the woods.

"I'm ready to go see Michael."

CHAPTER 12:

Valentine's Day

The black dress stretched to Sarah's knees, at which point stockings wrapped around her calves and disappeared into her heels. Taking a red sweater from the closet, she pulled on the sleeves and settled the collar around the gape of her neck. Glancing in the mirror, a favorable look reflected back as her hair continued to grow out.

As a knock came at the door, she gave a final look before heading downstairs. Paul, having arrived earlier for Emily, left Sarah to answer the door. "Come in, Michael. Take a seat on the couch if you like, and I'll be ready in a minute."

"No worries, we have time."

Sarah disappeared upstairs as he moved to the living area. Her preparation for the special night was nearly complete; however, she had forgotten the diamond earrings she planned to wear. With the pins threaded through her ears, she grabbed an overcoat for warmth against the night chill.

As she met Michael in the living room, he greeted her lips with a kiss, followed by another. She pressed her hand to his chest. "Easy, we want to make it to dinner on time. Here, I got something for you." Pulling a bag from her purse, she handed him the gift. "It's not much, just some candy. Everyone says Valentine's Day is for the girl, but I thought you might like candy as well."

"Ah, thanks! This will hold over my sweet tooth for a while. I have something for you too, but I left it outside." Michael slid his hand along her back, guiding her to the door.

As they settled in the car, he reached under his seat. "Close your eyes." Doing as she was told, Sarah squeezed her eyelids together and held out her hands in anticipation. Her fingers soon clinched around something soft and light. The fur that covered the object brought no surprise as she opened her eyes. "Oh, how cute! It kind of reminds me of Daisy."

"I figured since you don't have her here, a stuffed animal might be a nice alternative."

"That's really thoughtful. Thank you."

"You're welcome."

Michael shifted into drive as he tucked the bag of candy behind his seat. "I hope you don't mind, but I made reservations for the same place as our first date."

"That sounds great. It was a really nice restaurant."

"Yeah, it is."

As they drove out of town and the lights of Beval faded behind them, Michael steadied his left hand on the steering wheel while dropping his right to rest on Sarah's leg. He rubbed the covered skin below her dress before sliding above her knee. For a moment, she thought to move his hand from her thigh, but since he refrained from climbing higher, she instead laid her hand over his. Having him close felt comforting. She looked toward Michael, and he returned her glance with a smile. "Shall I move my hand, or is it okay there?"

"It's fine where it is," she smiled, grasping his hand slightly tighter. "So, what do you have planned for tonight?"

"I thought we would start with dinner, then maybe a movie at my place. I do have one other surprise for you, but it'll have to wait until we're at the restaurant."

"Oh really?"

"Yes, but try not to guess. If you're right, I'm not sure I can keep a straight face. I'm a dead giveaway when it comes to keeping secrets."

"If you insist, I guess I can wait a little longer."

Upon their arrival, Michael was greeted by Jason once again. However, instead of being seated in a back area, they were led to the main dining room. Awaiting them was a table for two, held with a "reserved" sign and a bouquet of twelve long-stemmed roses in the middle.

"These are for you," he said, placing them in her arms.

"They're beautiful, and a nice little surprise."

"I'm glad you like them, but here, we'll place them in the vase for now."

Sarah smiled as the waiter pulled her seat out and began explaining the menu.

"The dinner is a prescheduled meal of steak with roasted carrots and green beans. Each plate also comes with a side salad, then a chocolate dessert with custard to finish."

Sarah nodded as the man quickly disappeared, leaving the two seemingly secluded with a candle light that barely surpassed their table's edge. Michael reached across the table, taking Sarah's hands in his. She leaned forward, half relaxing and half anticipating a kiss to complete the mood. However, just as she became settled in the moment, the waiter returned with two main courses.

"So, why are you so fond of this place? Is it because you know the owner?"

"Umm, yes and no . . ." he hesitated. "It's also one of the nicest places around, but I like coming here because it has character."

"Character?"

"It's not one of those dopey chains that look like every other place you've been. I like things that catch my eye, draw me in, and keep me coming back . . . like you . . ." he smiled. Sarah placed her hand across the table and linked their fingers together, only for them to pull apart as each hesitantly reached for their knives to slice another piece.

Before the last bites of steak were consumed, a bowl arrived with a steaming brownie, covered with a lite topping, tiny morsels, and a dripping of chocolate sauce.

"I think they forgot to bring a second."

"Not quite," Michael laughed. "It's meant to be shared," he explained, handing her a spoon.

"When Emm and I split something, we always have to divide it through the middle. Otherwise, we'll race to get the last bite," she laughed.

"Whatever works for you."

Sarah sliced her spoon across the bowl before scooping her portion over to the side.

"Hey, yours is slightly bigger," Michael alleged.

"I said we divided it. I never meant that I was fair in doing so."

Michael found her leg under the table and gave a squeeze to the back of her thigh, causing a squeal to emerge from Sarah's mouth. Quickly, she bit her lips in embarrassment. "Michael! Don't do that."

"Think of it as me getting my missing bite," he laughed.

"Now that we are even, I wanted to ask you something. Would you want to come watch one of my races? It'd be a home meet, so you wouldn't need to travel far."

"I would love to. One thing though."

"What's that?"

"If I come watch then you have to promise you'll win for me."

"I'll do my best like usual," she negotiated with a grin.

"I'm going to need a win," he said unwaveringly.

"A win, huh? I'll give you a win, but you better be ready to hug me with all my sweat when I do."

"That should be easy enough. I think you forgot how we first met."

"Fair enough," she laughed.

Sarah took a few bites of her brownie as Michael watched with entertained eyes.

"How about we get a to-go box for the rest? Waiter!"

The sky lay crinkled like a blanket of stars with a full moon as they transitioned from the warm restaurant into the brisk night air. A line of couples still gathered past the entrance, awaiting a table. Sarah hurried Michael from the crowd as she fled to the car. The inside still felt warm in nature, but even so, the engine took a few minutes to revive the heater. Sarah nestled her head on Michael's shoulder while he threaded his arm around her, staying pressed together even as they left the parking lot.

"I have a few movies picked out. Do you prefer scary, or is romance your style?"

Sarah leaned her head up and kissed him on the cheek. "I don't mind. Either is fine. But can we watch it at my place instead?"

"Won't Emily and Paul be there? I was just thinking it might be more enjoyable to watch alone."

"Seeing that we just started dating, I rather watch it with them."

"You don't want to be alone on Valentine's Day though? You've already been to my place before."

Sarah sighed at his persistency, "Okay, you win, but just a movie. Deal?"

"You're a tough girl, but deal. Besides, we won't be alone."

"What do you mean?"

"Bessie will be there. Did you forget?"

"Ha, how could I," Sarah laughed, laying her head on his shoulder again.

Resting comfortably, Sarah could have nodded off, if not for the gentle touch of Michael stroking her arm. Without hesitation,

Sarah would have sat there all night; however, as they pulled into his drive, she found herself reluctantly leaving the warmth of his body.

"Make yourself at home while I stick this in the refrigerator."

Sarah sat on the couch, pulling a blanket from behind. A few moments later, Michael returned with a tape in his hand. "If I'm choosing then we're going with the scary movie."

Adjusting the television, Michael retreated to the couch where Sarah awaited lifting the blanket. As the movie played through the previews, they waited, enjoying the warmth between them.

The black screen faded to gray, then back to black. As a horrific scream blasted the speakers, Michael pounced his hand on Sarah, provoking her to emit a shriek of her own. After her heartbeat settled, the rhythm quickened again as he pulled closer to kiss her. He slipped his tongue between her lips and ran his hand along her breast. The feeling rivaled when she was last with Nigel, but different, better. She let his hand reside along the outside of her dress as his other hand massaged her leg.

However, Michael soon lifted his hand and began raising the bottom of her dress. As the hem rose, Sarah pulled away. "Easy," she said with a smile. Michael retreated his hand back to her leg, yet this time inching up the thigh. Again, she pulled her lips from his. "You're persistent, aren't you?"

"Maybe. Is that a bad thing?"

"Let's slow down," she said, turning her body away and resting her head against him. "I said I'd come over only for a movie, remember?"

"It's Valentine's Day, you know?"

"Well, you got further than I anticipated."

Michael sank into the couch, releasing a huff in frustration. Sarah countered by kissing him on the cheek. "Thank you for understanding."

"Understanding? If anything, I'd say being patient."

"Michael, just what exactly did you have in mind for tonight?"

"I don't think it's a secret. I want the same as any other guy. And you'd be lying if you said you didn't."

"Did I give off the impression I wanted to sleep with you tonight?"

"Not exactly, but you know things usually work to that, given enough time."

Sarah raised from the couch, folding her arms around her stomach, as if to shield her body.

"I'm not going to have sex with you. Not tonight, and not ever, unless you see a ring on this finger," she corrected.

Michael released a loud laugh, arching his back, embellishing his nonbelief. Sarah's face tightened in anger. The sinister expression returned his attention to reality. "Oh, you're not kidding?"

"I'm dead serious."

"Oh, come on, Sarah. Once you've slept with a guy, it's really not a big deal after that."

"I want to go home."

"Wait, unless you haven't?"

"I want to go home, now!"

"Sarah, calm down, I just thought . . . But wait . . . let me talk for a second."

"Whatever you have to say, it better be good."

"Okay, just hear me out. We've known each other for a while, right?"

"Apparently not long enough," she contended.

"Anyways . . . what about your knees?"

She sighed, "What do my knees have to do with anything?"

"When you started coming to the pool, I noticed they were red."

"So?"

"Seems to me you were pretty used to being on your knees, so I thought you might be one to venture around."

Sarah's eyes widened. She turned from the couch and marched to the door.

"Sarah, where are you going?"

"Home. And don't try following me," she demanded, slamming the door behind.

As best she figured, the walk home stretched a few miles. Under any other circumstances, the distance would hardly phase her, yet as she looked at her heels and dress, uncertainty fell within her thoughts. Walking along the drive to the sidewalk, she stopped only after losing sight of Michael's house. After a few glances to confirm he had not followed, she slipped off the heels and rolled her stockings down her legs and over each foot. Frozen concrete stung at her toes as she started the trek home. Wind rattled her hair as a lingering nip eased into her body. Confident that walking the entire way would pose more problems than relief, Sarah began to run through the abyss. Each foot landed hard and painfully along the sharpness of the stone-cold ground. Prickles tore at the skin along her feet, emitting pain even upon the dull feeling among her toes.

Forcing her legs to continue until all the feeling left her feet, Sarah stopped and began walking again. She bent over to examine her feet that pooled with blood on the small cuts across the surface. Lowering her leg, she noticed the rawness of her knees Michael referred to. *How dare he assume I'd have sex with him, or any guy, let alone work the skin from my knees while doing so.* A scream rang from her chest. The sound resonated down the road, but the sound appeared to emit not from herself but another lost soul.

Halting to the reality that walking home no longer remained an option, she sat down, bundling her body around her legs. Tears streamed down her face as hair stuck to the dampened sides. *God, why me? Why does this happen to me?* Within her cocoon, shivers took hold as her voice fell silent as if waiting for a verbal answer. Yet, only the lonely sound of the wind echoed. Trails continued running from her nose as she wiped her hand across to remove the mucus. *No. I'm not settling for this again.* Pulling up from the ground, Sarah headed in the direction of Michael's house.

More furious than upset, she marched to the door she previously slammed upon her dramatic exit. Without a knock, she barged through the door and into the living room. Michael raised his head from his finger laced hair upon her surprise entrance. "Sarah, I'm so glad you're back, I—"

Without thinking, Sarah silenced him with a slap that bashed the cheek closest to her. "Don't ever talk to me like that again!"

Michael rubbed his jaw, then slowly lifted from the seat. Inching closer, he towered above. Sarah crept backward as he continued to follow. She stopped as her back slammed flush with a wall. "You don't like how I assumed you're loose, I get it . . ." he said, raising one hand to her chest while tightening the other around her neck. "But you will never slap me again . . . Understand?"

An unknown fear shot through her body as his grip cinched her throat. Her head nodded in confirmation. As he retreated his stance, Sarah sank to the floor. Unable to comprehend what happened, her eyes merely fixed straight ahead on the television where the movie was still playing. Michael now situated himself on the couch as if nothing ever happened. Unsure whether to run out or try and defend herself, she sat and waited.

Sarah failed to flinch as the spooks from the screen filled her eyes, nor did she move from the floor until the credits had finished rolling. Only when he retrieved the VHS from the player and turned the lights on, did she find any movement returning to her body. Michael floated to the kitchen briefly before acknowledging her paralyzed stance on the floor.

"I'm sorry, Sarah. I shouldn't have assumed, and I can't stand to be slapped, but that's no excuse. Can I offer you a ride home?"

Sarah found her feet underneath her body as he lifted her upwards. Her head churned for another option but walking or finding another ride seemed implausible. "Please," she muttered.

"Very well. I'll get the purse you left."

Accepting the bag, Sarah followed him into the night air. Opening the car door, she remained close to the side paneling as they pulled into the street. Michael continued to talk, but the words he conveyed felt empty. With no questions directed to her, Sarah sat in silence. Both fear and confusion penetrated her gut. *Was this a bad dream or just their first fight?*

"Sarah, don't forget your roses," Michael said, pushing the bouquet into her arms. Unaware, they had come to a stop in front of her apartment. The flowers brushed her nose and she inhaled the gentle scent. Fresh fragrances filled her nostrils, suppressing the smell of Michael's house. As she reached for the door, Michael took hold of her arm, edging her close enough for a kiss on the lips. She offered little effort in the kiss and pulled away just as easily. Mustering a good night, Sarah walked to the door, never glancing at the headlights that peeled away into the night.

A continued darkness consumed her as she stepped inside, climbed the stairs, and disappeared into her room. Sarah unzipped the dress, half noticing the dirt ladened rear. Not inspecting the cloth for further damage, she dropped the garment on the bathroom floor. Leaning into the mirror, she swiveled her neck from side to side. A lite bruise formed where his thumb had buried into the skin.

Never had a man touched her in such a way. Never had a voice raised to the point of uttermost demand. She spoke up for herself in search for respect, yet his voice changed to a deeper, darker tone that scolded her heart. Sarah looked at the roses that lay on the bed, then again at her neck. Which was it, did his care for her surpass his malicious will, or was it the other way around?

Sarah changed into her pajamas before flipping off the lights and crawling into bed. A prayer whispered through her heart as she searched for answers blindly. During a relationship of hurt, prayer was the only comfort in which she found hope. Residing to her pillow, Sarah took a final look at the clock on the nightstand before realizing the closeness of Wesley's wedding.

CHAPTER 13:

A New Kind of Love

Sarah rubbed her sleep-ridden eyes as she stumbled to the bathroom. Sitting on the chilly porcelain reminded her of the failed attempt to walk home. Being hurt emotionally held no new precedents, yet Michael's actions reached a level of physical complexity she could not comprehend. Peeling her skin from the seat lid, Sarah shimmied her undies over her hips. Unsure if talking would help, the thought of having Emily to provide comfort brought renewed warmth.

To her surprise, Emily was awake and already in the kitchen. Pouring her own bowl of cereal, Sarah joined her at the table.

"Looks like you had a fun night," Emily teased.

"What do you mean?"

Emily stretched her finger toward the blemish spotting Sarah's neck, as she slurped milk from her bowl. Swallowing hard, Emily continued, "That hickey is something else. Michael and you must be moving along."

Sarah rubbed the bruise with her hand, subconsciously trying to conceal the painful night. Instead of allowing Emily to further question their evening, she changed the subject.

"So, what are you thinking for wedding colors? I know you have a while, but no use in waiting till the last minute."

"Sarah," she interrupted.

"Yeah?" she questioned, detecting trouble in Emily's voice.

"I had sex with Paul last night." Her gaze slowly lifted from her toast to Sarah, whose expression showered complete shock. "Are you going to say anything?"

"Wow . . . I mean . . . How did that happen?"

"We were so excited about our engagement, and well, we thought about waiting to our wedding night, but then again, we've waited so long not knowing if we'd even be together." Emily paused, longing for Sarah to show a hint of approval or unrest. "Come on, Sarah . . . Say something."

"What was it like?" she said, casting a slight laugh. Emily perked as she felt not only their conversation flame, but the familiar friendship they previously shared rekindle.

"Should we break out the nail polish for this?"

"I was thinking the same thing."

Sarah left the table, running upstairs to fetch the pedicure bag, and by the time she returned, Emily was in the living room, making her way to the floor. "I got it . . . Alright, what was it like? Was it weird? How did it start?"

Emily braced herself against the couch as Sarah began working on filing her toenails. Inhaling deeply, she exhaled a quivering breath. "It was the most amazing thing I've ever felt. At first, we were only kissing, but then I decided to straddle him. Oh Sarah, then there was this tremor . . . It teased and tensed my muscles like you wouldn't believe. He had to tug my pants off while I held tight to his shoulders. I tried not to laugh because of the situation, but we probably looked hilarious." She paused, relishing the memory before wincing at another thought. "The only thing was we didn't use a condom."

"Emm!"

"I know. Sex had come up in conversation before, but we were in such a hurry, that it slipped our minds. I'll tell you this, but don't let Paul know. We stopped soon after starting when we realized what we'd done. I rolled off of him for a second, then we said forget it, and he yanked me back on top of him. Instead, we decided to pull out beforehand . . . We were so afraid you were going to walk in on us."

"Wait, you were having sex in the living room?"

"Yeah. And be glad you weren't here. Apparently, I got really loud," she giggled.

"Did you have sex on the couch?"

"Uh sorry . . . We were too busy to move onto the bed."

"Well, I'll be sure not to sit there anymore," Sarah jabbed.

"Nothing except some bare skin got on it," she laughed. "But anyways, we had just finished and were catching our breaths when the door started to open. Luckily, the lights were off, and I guess you decided to go straight to bed."

"Yeah, I didn't even notice Paul's truck."

"Enough about that, how did your night go?"

"I think we had our first fight, or something."

"Huh?" said Emily, taking another sip of milk.

"This isn't exactly a hickey," she said, gathering her hair so the light could illuminate the mark.

"What is it?" Emily murmured through the milk.

"A bruise from his hand."

Emily spewed the cereal, spraying it across the table. "What did he do to you?" she demanded.

"He wanted us to have sex. Apparently, something's in the air."

Emily followed with a giggle, "That sounds kinky. So, he's into that weird stuff?"

"Emm. No. I said I wasn't going to sleep with him, then he pretty much called me a sleaze. So, I stormed out and started walking home. A little way down the road, I realized walking was a bad idea, so I went back, demanded he never talk to me like that again, and persisted he take me home. After that his voice changed, and he garnered my neck with his hand. Honestly, I got scared."

"Why would he get physical all of a sudden."

"I slapped him first, rather hard. But I've done that to Nigel, and he never approached me like that."

"Should we call the police?"

"What would I say? I threw the first punch. How's that going to look?"

"Does that matter? He's a guy, and a strong one it appears. Also, what about therapy? It's not like you can avoid him. Unless you drop us off and leave."

"Paul will be there, so I'll be fine." Sarah sighed as she recalled the rest of the night. "He apologized on the way home, so maybe it was a one-time thing."

"What do you want to do, Sarah?"

"Pretend it never happened . . ."

"That's not really an option, but maybe you should talk to Paul. Get his opinion."

"This needs to stay between us. And no offense, but I rather Paul not know my intimate business . . . Even though you spilled his," she caught herself. "Let's drop it for now. If something weird happens again, it won't be a surprise, and I can react better."

"Okay, I'll keep my mouth shut, but only if you promise to tell me if he touches you like that again. Slap or no slap, I'll come over and kick his rear."

"Thanks, Emm." Sarah lowered her voice, "Please tell me Paul isn't here."

"Ha. No, he didn't spend the night. We thought it would be too obvious that something happened. So much for keeping it secret," she laughed.

"Well, I'd hope we don't keep any secrets now . . . Are you not afraid of getting pregnant, Emm?"

"Not at all. I can't run, and we're planning on getting married this summer, so at worst I'll have a baby bump at the wedding. I've always wanted a little girl. Could you imagine me as a mom? That would just be the greatest thing in the world."

"Are you going to try and have a baby pretty soon?"

"Sometime after the wedding, but that's if it doesn't happen before. I asked Paul, and he didn't freak out like I thought he would. Instead, he said there would be more of me that he'd have to love."

"Emm, what would you name your girl?"

"Darlene," she said without hesitation. "It was my great-grandmother's name. I just love the way it sounds. What are you going to name yours?"

"I'm not really sure. I figured that would be something to discuss with my husband. I've thought about some old family names, but nothing really sticks. You know some people don't pick a name until the birth. Something about seeing the baby makes it easier. Mom said Sarah and Susan were the two names they picked out. Then, after the delivery while Mom was holding me, Dad leaned over and whispered, 'I think she looks more like a Sarah.' Mom agreed and that was how mine came about. Do you know where Emily came from?"

"Mom told me it was her childhood friend. They were inseparable until high school when Emily and her parents moved away. Mom was pretty devastated because they lost touch. Over the years, when she went to try and reconnect, she heard that Emily had gone missing from her parents' house, and was never located."

"That's terrible. Do you ever wonder about the original Emily?"

"I have in the past. But no one has seen her since before I was born. After delivery, my head was already covered in blonde hair. Seeing me, the name Emily flooded her mind and when she told my father, he loved it. They had picked out Marie, but when Emily was presented, they officially put Emily Marie Ellis on the birth certificate."

"Well, Sarah and Susan were just two names drawn from a baby book I suppose. Olivia on the other hand was a name used somewhere down the line in my family, but I couldn't tell you which great-great relative it was. But, Emm, what if it's a boy?"

"I've never considered boy names."

"Well, there's a fifty-fifty chance that it could be a boy. I guess Daryl is an option if you wanted to go that route."

"That doesn't sound like a baby's name," she laughed. "I might have multiple girls, but as far as a boy, I don't think that will happen."

"Why not?"

"It's a feeling I have. But if I do then maybe Emmitt would be good. But let's talk about something else. All this baby talk makes me want to get Paul and—"

"Emm!"

"Sorry. My body is aching for him now."

"Maybe we need a system. You know, so I don't walk in while you two are . . ."

"Wrestling?" Emily proposed.

"Eww, no. That gives me a terrible mental image. How about singing?"

"Ha, ha. Sarah, that sounds like a winner. La . . .!" she yelled.

"Okay, okay, I get the picture," Sarah laughed.

"So how can we let you know we're 'singing' without catching us in the act?"

"A sock on the door is too obvious. We need something less conspicuous."

"I know what we can do. First check and see if Paul's truck is here. If it is, that's clue number one. The next clue is I'll flip over the door mat."

"Okay. If I see both, I'll give a few knocks on the door and come back in what, twenty minutes?"

Emily laughed at the estimate. "Is an hour too much?"

"An hour? Really?"

"Well, I rather not have to rush. But yeah, you're right. An hour is too much. We can stick with twenty minutes. Just remember we may not be fully dressed."

"Nothing we haven't all seen before," Sarah reminded.

Switching the conversation, Emily shrugged, "So, are you excited about the first track meet?"

"I am, but I invited Michael before all this happened, so who knows if he'll show or not."

"Who cares? You're going to do great, and if he does, that will teach him that he has no authority over your life, and you can be confident with or without him."

"Yeah. I need a win to get the momentum going and he's not going to control that. Are you coming?"

"Don't worry. I'll be there, and so will Paul. If there is any singing today, I figure that will come later tonight."

"Question," Sarah interjected.

"Yeah?"

"Are you two only going to sing here, or will the music take place at Paul's as well?"

"Possibly. Or it could be wherever the beat gets started."

"Emm, you're impossible, you know that?"

"I am, but seriously, this is all new to me. Now that we have the first time out of the way, I'm ready to try again. There's something about it. I've never felt such closeness and it makes complete sense to follow the desire. I wish we were already married, because I know it's sinful. But after almost dying, I consider it more of a blessing to enjoy life with someone who loves me."

"Perhaps don't tell the whole world."

"I wasn't planning to, but what makes you say that?"

"You know how coach is about dating, even though you're engaged."

"Right. It's not like I want everyone to know my saucy side of life, but you're my best friend and I had to tell someone."

"Honestly, I'm glad you did. And I promise I'll try not to be a dead giveaway when Paul is around. I'm sure he rather me not know."

"Don't worry about Paul. I'll tell him that you're going to be in the loop."

"Are you not afraid that he'll talk to his friends?"

"Who's he going to tell?"

"Good point. I know he won't tell Nigel. And Ralph. Ha. If he told Ralph then everyone, and I mean everyone, would know before the day was over."

"He knows better than that, so I'm not worried."

"One last thing, Emm, and I won't ask any other questions. . . Is Paul a good lover?"

"Ha. Yes, he's so gentle, but firm when I want him to be. Also, he has this little birth mark on his upper thigh. It's kind of a cute turn on."

Sarah rocked back in her chair before gathering their bowls to soak in the sink. "I'm going to grab a shower. Do you need anything?"

"No, but I'll wipe off the couch cushions, to ease your mind."

"Ha, thanks, Emm. Maybe we won't have to burn the cushions after all."

Leaving Emily to clean the couch, Sarah found herself alone in her bedroom. Picking her purse up from the floor, she sat along the bed. Wrapping her legs around the bag, she leaned over digging through the contents in search of a particular item. Her hands fumbled over most of the contents, pushing them aside, as she knew exactly where the piece of paper lay. Much like the first time she found it, her fingers took hold of the precisely folded parchment. Seeing her name etched across the front drew a single tear, followed by another. Why she kept it even just this short time was not so odd, because she knew why. However, the time had come. Unfolding each crease carefully, Sarah flattened the unsmeared letters across her lap. Again, she read over the words in the same careful manner. Then, as she reached the end, a stream of tears formed from her cheeks and dripped on the note below. The hurt that stung her heart was twofold. She had lost him to someone else and felt unsure that she would ever have that connection with another guy. Her head hung low to the weight of her heart. Doubtful that the sobs carried downstairs, she cared less if Emily could hear. She never imagined love being this hard, nor that the burdens of life would weigh so immense. What would it take for someone to love her enough to ask her to marry him? The question lacked meaning, knowing this once perforated into a proposal, yet she fell short, somehow, someway.

Sarah's voice quaked as she attempted to pray, but she felt lost and broken. No love could fill the void within. Wiping her runny nose with the arm of her robe, Sarah sniffed back the drainage and dammed her tears. Looking hard at the name printed at the bottom of the note, she shredded the letter from top to bottom, being sure to splinter the lines that included both her name and Paul's.

CHAPTER 14:

Two of a Kind

The sun broke the clouds of the afternoon sky as Sarah slammed the car door. The tips of her hair, peeking out of her hoodie, flurried in the wind as she made her way to the track. Waiting to join the team until race time was by far untraditional, but under Coach's instructions, she was to remain inside and warm for as long as possible. However, stepping into the sun alleviated the tensions leading up to the race and a renewed hope hung in the balance.

Paul and Emily hugged Sarah for good luck as they departed for seats on the field. After checking in with Coach Cavlere, Sarah disappeared from the track and into the back fields to complete a warm-up. She had been here before. A world of promise, turned sour, and eventually crashing, were nothing new.

Looping around the beaten grass boundary, Sarah joined Abby as they talked through a race plan. Only the appearance of

Nigel briefly interrupted their conversation as they acknowledged his presence, but pleasantries aside, Sarah remained focused on the fifteen-hundred meters.

Within her mile warm-up, the continued sunshine heated the surrounding air, while each step felt easier. Falling into strides and stretches, Sarah resided into her normal prerace mindset.

Abby and Sarah left the field as the announcer made a second call for the fifteen. Joining Coach near the start, they stripped to their racing attire as he listed their final instructions. "You got this, kid," he said as Sarah gave an understanding nod while squatting to check her spikes a final time.

Jogging to Abby's side, Sarah whispered into her ear, "Stay with me." In the next moments, the announcer stood ready to fire the starting pistol, while the girls toed the line.

Hearing the blast, her muscles jolted forward, rushing to work toward the inside lane. Even with a straight one-hundred-meter start, hands and elbows clashed along her side and back. She could see Abby from the corner of her eye, dealing with the same issues. The outside lanes were collapsing inward, and soon they would all be forced into the turn. Sarah moved forward, starting to edge out the other girls, hoping Abby would follow.

Reaching the curve first, Sarah leaned inward to sling around to the two-hundred mark. Uneven strides could be heard as the fight for places still persisted behind her. A desperate cry followed as one girl skidded across the track after an unfortunate stumble. Unable to see Abby, Sarah's eyes remained ahead as somehow, she knew the breath behind her belonged to the younger teammate.

Breaking into the straightaway and approaching the impending finish line, the group settled into a favorable rhythm. Enough space formed between individuals to avoid collision, but not enough to ensure complacency.

Coming around to the start of the first lap, Sarah heard her time straining from Coach's mouth, "A minute eighteen!" Sarah tried to configure the pace in her head, but at the same instance, the desire to pace was missing. Her legs were starting to burn, but that mattered not either. She knew he wanted her to slow the pace; however, she felt Abby behind her and that going faster was obtainable.

Cranking across the back stretch, Sarah could hear another girl challenging from the outside. Without a doubt, it was a rival trying to take the lead. Hoping to hold off the girl until they reached the curve, Sarah upped their speed again, yet a girl from Hullensail, whom Sarah knew to be Amy, began to pull past her. Amy's form looked sharp and poised, but irritating. The bounce in her stride and confidence in her movement rode intensely in Sarah's thoughts. No preconceived notions brought her to hate Amy, yet the single move proved humiliating.

As they flashed around to the halfway mark, again Coach's voice arched her ears, "You girls stay with her." *Stay with her, as in we aren't good enough to leave Amy behind?* she thought in protest. Sarah spit a dry phlegm that clabbered her mouth and thrust her hips underneath her, making a bid as she pulled into the second lane. Forgoing better judgement, Sarah headed into the curve from the outside. The wind stung her face as she broke through the air and past Amy. Roars from the spectators livened the stands as both Sarah and Abby retook the lead spots.

Entering the homestretch for the second to last time, Sarah's eyes strayed from her forward focus toward the stands. A raving Emily and Paul cheered while chanting along with the crowd.

A mental smile pasted her face, adoring their love and friendship. Then as she started to return her eyes to the track, the bleak shape of Michael caught her eye. However, with the passing second she saw him, Sarah could not tell for sure.

"Ding, ding, ding!" The sounding bell lap drew her from any persisting thoughts of the man as she leaned into the final lap. Her pace quickened with each step as she transitioned to a premature kick. There would be no possibility of Amy reaching her with the momentum built along the back stretch. Abby continued to follow, which Sarah confirmed with an overlooking shoulder glance upon the final two hundred meters.

Sarah dug her spikes deeper into the rubber as she lifted on her toes for the grand kick. Her legs sewed between the hem of her shorts as she propelled forward, reaching her highest gear. Pandemonium filled the air as she closed her eyes through the finishing tape. Her body's ache of soreness and drain was dismissed as she turned blindly and wrapped her arms around a winded Abby, who cleared the line mere seconds later. Together, they exhaustedly embraced in excitement. "Four fifty-eight, Sarah," quothed Abby.

"That's amazing!"

"No, that's your time. Five seconds under your goal pace."

"See, I told you to stay with me," Sarah murmured as they departed from the track.

Awaiting beyond the fences stood Emily and Paul. Disregarding the sweat-laced uniforms, they coupled around Sarah and Abby, embracing their win. "Sarah, you looked better than ever out there. And Abby, it's like you've just become a star."

"Thanks, Emm. Hearing y'all cheer makes a big difference, and that's no lie—"

"Sarah?"

Sarah turned to the sound of her name, but immediately wished she had not. Both she and Emily shared similar stares that could cut glass as Michael appeared.

"You're a completely different runner on the track than on the trails; that's a stellar time too."

"Thanks," she offered halfheartedly.

"Do you have a minute? I was hoping we could talk."

Sarah looked around to Emily, who awaited her confirmation of whether she and the others needed to leave or stay.

"Umm, maybe later. I really need to cool down and get back into my sweats."

"Oh, okay, that's fine. I'll see you at the pool then."

"Yeah, the pool," she resonated as she started walking away with the others, leaving Michael unaccompanied and unmoved.

"I can fetch your sweats if you want to stay with Michael," Abby offered.

"That's quite alright. I want to enjoy our triumph right now," Sarah smiled, looping her arm around Abby.

"What do you suppose he wanted?" Abby questioned.

"Nothing important. I'm sure it can wait," she answered dismissively. "Right now, I need to change and get something to eat."

"Sarah, can we take a detour to the bathrooms first?" Emily asked.

"Yeah."

"I'll get your clothes, Sarah."

"Thanks, Abby."

Sarah followed Emily to the brick-and-mortar restrooms tucked behind the stands. A frail heater baked the walls, emitting much-needed heat. Sarah absorbed the warmth but turned around when she noticed Emily was not heading for a stall.

"Didn't you have to go?"

"No. But I need to tell you something."

"Emm, if it's about Michael, I rather not right now. I feel so good, and don't care to come off my high."

"No, it's something else, or someone—"

"Not now. I really don't have the energy or the care to deal with anything. Okay?"

"If you say so. I just heard something and didn't want you to—"

Sarah waved her hand. "Come on. Let's find Abby and Paul, then some food. The eight hundred is in a couple of hours."

Rounding the track, Sarah watched as the sprinters prepared their blocks for the two-hundred-meter sprint. She wanted to stay and help cheer on her teammates, but Coach was taking extra precaution. Working her way into the stands, Sarah grabbed a bar from her bag. Peeling off the wrapper, she chewed on the less than tasteful bark as she tucked her spikes into the side pocket. Sarah gave a passing glance over the field and rows of spectators; however, Michael was nowhere in sight. *I guess he left, but that's fine with me. I may have been a bit harsh, but talking would have to wait.*

Bouncing down the spongy steps, Sarah dropped her gym bag at Emily's feet, as Abby handed off the now cooled sweats. The fabric slid over her head and chest, both easing the chill through her body while bringing a subtle nip as the cold bundles adjusted to her body heat. Carefully, she slid through the legs of the pants and crept the waistband over her hips before tying the string.

"Are we heading back to the gym until they give first call?" asked Paul.

"Yeah, it'll be a few hours, so you don't have to stick around."

"We'll stay with you," countered Emily.

The four of them stuffed into Sarah's car and drove around to the back entrance of the gym. Inside, many athletes sought shelter from the wind and were sprawled about the floor. Some bundled in groups while others secluded themselves in the corner. Sarah located a spot along the wall where they could wait without being trampled.

Settling on the hardwood, Sarah laid her head on Emily's lap and closed her eyes. The low conversations met by the stroking of her hair lulled her to sleep.

Visions of the race flashed within her dream. Every instance mirrored the race that previously took place. However, instead of only seeing Michael on the last lap, his face appeared distinctly in the same spot on each turn. Seeing him, she no longer felt the presence of Abby and the other runners, and all the spectators became blurry with the background. Again, she won the race, but lost sight of Emily and Paul. Hungry, cold, and with no one else nearby, she turned to Michael. He tossed his jacket over her bare shoulders and walked her to the car.

Inside the engine idled as the heater broke through the air and fog clanged to the windows. "Let me make it up to you . . ." he said. ". . . And I'll make love to you."

Sarah felt her head nod as he began removing his clothes, followed by hers. "Sarah," he whispered into her ear as he reached to pull off her bra.

"Sarah, Sarah," Abby called pulling her from the dream. "Wake up, it's time for the next race."

A dreamy-eyed Sarah lifted her head from Emily's lap, unaware of her surroundings.

"What?"

"The eight hundred is soon."

"Oh," Sarah said, brightening her eyes. "How long was I asleep?"

"An hour and a half."

"That long?"

"Yeah. You passed out as soon as you laid down."

Sarah gathered her gear, leaving the dream behind as they walked to the car and drove back around. Pulling into the adjacent parking lot, a noticeable drop in attendance was apparent from the remaining cars. The eight hundred had been pushed to the second to last event, followed by the four hundred.

Emily pulled Sarah aside once again, allowing Abby and Paul to continue ahead. "Sarah, I've got to tell you this, and now."

"Okay, Emm. What is it?"

"While we were waiting for you to start the mile, I overheard some of the girls. At first, I couldn't tell who they were talking about, so I walked by to eavesdrop. It was Jenna. I don't know if you've noticed, but she isn't at the meet today."

"Yeah, I guess. I wasn't really looking, but Nigel wasn't cozied up with her, so that makes sense."

"Do you know why she isn't here?"

"Maybe she thought she was too good for a small meet. But, Emm, I've got to get ready. Jenna is the least of my concerns right now."

"Sarah, wait," said Emily grabbing her arm. "The girls that were talking about Jenna, said something about her being pregnant."

"That's ridiculous, Emily. Have they even been dating that long?"

"Dating or sleeping together?"

Sarah realized Emily was right as her stance remained strong.

"Maybe I heard wrong, but clearly they said she was having morning sickness this past week."

"Good for her . . . and Nigel," she said, dismissing the conversation.

At this point, Nigel was gathered with Ralph, awaiting the men's race. Hearing the news bore hard to swallow. Seeing his undeterred focus on the race, she wondered what also ran through his head. *A baby? What am I going to do? Is it really my problem or Jenna's? No, it's not my fault. That's something she'll have to handle.*

That pig. Jenna may be a rounder, but I know how she feels. That could have been me, and almost was. I'm so thankful it wasn't. Handling one heartbeat is tough enough, let alone two by yourself.

The gun resonated over the field as the men's race commenced. Nigel broke from the pack within the first two hundred, followed by a rival, then Ralph. His face bore the same determination Sarah had seen time and time again.

Sarah looped around from the warm-up to find her bag that remained with Emily. Neither her nor Emily spoke while she rotated through the traditional stretch routine. Instead, they watched as the guys circled around for the bell lap.

Abby's voice echoed over the crowd as she cheered on Ralph, who moved into second place. Seconds later, Abby appeared beside Sarah as she awaited the walk to the starting line.

Sarah stood from tying her laces and gave Emily a hug. "Good luck, Sarah!"

"Thanks, Emm. This one is for you."

Striding outside the fence, Sarah and Abby continued to watch as Nigel and Ralph began battling for the front spot. Entering the final stretch, the grit upon their faces bore harder with each step. Only upon the last ten meters did Nigel regain a slight lead to edge out Ralph for the win.

Abby ran to Ralph, wrapping her arms around his neck as he worked to slow his breathing. Nigel pulled off the track and headed straight through the gate. In passing, Sarah offered a two-sided congratulations that received an equally enthusiastic thanks.

The grasp Abby had around Ralph only loosened as the last male crossed the finish line and the women were called to the start. Sarah studied the line as she controlled her breathing. Looking up, she saw Michael had rejoined the few observers that awaited the last two events. Avoiding his eyes, she acknowledged her coach for any last-minute instructions before they separated.

With all pent-up determination and emotions inside, Sarah released them as the race commenced. The pace rose immensely as she fought for a top spot inside the first curve. A few girls collided with her, pushing themselves ahead and almost knocking Sarah over the edge. Frustrated, Sarah rounded the corner and slid to lane two.

There were only two laps this time, meaning a different race with a different strategy.

Sarah fought the entire backstretch before pulling to the inside lane behind the lead girl. As they exited to the other side, she again moved outward. Meeting the bell with a 1:11 split, she found herself choosing to challenge from the outer lane or fall in line. Deciding to wait for the final kick, Sarah followed the lead girl through the five-hundred-meter mark and halfway down the straightaway. Upon the last two hundred, she transitioned her legs for a finishing kick.

The lactic acid residing from the first race resisted the change, yet she demanded her legs increase the pace. Bearing down, she felt her body sling forward and alongside the leader. Working the final turn, Sarah and the other girl exchanged brief looks of struggle. Sarah pressed forward, counting down a fictitious timer inside her head. Words of persistency followed, carrying her the remainder of the race. Sarah tilted her head forward with a lean as they approached the finish. Eyeing the clock and the line, Sarah's chest clipped the tape just moments prior to her rival.

Steam boiled from her skin as Sarah hitched her hands on top of her hips. She watched as the second girl doubled onto the ground, aiding a cramp. Seconds later, in third, Abby collided into Sarah with an exchange of congratulations. Following the cumbersome embrace, Sarah reached to offer the other girl a hand. "Awesome job. That was intense."

"You too. It was quite the race."

Long after the finish, Michael awaited as she transitioned to a cooldown. Sarah wondered how long he would stay as she dallied watching the first heats of the four hundred. Deciding that he would not budge from his spot until she left, Sarah waited until the third group had finished before walking across the track.

"Hey. That was amazing. You even won both races, just like you said."

"Thanks."

"And, the last one . . . that was a nail-biter."

"Yeah, I like the close ones better."

Sarah stood looking at him, then peered off into the distance. Emily and Paul could be seen talking with Abby, obviously lingering, waiting for her to join them.

"So, can we talk now?" asked Michael.

"What about?"

"The other night. Things got a little—"

"Maybe later," she interrupted. "My friends are waiting on me," she said defiantly.

With no further acknowledgements, Sarah left. She could feel his eyes examining her body the entire distance. Even with her baggy sweats concealing her curves, she considered his imagination fulfilled what his eyes could not see. Recalling the earlier dream, she resisted the temptation to look around and confirm if he was still there.

Exchanging her spikes and shoes, she shot a brief glance down the path she came. To her surprise, he was no longer lingering. Instead, stood Nigel with Jenna, who was dressed in lose-fitting street clothes.

CHAPTER 15:

What Hurts the Most

The waiting room remained quiet as the first patients trickled in for their eight o'clock appointments. Most of them were older women, likely in their forties and fifties, either in pre- or full-blown menopause. She scanned the room, but there were no other young girls.

A bundle of magazines rested on the coffee table just above her feet. Sarah leaned over to flip through the assortment, settling on a copy of "Women's Health Discussion," with a cover depicting women running on the beach. Sarah arched into the chair as she flipped through the pages. A few articles caught her eyes, offering tasteful and nutritious recipes, but those failed to fully capture her attention. About halfway through, a picture of a teenage girl took focus in the shadow of another person. Anguish and pain sculpted her face, while her body told a story of abuse.

The header stretching over the article read "Sex Trafficking: A Silent Killer," a volatile expression that stroked fear and remorse into the imagination upon rendering its meaning. Curious, Sarah read the lines portraying how the livelihoods of young women, or often girls, are broken from their families and then sold for sex. The staggering statistics that fabricated the side bars of the magazine stood so high, that the reality felt more of a fantasy than an unnoticed truth.

Reading a line containing a rape encounter of the pictured girl, left Sarah clinching her crossed legs. Forcing herself to finish the article proved difficult, but seeing the girl's story of escape brought enough relief to close the magazine and place the piece on the table. Even though the mistreated girl's face now lay among the stacks of papers, the battered eyes that endured years of heartache from such a young age continued to reside in Sarah's mind.

"Sarah Mills?" a nurse called. "We're ready for you in exam room C. Follow me, please." Sarah took a final glance at the *Women's Health Discussion* cover before departing. Walking down the hall, Sarah turned into a room which she had yet to visit. The posters and machinery that marked the space, however, were all too common. By glancing around, Sarah could tell the area was dedicated for expecting mothers.

"Excuse me, miss, but I'm not sure why we're in here. I'm in no way pregnant," she passed off lightly. Thumbing through her chart, the nurse panned the records for clarification.

"The doctor mentioned a pelvic exam may be offered at the next visit. He'll be in shortly to discuss if this is something you would like to pursue." Sarah pinched her legs together, imagining someone poking around her insides with undoubtedly cool metal. Before

Sarah began to reply, the nurse shoved the file into the door cubby and dismissed herself.

Looking about the room, pictures of new mothers draped the nearest wall. Arching her back, Sarah pushed her belly outwards with a deep gulp of air. Then, rubbing her well-formed stomach, she imagined how she would feel if a fetus was growing inside.

Within a few minutes, the doctor entered while simultaneously reviewing the notes from the door. Today's visit left him lacking in personality with a straight face replacing his usual greeting smile. "Good morning, Sarah. How are you?"

"Pretty good actually. I've been feeling like my normal self lately."

"Good to hear. And your period is on track now?"

"For the most part. It's off a little, but I figure that's expected." The doctor nodded before taking a seat on the stool angled in front of the table.

"Sarah," he continued without delaying the cause of his seriousness. "I'm glad to hear you're doing well. However, in your blood work, I found something that raises concern. We don't want to get too excited right now," he insisted, seeing her facial expression change. "Initially, we thought the loss of your cycle was due to the ferritin levels. And that was likely the trigger at the time. Over the past few exams, I've noticed another irregularity in the blood work. The concern is, I believe they're related."

"What is it?"

"Typically, I see this pattern in females that, well, have trouble conceiving. Do you know if there is any family history?"

Sarah searched her brain trying to recall anything that stuck out from talking with her mother. "Not particularly. My mom had me, then my brother."

"Was she young when you were born?"

"Yeah, then Matty came about eight years later, but he wasn't planned."

The doctor tucked his lip, pondering over the circumstances. "With what you're telling me, and what I've seen, there's a high probability that you may not be able to conceive."

"You mean, I can't get pregnant? But I have my period now and—"

"Pregnancy often is overfocused on having a normal period, but many women are not aware of underlying issues. In your case, I'm concerned you may have fibroids."

"Fibroids?"

"Yes. They're spots that can develop on the uterus, an although you might have a normal cycle, they may reduce or eliminate the chances of having children."

"Are you sure I have them?"

"Like I said, I don't want you to get excited, because we won't know for sure until we do a pelvic exam, or possibly they can show up on the ultrasound. Seeing this is so new to you, perhaps we start with a scan. Then, later we can proceed with an inside exam."

"I think I would rather try that first."

"Okay. If you would go ahead and lie on the table, then I'll need you to pull your shirt over your stomach and unbutton your pants."

Sarah scooted until her knees met the edge of the seat, and then reclined fully onto the table. Her shirt grazed her stomach as she slid the bottom up to her chest. Unbuttoning her jeans, Sarah lifted her hips, pulling them below her waist.

"I'll rub some gel where your uterus and cervix are located. But don't worry, it'll be warm," he said, ensuring her to relax.

With the topical ointment spread over her skin, he reached for the handle of the machine that emitted the sound waves. Guiding the head of the device up and around, Sarah lay watching the screen, half expecting a heartbeat to appear. Her eyes remained intently locked with each pass, as if to catch anything abnormal prior to the doctor making mention.

Just as Sarah assumed they were about to finish, the doctor revisited one location, stopping and stilling the picture on the screen. "Sarah, do you see that small speck? It looks almost like a ball."

"Barely, but yes, I do see it."

"That's what we call a uterine fibroid."

"Is there just the one?"

"I saw two, total, but this one is more prominent."

"Does that mean I can't—"

"It doesn't mean a whole lot at the moment," he interrupted. "Now that we see them, we can start deciding a plan of action. Sometimes fibroids show up and have no effect, while other times they cause issues. Given your prior problems, it is a concern, but not a for sure."

"What do you recommend?" Sarah asked, still focused on the grainy screen.

"I want to schedule an exam to go inside for a look. Once we do that, I'll have an idea of issues and treatments. I would tell you not to worry but with multiple occurrences, we need to be cautious."

His words rung in her ears. She was in the best shape of her life, yet here she was, receiving news that her body's health was solely an outward appearance. Unable to comprehend the situation, she rose from her position hastily.

"I think I want to go home now, if that's alright."

"Of course. Here," he said, handing her paper towels to wipe the gel from her skin. "Get dressed, and we'll walk down to the office."

Sarah gobbed the goo from her skin without a second pass before shimmying her pants over her hips.

"I'm going to recommend we do the pelvic exam at your next appointment. Ideally, I'd like to see you after track is over and your body has had time to rest. If you feel more at ease, your mother or a friend can accompany you. Either way, a female nurse will be present."

"Thank you."

Sarah followed the doctor to the front before bundling in her coat and heading outside. Her mind felt numb to the news, almost immune. Infertility was something that happened to other people, not her. And fibroids, that was not something found in healthy, fit girls.

Returning to the apartment, Emily greeted Sarah by flashing her swimsuit under her robe. "Are you okay with taking us to the pool today? If not, I can get Paul to ask Ralph. I didn't know if you were fine with seeing Michael."

"Actually, if Ralph can take you, that would be best. And, it's not Michael."

"Oh, what's wrong?"

"The doctor thinks he found something."

Emily's smile faded with the screeching sound of bad news.

"What?"

"It was. . . I mean. . ." said Sarah, shaking her head. "It could be nothing."

Emily's tenseness relaxed at Sarah's almost hopeful proposal. She joined Sarah with a hug.

"Maybe they made a mistake."

"Perhaps, but I think I'm going home. I want to talk to Mom and see what she says."

"Do you want me to go with you? I don't mind skipping therapy if you need me."

"That's alright. I may not be back until late or possibly tomorrow morning, depending on how I feel."

"I'll let Coach know. I can tell him you're not feeling well."

"Tell him I needed to return home and can explain later, but not to worry."

"Whatever you say, Sar."

Shutting the front door, Sarah hopped into her car and headed out of town. With each mile, she hoped the sound of the doctor's voice would fade into an ill-conceived dream. However, the closer she got to her parents, the more real the situation felt.

Pulling into the drive, Sarah sat a few minutes before gathering the courage to go inside. Instead of letting herself in, she gave a knock, hoping not to startle her mother. Following the sound of footsteps, Megan's face appeared at the door.

"Sarah? What are you doing home?"

"I needed to see you," she said, anchoring her arms around her mother's waist.

Megan leaned into the hug while patting Sarah on the head. "Come in and tell me what's going on."

The quietness that sounded from inside affirmed Matty was at school, while her dad was at work. Sarah took a seat on the couch beside her mother. Unable to look into her eyes as she pondered the question, Sarah instead hung her head.

"I just left the follow-up with my doctor. He did an ultrasound and found fibroids on my uterus."

Finishing the sentence, she peered up to read the expression on her mom's face. Anguish and fear were the first thoughts that came to mind as she continued.

"He said it might make me unable to have kids."

"Oh, Sarah." Megan paused for an unprecedented amount of time, but Sarah already knew what she was about to say. "I didn't think this would come up so soon, but those run in our family. I'm so sorry I didn't warn you before, but I thought you might not have to worry about it. You see, I didn't know I had them until you were born. The doctor found one when I was pregnant. He said, if I wanted to have another child, then I should do it soon. Your father and I decided if we were blessed with another, that was fine, but we wouldn't fret over the situation. Matty as you know didn't come until later. So, the eight years in between, I was never able to conceive. We figured it best we wait until you were to the point of getting married, then we'd tell you."

Sarah leaned her head on her mom's shoulder as she sniffed at her now runny nose.

"So, if I don't get married early, and have kids soon, I may not ever have any? Or even if I do, there's still a chance I may not?"

"The way they explained it was there's a lot of circumstances and chance. The doctor also advised they could be removed, but there was no guarantee of a fix."

Sarah began to cry as the possibility of never holding her own child sunk in. The thought of bearing children of course was something she wanted and thought about at times, but never was the possibility of having fertility issues a concern. Getting married, having sex, and bearing children were what women did, and without the last part, what would be the overall point?

Sarah sobbed and gagged back the urge to throw up as pools of water seeped into her mom's shirt. Her own body had once again revolted.

"Would you like me to fix you something to eat?" her mother offered in hopes of comfort.

"Thanks, Mom. I would." Sarah lay on the couch as her mother went to the refrigerator. "Mom."

"Yes, Liv?" Megan said, reappearing around the corner.

"On second thought, do you have any ice cream?"

Without questioning, Megan smiled and revisited the icebox. As she returned, Sarah was greeted with a carton of chocolate fudge brownie ice cream and two spoons. "Care if I join you?"

"Not at all. Are you having a rough day too?"

"No, but I figured we could talk some more."

"What do you want to talk about?" she replied, shoveling a scoop into her mouth.

"I know that the news you received this morning was tough to hear. I already had you when I was told, but the thought of not being able to have another still left me feeling empty, almost useless. In fact, I cried for the first week. I'm not sure why. I had a beautiful baby girl, while Cliff and I had never felt closer." She paused taking a bite herself. "But I can't help but ask how everything else is going."

How her mother knew that more was bothering her, she would never understand, but this time she was relieved in her concern. "There's a lot going on. Emily and Paul are engaged, and plan to get married this summer. Not to mention, you already know Wesley is getting married. It seems everyone has someone, and here I am finding out my body is actually broken."

"Liv, I know. You're in a difficult spot in life. Many people get married after college and it's a trying time when you're single."

"Well, that's another thing. I've started seeing someone."

"Oh really? Tell me about him."

"His name is Michael. We met at a race a few months ago, but as it later turned out, he's Emily's physical therapist."

"Are you afraid now that you will have to share the news with him? I mean, if you just started dating, and you don't know for sure yet, this would probably be something to mention much later."

"I don't know what we are. The thought of sharing my fertility with anyone, scares the life out of me, but we're nowhere near that conversation. Actually, I've kinda been putting him off. We had a fight of sorts."

"What about? Or if you rather not—"

"Yeah, I don't want to think about it right now. However, he came to my meet and tried talking to me. But you know how I am after running."

"That's fair. He should respect that . . . So, are you going to call it quits?"

"I really thought I would. However, I already invited him to Wesley's wedding. If I break up with him, I'll be without a date."

"What do you want to do?"

"I want him to go with me. I've had enough bad news that I just need something in that department to go my way."

"Then take him to the wedding. If it goes well, you might have your answer. If not, then Emily will be there. Right?"

"Her and Caroline both will."

"Good. I hate seeing you upset."

"Thanks, Mom."

"Are you planning on staying here for the wedding?"

"I'm not sure. The others might be getting hotel rooms, but again, how's that supposed to look if I share a room with Michael?"

Megan raised a brow adhering to what Sarah meant. "You know, there are many times in life where you will face decisions like that."

"I know, but what do you do in that instance? I don't want to miss being with the girls, but that leaves me with Michael."

"You're right, it does. Just remember, as a girl you must set the tone of the relationship. I believe I've raised you to do what's right, and you'll have to answer that question on your own."

"So, I shouldn't get a room and stay here instead?"

"How about this? If that's what you want then everyone can stay here. We can put the guys in Matty's room and the girls in yours. That way, there's no pressure to break away from the girls and you have a place to stay without, you know."

"Yeah, but will anyone go along with that?"

"If they're your friends, and you tell them why, then they will."

CHAPTER 16:

Answers

Sitting in the Lounge alone, only subtle noises from the stairwell dared to funnel down the hall. The last of the nappers had woken and stumbled to class, still under the spell of the recliner. Sarah tapped her thumb on the table, waiting for the change of classes in anticipation for any students to wander inside.

The ten-minute gap between classes had long faded before Sarah pulled a book from her bag. As she began to read, her eyes skimmed the words, yet her mind was elsewhere. Caroline and Emily were easily convinced to stay the night at her parents' house. Each of them ensured Sarah that their respective boyfriends would agree once they had the chance to inform them. Peace of mind followed with the assurance, yet she needed to talk with Michael. Placing the book down on the table, she acted out how the conversation would go in her head.

If he said anything to downplay or hark at the fact that she wanted them to stay with her parents, she would end the relationship then and there. The night of terror he caused warranted no further instances. Two strikes, and he was out.

On the other hand, if he cared enough to concede to her wishes then perhaps that night meant nothing more than a fight. Considering the two options, she felt more temptation to wager on the first outcome and find another date. However, at that moment, there were no other options.

Again, Sarah returned to the pages, merely going through the motions. Her shift would end in another forty minutes. The opportunity would then come to talk with Michael. On some level, the instance weighed similar to visiting Nigel, hoping for something, but not knowing what she could possibly expect.

Another exchange in classes brought freedom from the imprisonment of her thoughts. As she walked to her car, Sarah considered the likelihood of Michael not being at home. Being the middle of the day, the probability appeared small, yet her proposition needed resolve.

Settling into her rehearsed conversation, Sarah drove the roads that led from campus to Michael's house. As she rang the doorbell, the barking of Bessie was followed by scratching from the inside. Within a few minutes, the lock on the door slid open, and Michael's face peeped through before he slid through a narrow opening. "Stay inside, Bessie," he shooed inching the door closed behind him.

"Hey Sarah. What a pleasant surprise to see you here. I would offer for you to come inside—"

"That's alright, I just wanted to stop by for a minute."

"Look, I'm really sorry about what happened the other night. To be honest, I can't stand to be hit, so when you slapped me, I visited a dark place in my head."

Sarah's chest sank as the air rushed from her lungs. "I didn't know. I really shouldn't have."

"That's alright. You were right to be mad. Can we call a truce, now that we know better?"

"Yes, of course."

"Good, so can I consider we're still on for the wedding?"

"Actually, that was another reason I stopped by."

"Oh?"

"It's nothing bad, but I would feel better if we stayed with my parents. Two of my friends and their dates would be sleeping there too."

"Sure. Whatever makes you happy," he smiled. Michael leaned over to give Sarah a kiss on the lips, followed by a light slip of his tongue. Sarah wrapped her arms around him as he cradled her in his. "We should get dinner one night."

"Okay, but can we go somewhere in town?"

"Yeah. I'll let you pick."

"I'm free tonight if you want to go for Mexican."

"I can't tonight. I have a friend passing through town and will be staying here. I took a half day at work, so I could be around when they arrive. How about tomorrow?"

"It's a date."

"Good. I'll pick you up at seven. I've got to finish cleaning and check on Bessie before she tears something apart."

"I'm about to head to practice anyways, but I'll see you tomorrow night."

Sarah pushed up on her toes for another kiss. Michael slid his hand down along the back pocket of her jeans, before settling them on her hips. The load that bore on her shoulders had now lightened upon Michael's confession. She thought to ask him why the slap tormented him, but resolving their own struggles brought a light she rather not dim. Finally pulling away, Michael watched as she walked to the car. Only as Sarah turned the key did he usher Bessie away from the door and return inside.

Emily stood half-dressed by the time Sarah returned to the apartment. Her shoes remained strown across the floor while her hoodie lay sprawled across the couch, but pausing amidst the chaos, questions quickly rolled off her tongue.

"Were you talking to Michael? Did you set him straight? Or did you break it off?" she chattered, moving from excitement to comfort in the same breath.

"I did. And no, I didn't. It was just a misunderstanding."

"How's getting physical a misunderstanding?"

"He admitted slapping him drove him to a dark place, and that was how he responded. I didn't question him, but it sounded like he suffered from a troubled past. Either way, he seemed very sorry and said it wouldn't happen again."

"Oh . . ." Emily retreated. "What about the wedding?"

"He said whatever made me happy."

"Sar! I'm so excited you were able to work things out. You need a man in your life."

"Thanks, Emm," she laughed.

"I'm serious. Not for sex, but in general. Everybody says to find a man in college, because once you graduate, there's only slim pickings, which I'm not fond of."

"Nice old-maid pep talk, Emm. Hurry and get your shoes on, or we're going to be late."

"You're not helping my point," Emily teased.

"Well, we could always leave Paul at home. That would make up some time." Emily quieted as she refocused on finding her socks and rushing to the door.

"I'm ready. Let's go," she countered, still working the sweatshirt over her head.

"I thought that would get you moving."

Emily slanted her eyes before laughing at her own peril. "Speaking of moving, you never told me what the doctor said when you rushed home the other day."

The smile across Sarah's face turned to a soured expression, followed by a gloom that dusted her eyes.

"You don't have to tell me. I just thought I'd ask."

"No, it's okay. I want to tell you," she said, followed by an extended pause. "Remember how I said the doctor discovered something when I had my check-up?"

"Yeah. Oh Sarah, is it worse? Is it—"

"Calm down, Emily. I'm not dying, but I didn't tell you the whole truth. They discovered some fibroids during an ultrasound. Two to be exact. He wants to do an internal exam and see if there are any more and hopefully provide some details."

"Fibroids? Are those cancerous?"

"I'm not sure. He didn't mention that part, but what he did say is what's bothering me." Sarah struggled to form the next sentence.

"What did he say?" Emily encouraged.

"He said I might not be able to have children," Sarah admitted, lowering her head.

"Sarah, I'm so sorry." Emily lifted Sarah's chin before giving her a hug. "I didn't realize. . . And, the other day I kept talking about getting pregnant. I—"

"Neither of us knew then, but yeah, I'm afraid I may never be able to. I've been thinking about it, and I could always adopt, but that's a lot of money, and you miss out on carrying them in your stomach, and breastfeeding. I feel useless and broken. Like what guy would ever want to marry a girl that can't conceive. Sure, they wouldn't worry about getting me knocked up, but that invites guys looking for a one-night stand."

"You wouldn't go around advertising it, Sarah."

"I know. But can you imagine? What if I date a guy, we fall in love, and marriage becomes a topic of discussion? At that point, I would be obligated to tell him, if not before becoming so serious. Next thing I know, he decides that's not the life for him, so he walks out."

"Then good riddance to that jerk," Emily insisted.

"Of course, but then you know his friends will ask what happened, so he tells them I'm only good for a night in the sheets, but not marriage material." Tears somberly trickled down Sarah's flushed cheeks. "When word gets around, that's all I'll be."

"No, you won't. I'll give whoever talks bad about you a kick to the groin, then he can see what infertility looks like."

"Ha. Thanks, Emm," Sarah choked.

"I think you're looking at this the wrong way. Not every guy will have that outlook. And you're forgetting, some guys can't get the job done either. You might get lucky and find one of them. Or you could just tell them from the get-go that you don't want to have kids."

"But that's just a lie at best."

Emily shrugged her shoulders, trying to figure out a believable story. "You still have a period, right?"

"Yeah. And I thought everything was fine when that returned."

"So why can't you if the period is regular?"

"Something to do with the uterus being able to host the egg."

"Well, you don't know for sure though, right?"

"Not yet."

"Then, what are you worried about?"

"Wouldn't you be worried? Imagine not being able to hold your Darlene. How would that make you feel?"

Emily sunk her shoulders. "I have. Or I did while I was in the coma."

"Look, Emily, I don't want to start anything. The whole ordeal arose so suddenly, my emotions are a wreck."

"We've had our ups and downs, but we'll always be there for each other."

"That's why you're my best friend."

Emily joined Sarah as her eyes welled with tears. The harder Emily cried, the more Sarah sobbed, until their ducts appeared to run dry.

Choking back the last of their sentiments, Emily pulled away, stretching her arms out to Sarah's shoulders, as if examining her. "Sarah. Look at me." Sarah cast her eyes upward to a now smiling Emily.

"What's so funny," she sniffed.

"I know what we'll do."

"We?"

"Yes, we," Emily corrected. "Sarah, I'll be your surrogate."

"You would do that for me?"

"You and only you," she laughed.

"Oh, Emily. That's the nicest gift anyone has ever offered me. But what about Paul? How do you think he'd feel? And your body takes a beating from pregnancy. He might not like that."

"Paul will be fine. He wants like five kids, so what's an extra one to him?"

"Five? Are you okay with so many?"

"At first, I was shocked, but after thinking about it, I decided I wouldn't tell him no."

"Why not?"

"I can't refuse the love of my life's desires. If that's what he wants, I want to give him that and so much more. Besides, that means more sex, and I think both of us can come to terms there," she laughed, easing the tension.

"Emily, you're a card."

"I know. But oh me, we better get a move on. You're late for practice."

"It's okay, I'll tell Coach I had some girl problems to take care of again."

"Does he ever question that?"

"Not after the hospital ordeal."

Walking out the door, Emily turned, forming an expression of plea, "Can we still get Paul?"

"Ha. Don't worry. We will. It's a distance day, so I won't fret over starting late."

By the time Sarah pulled into a spot next to the track, the sprinters had already split into their groups. Looking around, the distance team was nowhere to be found, indicating they were likely on the trail. Coach Cavlere stood along the bleachers, clearly waiting for Sarah before starting a run himself. As she approached, he crossed his arms, indicating his irritation.

"You're late, Sarah."

"I'm sorry. I've been having some girl issues lately."

"So, I hear. Is everything alright? You know you have to keep me updated if you are no longer cleared to run."

"I know, and it's not that."

"I think I need to ask what the trouble is then."

Sarah looked around, as to see who might hear her. Nigel and the others were long gone, and yet again, Jenna's absence persisted at the pole-vault. Only a few sprinters lingered nearby, but they too were fully emerged in their own conversations.

"It's nothing that will affect my running, I promise." However, his unwavering appearance required her to continue. "I'll tell you, but this is confidential."

"As always," he agreed.

"The doctor wants me to have a female exam because—"

Coach held up his hand, "Maybe it's best I don't know. But you can assure me that over all you're healthy?"

"One hundred percent."

"Good. I don't want to face the rest of the season if I can't count on you to lead the girls. Now hop to it. The team has already left, but Abby said she would circle to check if you were here."

"Thanks, Coach," she said, as she transitioned into a jog.

Keeping to the track, Sarah looped the edges of the paved surface for two laps until Abby appeared outside the gate. Seeing her bright smile, Sarah could not help but fixate on the jovialness Abby emitted as she strode across the field. Her auburn hair danced behind her as she glided closer, only pausing as she turned to join Sarah.

"I told Coach you would be here."

"Hey, sorry I'm late."

"Better late than never if it means I get to run with you. Is everything okay?"

"Yeah, Emily and I got to talking and I didn't keep an eye on the time. . . Which way do you want to run?"

"I figured we could do a version of the out and back."

"Is that where everyone else went?"

"No, they're on the short loop, but I figured you might want to end the same time as everyone else."

"The out and back works for me. It will give us a chance to talk without Nigel and Ralph hanging around," Sarah insisted. "How are you and Ralph anyways?"

"Fine. I took your advice and since we've slowed down, I think we've connected even more."

The two continued along the trail amongst the evergreens, winding along the mountain side. The glare of the sun soon gave way to the shadows of the mountains and the trees as they reached the turn around.

"I'm not sure what I'm going to do without you and Emily next year."

"What do you mean?"

"Who am I going to run with?" Abby laughed.

"I guess you will be the top girl, so you make a good point. You might have to run with the guys."

"Yeah. I just don't like running with them. It's kinda awkward. They always have their own conversations, and being a girl, I don't contribute to them. I might as well run by myself. Like one day, Nigel was mouthing off about—" Abby broke her sentence, realizing the sore subject she was touching on. "Sorry, it's nothing you would want to hear."

"You don't have to censor the conversation around me when it comes to Nigel," Sarah said, half curious if the story pertained to Jenna.

"Well, if you're sure."

"Go on."

"He was talking about how he was debating breaking up with Jenna."

"Why?"

"Something about he thought he could do better. I honestly started tuning him out."

"That's a harsh thing for him to say," Sarah muttered.

"Oh, I know. I didn't realize guys were that heartless when talking about their girlfriends. Do you think Ralph talks that way about me?"

"I doubt it. He isn't the jerk Nigel is. Ralph is too crazy about you for that. Besides, if he did, he'd probably be talking to Paul, and Paul would tell Emily, who would tell me, and that hasn't happened . . . Abby?"

"Yeah?"

"When was Nigel running his mouth about Jenna?"

"This was weeks ago."

"Did he say anything about them sleeping together?"

"No, but I got the drift that at that point they weren't."

"How so?"

"The manner in which he said he could do better sounded like frustration."

"Have you heard anything about why Jenna hasn't been at practice?"

"I noticed she has been gone, but no one ever mentioned it. I guess since she is a pole-vaulter, it doesn't really matter."

"I'll tell you something, but don't repeat it. The details will eventually be divulged, but I heard she's pregnant."

"Oh, wow. That would make sense. I can't see vaulting being good for a baby."

"Yeah, and she was at our last meet, but in street clothes."

"So, you think that's why they're staying together?"

"It makes sense. Although, maybe it was the fact that she started putting out, but I thought she wasn't one to hold back in bed."

"Now that you mention it, he said she had something special planned for him, so he would wait it out a little longer, to make sure."

CHAPTER 17:

The Rehearsal

After an hour's long battle to decide on which dress to wear, Sarah settled on the rose-colored one with black inlay. The material sculpted nicely to the curves of her body, yet without bunching at the stomach. Nothing felt worse than appearing bloated on any given day, but more so at a wedding.

Paul awaited downstairs as Emily resided in the bathroom with Sarah. With each change in appearance—style of hair, choice of shoes, and inquiry of jewelry—Sarah prompted Emily for her advice. No detail went assumed as Sarah intended to look her best.

"Sarah, you need to get a grip on yourself. Who are you trying to impress anyway?"

The onset of panic diminished upon hearing the question.

"Are you thinking about Michael or Wesley right now?"

Pulling away from the mirror, Sarah looked Emily dead straight in the eyes.

"I'm thinking of both."

"Sarah, why? I thought you were over Wesley. I mean, how many years has it been?"

"I know. And I was. This wedding is playing with my head though. Who wants to see their ex live happily ever after, while—"

"While what? You have Michael. You said yourself the two of you had resolved the fight from the other night."

"I do. I do have Michael, but Wesley will always be my first love."

"If it's only nostalgia, then put on your big girl panties and keep moving on with Michael. I'm convinced it's your body talking and not your heart. However, if you're still in love with him then we don't need to go. Which is it?"

Sarah turned to the mirror, deliberating the question, while trying to listen to her gut.

"We should go. I want to be his friend more than anything. If we don't, then that'll end those chances."

"Good," Emily said smiling. "We've spent the past few hours getting ready, and I'd hate for us to let that go to waste. No matter what you're thinking, I say we look mighty hot."

"Ha. We do."

"Are you ladies almost done?" called Paul from below.

"Just a minute. We'll be ready in a few."

"Oh, I almost forgot," said Emily, shuffling out of the room. She returned holding two boxes, which Sarah knew all too well. "These studs or the diamond earrings?"

"You should wear the diamonds, and I'll wear mine. Also," Sarah said, retrieving a box from her nightstand, "I'll wear the cross you got me."

"You're sure I shouldn't wear the studs?"

"You wear them all the time. You need to enjoy the diamonds," Sarah laughed.

Emily threaded the needle through her ears and fastened the clasp in place. "All set. Are you ready?"

Sarah took a final look in the mirror. "Yeah, I am."

Paul awaited at the landing below. His eyes widened as Emily made her way closer. "Wow! Who's the lucky guy who gets to take you out tonight, Emm?"

She smirked before giving him a kiss. "I'm not sure, but you got that right; he's lucky."

"And, Sarah. You look amazing. I dare say you girls outdid yourselves."

"Worth the wait, wasn't it?" Emily joked.

"Always is . . . Sarah, did Michael say he was meeting us here?" Paul asked.

"Yeah. I told him to be here by half past. What time is it?"

"It's a quarter till now. Maybe we should swing by and pick him up?"

"We might pass him if we do. Maybe you and Emily should go on, save us a seat in case we're late. Are you okay to drive that far, Paul?"

"Yeah, I've been driving the past two days with no issues. The doctor didn't mention any restrictions when he released me to drive. I think it was mainly a precaution before."

"Alright. Go ahead of me. I'll pick him up and see what's taking so long."

Following them outside to her car, Sarah headed along the road toward Michael's as Paul and Emily turned the other direction. She kept her eyes peeled for any sign of his car, hoping not to double back. Her mind considered what might be detaining him, but mainly her concern centered on them being the last to arrive, leaving all eyes to watch as they entered.

Reaching Michael's driveway, she relaxed the grip on her steering wheel. The lights inside shown through the living room and his car remained in the drive. Hustling to the door, Sarah knocked, withholding any frustration. Following a second knock and a few more minutes, Michael opened the door.

"Sarah, I was just about to leave. Come in for a second."

"We really need to get on the road."

"I know. I'm sorry. Bessie got sick and I was trying to clean and make sure she was alright before leaving."

Stepping inside, Sarah was met by the smell of vomit in the absence of Bessie's greeting.

"I just put her in the crate, but I think the smell sunk into the rug."

Sarah withheld a gag upon inhaling a full whiff of regurgitated dog food. "Poor thing. Is she going to be alright?"

"Yeah, I switched brands, and I guess that set her off. Come on, I'll throw the rug outside and we'll go."

Sarah waited at the door as Michael rolled the carpet into a cylinder and lugged it through the house. Given the outfit she wore, she was in no position to help, neither did she think she could stomach the stench to do so.

Water running from the bathroom was followed by the sloshing of his hands. Joining her once again, Michael ran his mouth from her forehead to her lips. Sarah leaned into his body, closing her eyes to the softness of his touch.

"Better to start the night on a good note instead of dog patrol," he laughed, inching his face away from hers.

"Will she be alright staying here alone for that long?"

"I have a friend checking in, so I left a note about the food. She'll be fine as long as she doesn't eat anymore of the new mix."

Taking her hand, Michael led her to the car.

"I'll drive," offered Sarah.

"Are you sure?"

"Yeah, I know the way and after all, I asked you to go with me, not the other way around."

"If you insist."

The Volkswagen sparked to life as Sarah turned the key. Heat still loomed in the air vents, warming the cabin quickly. She adjusted the thermostat as to not have to slide off her coat, while still keeping warm.

"Do you want some music?" Sarah asked.

"Not really. Maybe you can tell me what to expect. I doubt I'll know anyone but Paul and Emily."

"Yeah, also two of my other friends from high school, Caroline and Bryant, will be there. They've been dating since my sophomore year."

"Sounds pretty serious. Are you the only one that's not engaged?"

"They aren't. Just Emily. Although, I can't figure out why they're dragging their feet, unless he's saving for a ring."

"That's always a safe bet. What's the rule, three months of your salary?"

"Something crazy like that. Honestly though, she'll graduate this spring, and then I can see them getting married soon after. It seems pointless to get engaged if you've been together that long. Most people already consider you married anyhow," she laughed.

Considering their looming future, Michael interrupted. "What are your plans after college?"

"I've actually been considering that more seriously lately. My old teacher wanted me to visit her classroom, so I finally went. She even let me help with one of the lessons. They were so much fun. Dad had mentioned last semester she was getting ready to retire, so when I left, she walked me to the front office to talk with the principal about the opening. I haven't heard anything yet, but it's still exciting."

"Oh really. Are you qualified?"

"Not yet. However, with my core work, getting certified won't be hard."

"So, you're planning on returning home?"

"I mean, I guess. Nothing's set in stone. There's still a lot of unknown—"

"So . . . where does that leave us?" Michael persisted.

"It really shouldn't change anything. I'll be further away, but if we're both working then we can see each other on weekends, or even meet somewhere during the week if we wanted."

"Perhaps."

"Are you upset?"

"No, just surprised. I wish you would have told me about this before."

"The possible teaching job fell into my lap recently. I guess I could have told you, but this is the first instance we've had to talk since then."

"Fair enough... Let's talk about something else to clear the air. Who's the bride and groom, and which side will we be on?"

"The couple getting married is Wesley and Haley, but we'll be on the groom's side of the aisle."

"Oh, you are friends with the groom? How do you know him?"

Sarah realized the corner she was painting herself into. She had failed to mention the situation to Michael, on some level hoping he would go along for the ride and everything would play out smoothly. But at that moment, she realized the necessity of being open in their relationship.

"Don't freak out when I tell you this, because it was a long time ago. Wesley and I dated in high school. Caroline's boyfriend and he are best friends. Since Bryant is going to be in the wedding, Caroline wanted me to go."

"So how did you get invited?"

"I ran into his family at Christmas. In fairness, this was before you and I got together, and why I wanted you to come. I thought it would be better than going alone, and a good way for us to spend time together."

"I'm following so far, but I have to ask, did you screw him?"

"No. Absolutely not."

"And I'm not insinuating anything, but if you had, that would make this wedding really weird." Michael laid his hand across Sarah's thigh, patting her leg. "That makes me feel better though."

Sarah mirrored her hand along his leg.

"I agree completely, but no, we dated for maybe a year and a half."

"Wait, you dated that long and never slept together?"

"Yeah, what's wrong with that?"

"That's a long time to go without at least getting curious."

"We didn't have that kind of relationship. Sex was something we wanted to experience after marriage." Hearing the words leave her mouth, Sarah tensed, wishing she could retrieve them from the air.

"Sarah, have you never slept with a guy?"

She straightened her back in the seat, affirming her next words. "I have not, and there is nothing wrong with that."

"I wasn't going to say anything. But I guess I was far off when I assumed previously."

"You were. And that's why I was so mad. I'd never been humiliated like that before."

"Well, I'm sorry, and I understand now," he said, lowering his hand from her thigh to her knee. "Are you still wanting to save sex for marriage?"

"Yes . . . But can we change the subject again?"

"You said we're attending the rehearsal dinner tonight and then the wedding tomorrow?"

"Yeah, and I know what you're thinking. We aren't family. Apparently, some of them cancelled, and the meal was already paid for. You're okay with getting a free dinner, aren't you?"

"I won't argue with that. I packed two suits, just in case . . . What did your parents say about me spending the night? I've never stayed over at a girl's parents' before."

"It was my mom's idea, to save on hotel rooms," she half fibbed.

"Are they as conservative as you?"

"You and Paul will sleep in my brother's room, if that's what you mean."

"I figured as much."

Arriving at the venue, Sarah spotted Paul's truck parked separately from the cluster of cars. She pulled in beside him, noticing they were still waiting.

"Everything alright?" Paul asked.

"My dog got sick and you can imagine the rest," Michael offered.

"I rather not before we eat," interjected Emily. "Let's go; they are probably about to start."

Entering the church, the four found an open seat where Caroline sat alone. Sarah scooted down the bench, tucking her dress under her legs to slide easier.

"Hey, Caroline. So good to see you again."

"Sarah, I've missed you," she said while exchanging hugs. "Who all have you brought?"

"This is my date, Michael, and beside him is my roommate, Emily, and her fiancé, Paul."

"Good to meet you all. We're going to have so much fun this weekend," said Caroline before turning to Sarah. "He's a cutie. You'll have to tell me where you found him."

Embarrassment streaked her eyes, knowing that Caroline's voice naturally flowed loud enough for the others to hear. "Caroline," she whispered.

"What?" she questioned, before leaning over to address the others. "That's my boyfriend standing next to the groom. Bryant's the best man, but he'll be joining us for dinner."

Sarah sat and watched as Wesley and Haley went through the motions of the ceremony. The idea of him getting married bore easier seeing the wedding play out before the actual exchange of vows. However, she clasped her hand in Michael's as they reached the traditional "you may kiss the bride" presentation.

Michael leaned closer as they held the embrace. "Do you think they've done it yet?"

Sarah responded with a slight shake of her head.

"Usually, most girls put out once they get engaged," he continued.

Sarah tightened the grip around his fingers, hoping to silence his commentary, but also in a sudden fear. He was right. Emily and Paul were a prime example of breaking that barrier before the wedding. She was naïve to think differently, but also, she knew Wesley, knew him on a level no one else but Haley would. Even though the wife-to-be unquestionably knew him better, there remained a piece of him that only Sarah would ever know.

At this point, Wesley and Haley started their procession down the aisle. As they approached the back row where her group sat, Wesley poked a smile in their direction. After grazing the last bench, they turned and rejoined the wedding party at the front.

Sarah could hear the final preparations being made between the preacher and the others. Agreeing on the last of the arrangements, the bridesmaids and groomsmen trickled from the altar, leaving Wesley and Haley behind. Taking note, the guests left the chapel soon after, as they headed a few blocks away for the rehearsal dinner.

As Sarah and the others made their way to the door, a hand caught her shoulder. "You made it," said Wesley.

"Hey. We did, and congratulations to you two."

"Thanks, Sarah. And who has the honor of escorting you tonight," he said, turning toward Michael.

"Hi, Michael's the name. Thanks for having us."

"Of course. Any friend of Sarah is a friend of mine. You'll have to excuse me though. I have to loop back with the wedding party, but I wanted to personally thank you all for coming while I had the chance." Without further reservation, Wesley rushed down the aisle to the awaiting Haley. Sarah watched as they joined hands and Haley gestured a smile, accompanied by a wave. Lifting her hand, Sarah did the same.

"What do you think so far?" she asked Michael.

"Nice guy. I guess some people can be friends with their ex. I never had such luck."

"Hey, Sarah, I'll meet you at the restaurant," called Caroline. "I'm going to ride with Bryant."

"Alright. I'll see you there!"

Walking out to her car, Sarah settled inside before she continued the conversation. "You know, I've told you a lot about my past, but you haven't shared anything with me."

"Ha. The past is the past. What's there to share?"

Sarah raised her cheeks and took his hand, signifying that she longed for more.

Michael exhaled loudly, "What do you want to know?"

"Do you have a lot of ex-girlfriends?"

"I dated a girl pretty seriously in college. She ended up breaking things off, and that crushed me. We were together for two years, on and off."

"Did you give up on dating after her?"

"I still dated, but I've always been cautious."

"Did you love her?"

"Of course. She was my world."

"I take it you slept together?"

"About six months in, we started having sex. I think around that time is when the relationship got rocky. I'm not sure why; I've drowned out the details. And yes, she was my first."

Sarah looked down at the steering wheel and began reaching for the gear shift before pausing. "Is she the only girl you've had sex with?"

"Sarah, once you've had sex, you can't turn off that desire so easily."

"But I thought you said she was the only serious relationship you've had?"

"After we broke up, I spent the rest of college trying to heal those wounds. That's a tough mental game, which led to a few hookups."

"How many?"

"Uhhh. . ."

"How many girls have you slept with total?"

"Sarah, I honestly don't think that matters anymore. So, I wish you wouldn't harp on it. And I wore protection, so it's not like I have any kids."

Forfeiting the conversation, Sarah lifted her hand to the shifter and started down the road. The ride fell quiet the entire way, pushing a void between them.

When they arrived at the restaurant, Sarah unbuckled, then reached for the door handle in silence. Before she could open the door, Michael caught her by the arm.

"Five. I've been with five girls. Is that better?"

"Yes, thank you."

CHAPTER 18:

Wedding Bells

Neither the sound of Emily's snore nor the murmur of sleep-talking woke Sarah that night. Instead, her face awoke to a glob of slobber sticking her cheek to the pillow. All three girls had managed to fit into Sarah's bed comfortably, while the guys all settled in sleeping bags on her brother's bedroom floor. When her eyes casted open, the deep sleep proved refreshing; however, the dread of what the day held soon presented itself.

Rolling to her back, Sarah checked to see if Emily and Caroline were still asleep. There were better ways to savor the morning, but instead she chose to peel the covers back and face the day.

In the hall, she pulled the door shut, then paused to listen for any signs of life coming from her brother's room. If Matty had stayed with the other guys, their sleep would have been interrupted earlier than usual. However, his placement on the couch left the upstairs completely quiet. Only hushed voices from the kitchen could be heard.

To her surprise, the three people occupying the downstairs were not just her family. Matty having moved to her parents' bed early that morning, left Cliff, Megan, and Michael circled around the table, enjoying coffee.

"Good morning, Sarah," Michael said cheerfully. "How'd you sleep?

"Apparently, like a rock. Emily sometimes talks in her sleep, and I didn't hear a peep last night. How about you?"

"Once I got settled, I did pretty well. I might have woken up once to adjust my pillow."

"Liv, can you help me in the kitchen for a few minutes," her mother asked, rising from the table. "If you'll knead the dough for biscuits, I'll start the sausage and bacon."

"Liv?" Michael asked.

"As in Olivia," Sarah smiled. "That's my middle name."

"Hmm, I like it."

Leaving her father to entertain Michael, Sarah headed to the kitchen where her mother waited eagerly.

Sarah looked around, noticing the biscuits were ready to pop into the oven, while the meat laid next to the frying pan. "You already—"

"I know. I just wanted to talk to you about Michael."

"Oh."

"He seems like a really nice guy. But why didn't you tell us that he was thinking about moving here after you graduated?"

Sarah's eyes widened. "Wait, he said he was? He never mentioned it to me."

"Really? The way he talked, it sounded like you helped plan the details."

"No, I had suggested our relationship would continue as normal. If I'm living here, and he is in Beval, we could make the drive in an afternoon if we wanted . . . Did he mean he would be living alone, or did he infer that I would live with him?"

"Just him. I think we raised you better than to move in with a guy. But I thought it was sweet of him to consider extending his commute to be closer to you."

"That would make dating much easier. You know how well I handle distance," Sarah laughed.

"So far, I like him. He's very respectful, and as soon as we met, Michael gave me the impression he wanted to fit in, and he appears to be doing so . . . How are you feeling about the wedding today?"

"I'm fine. We talked to Wesley last night, and he was really glad to see us."

"What did you get them for a wedding gift?"

"Mom! I completely forgot. What should I—"

"Get your ex for a gift?" she finished. "Don't worry. I figured that would be the last thing on your mind. I bought a set of ceramic bowls that were on the registry. You can take those if you like."

"Thanks, Mom, you're a lifesaver."

Megan bent down and pulled a box from the cabinet, setting the bowls on the counter.

"There's wrapping paper upstairs. Do you have time?"

"I can handle it. I'll go dig the paper out of the closet."

"One more thing, Sarah. If you and Michael want to visit for another weekend, he is welcome anytime."

"Thanks. Judging from how well he's taking to you and Dad, we probably will."

Outside the kitchen, Cliff and Michael's discussion now focused on this season's baseball projections. Sarah walked to Michael's side, where her hip butted up to the back of his chair. Breaking into the conversation, she placed her hand on his shoulder.

"Are you two having fun? I forgot to wrap the wedding present."

"Yeah, just discussing sports, but I can help you."

"That's alright."

"I insist. I've been told before that I'm handy with the tape and scissors."

"Oh, by whom?"

"Possibly my first-grade teacher, but I doubt she would have lied to me."

"We shall see then. Come on. Everything we need is upstairs in the closet."

Michael followed Sarah as they tiptoed up the stairs. Eyeing her flannel pajama pants, he gave her a gentle smack on the behind, causing her to double step. Sarah turned and smiled. "Easy, boy," she said, giving him a kiss. Turning around, they continued to the hallway. Sarah flipped on the light, instructing him to wait while she went to the closet.

Inside, a box sat flat against the wall, holding wrappings for any occasion. Sarah examined the assortment, looking for a pattern fitting for a wedding. Settling on a white background with silver stripes, she fished out the scissors and tape before flipping off the closet light and returning to the hallway. However, instead of her eyes seeing Michael, her pupils dilated to the surrounding darkness.

"Very funny, turned off the lights, didn't you?"

"I did," Michael said, his voice coming from the floor.

Sarah felt her way along the wall, until she reached the spot where she heard Michael. His hand caught her by the calf, tugging at her to join him below. Sliding down the wall, Sarah felt his hand glide up her leg. As she came to rest beside him, his breath trickled from her cheek to her lips. Michael's hand continued to progress higher, coming to rest at the top of her thigh. Just as their lips met, he adjusted his hand to cup around her. Her body tightened as her heartbeat intensified. Sarah leaned into him, guiding her hand to his face.

"We've got to stop," she whispered.

Michael peeled away his hand and reclined his head onto the wall. Breathlessly, Sarah buried her head into his shoulder as he stroked her hair. "Are you sure?" he asked, but the question went unanswered.

Their heads lifted and eyes dimmed as Sarah's bedroom door opened. Emily stood above them, offering judging eyes. "Am I interrupting something?" she laughed.

"We were about to wrap some bowls," Sarah suggested, pulling away.

"If that's how you do it then maybe I could learn," said Emily, flipping on the lights and easing herself to the floor. "Sarah, what time are we supposed to leave?" continued Emily, dispersing the tension.

"The ceremony is the same time as last night, but I would say we need to get there at least thirty minutes early."

"What are you going to do while us girls get ready?"

"Bryant said they planned on playing a softball game at the park around lunch time. They invited Paul and me to join."

Sarah unrolled the paper, then handed the scissors to Michael. "Your turn."

"So basically, I have to wrap the present?"

"You were the one talking a big game earlier. Let's see what you can actually do."

"The folding and ribbon are all you. Just tell me where to place the tape."

"Typical guy," Emily huffed. "I'm going to get a shower before everyone uses all the hot water."

Sarah finished the present with minimal assistance from Michael, as he soon found his way downstairs. As she positioned the final piece of tape in place, she examined her work for possible snags. Satisfied with the outcome, Sarah checked on Emily before heading to the living room. It was not until the guys left for their game, did she venture back upstairs and into the shower.

A bustle of commotion arose some hours later when the three guys returned to the house. Each lathered and rinsed quickly, transitioning into their suits before their dates finished their final touches.

With Caroline and Emily crammed into her bathroom, getting ready proved much more challenging. One mirror, one sink, and three women made a tight fit, but none wanted the luxury of their own amenities while missing out on the laughter.

The excitement carried unceasingly until they finally considered themselves ready. Megan awaited in the living room with her camera, insisting they each pose for pictures, with one final group photo before leaving.

The couples split en route to their cars, leaving Sarah and Michael alone. He waited until they pulled from the driveway before addressing what was on his mind. "We don't have to stay and watch the wedding if you don't want, Sarah," Michael said as they followed the other two cars to the church.

"Why wouldn't we?"

"I figured you might not be up for it after all. Like you said, you want to be a good friend, but do you want to at your own expense?"

"Well, it may not be easy, but there is no use in turning around now."

"I wasn't suggesting turning around and going home."

"What did you have in mind then?"

Michael pulled a card from his chest pocket and handed it to Sarah. "If things get bad and you need an escape, I booked a room at the motel across the street. Apparently, you only have the one in town, but it would beat breaking down in front of everyone."

"I doubt I'll get too emotional. It's natural to shed a few tears at a wedding, but aside from that, I'll be fine."

"You might as well hang on to it; I won't be needing it."

Sarah wedged the key into the side of her purse. A few troubling thoughts crossed her mind as they drove, but with Michael and the girls by her side, there stood no reason for nervousness. If anything, she felt elated. There were no feelings of hate, but instead only love from Wesley and Haley.

The front doors opened to the smell of fresh flowers within the air. The two shades of blue that coordinated the bride's color choices adorned every door, bench, and rail, as an elegant arrangement centered the guests' attention to the altar. Within the staging stood three candle holders, two with smaller white sticks, and another undoubtedly clutching the unity candle.

Tucking herself into the bench, Sarah allowed Michael the far inside seat, followed by her and Emily. Considering if she hid within the pews, unable to move left or right, there would be no motive to leave or make any other movements.

Inside each bench, seats were distinguished by simple portraits of the couple. Since the photo, Wesley had clean shaven and tidied his hair. The smile etched across his face mocked Sarah's memory of when he once looked at her the same way.

Emily's voice sounded in her ear, speaking of how she might incorporate some of the same designs into her own wedding. Sarah spoke inattentively, resounding reassurance in her choices. Blue felt odd for a spring ceremony, and knowing Emily had another scheme in mind, she broke her trance.

"Why do you think she chose blue?"

"Her favorite color I suppose."

Relaxing back in her seat, Sarah eased her mind. Arriving early bore its own perks. Finding their seats before others and avoiding greetings and formalities at the front door meant no awkward conversations, introductions, or running into either set of parents.

Looking at the picture again, she recalled the night she met Haley. They not only struck a similar appearance but also felt like friends themselves. No jealousy from either party, only admiration. Deep down, she was happy for them both. Looking to Michael, Sarah considered there was no reason not to be. They both had someone in their lives with the promise of a sound future.

Confidence built as groomsmen began to usher in the families. Of the party, the only one she recognized for sure was Bryant. Even if she had forgotten his face, the fact that he acknowledged Caroline at every trip he made down the aisle would have given him away.

"Sarah, can you come to the bathroom with me?" Emily asked. Sarah's face portrayed her reluctance to leave, but Emily persisted. "I don't want to hold it the entire time, and if I wait any longer, it'll be too late."

"We'll only be a minute," Sarah instructed as she pushed past Michael to the outside aisle.

Emily followed Sarah along the side and into the foyer. The wedding party quickly formed from a bustling crowd, as someone advised only ten minutes remained until the start. Hurrying through the restroom door, Sarah turned to Emily, "Make it quick."

Rushing to the stall, Emily wasted no time making the two-sided purpose of the trip known. "Are you still okay?"

"Did you pull me out here just to ask that?"

"No, my bladder was about to burst too, but I also felt like asking when you weren't sitting next to Michael."

"I'm fine, but I'd be better if we weren't the last guests to get our seats."

"You heard the man, ten minutes," she said, flushing the toilet.

"Can we go now?"

"Lead the way."

Pulling open the door, Sarah stopped as a mass of white formed in the foyer. Haley's dress, which lay bunched in her hands, fell to the floor as her maid of honor worked to fluff the sides. The veil hung loosely over her face, yet the garment created an illusion in which Haley resembled Sarah. The stopping of time along with the beat of her heart rendered Sarah motionless. The image of herself in the wedding dress not only felt real but unquestionable.

Emily jarred her shoulder. "Are you coming?"

"Umm . . . now I have to go," she said, retracting her daydream. "I'll meet you inside."

"You're the one that has to hurry now, but okay, I can't walk as fast as you, so I'll head in."

Sarah retreated to the far stall and hovered over the toilet, unsure if she would vomit or faint. Her legs weakened, causing her to stumble backwards against the partition. The time to decide had subconsciously been pushed to the last possible moment: run down the middle of the church to stop the wedding or sit quietly with her friends as she watched the only man she ever loved marry another woman.

A feeling of dry heaving lured her head to the porcelain rim. *I can't. It's too late. And if I watch . . . I might as well vomit in here. So, I'm just going to stay and wait it out?* But there was a third option. Recalling the motel key Michael slipped her earlier, Sarah pulled the card from her purse. The Amply, as he said, was just a short walk across the street. Staying there for the ceremony then mingling during the reception would require little effort. Her friends would notice she was missing, yet once the procession started, they would be stuck. She could even manage a lie and say she fell in behind the bride and snuck in the side. Besides them, no one else would know, better yet care.

Sneaking to the sink, the stall door shut with a slight clatter. Checking her appearance in the mirror, Sarah gathered her courage before easing the door slightly open. Her eyes focused through the gap, patiently waiting until the white dress left her sight.

Processional music suddenly echoed through the chapel and foyer. Rushing to the double doors, she peeked through the crevice created from the missing center door jam. Haley's dress blocked much of the view; however, she could see part of the row where Caroline was perched on the edge. Waiting until Haley finished the enduring journey, Sarah mustered a final look as Wesley joined hands with his bride.

Pulling away, Sarah rushed outside. Realizing her sudden outburst might draw bypassers' attention, she slowed her steps until reaching the road. Her heels clicked as they bounced over the pavement; however, the flopping against her feet did not cease until she was concealed by the motel walls.

Room seven entailed a king-size bed, a small refrigerator, and about as standard of a bathroom as they came. Settling on the corner of the dated bedspread, Sarah ran the card through her fingers. Images of Wesley undressing Haley and confining their bodies to the bed of some honeymoon suite flashed before her eyes. The same hands that once held her, the same lips that once kissed her, the same love he once showed her, all being showered over Haley. Her heartbeat fluctuated to the surges of passion she felt being exchanged between the two.

With her head drooped, Michael's words echoed from within. He was probably right. The marriage was only a formality. Since becoming engaged, the two had likely made love. Sarah wasn't losing Wesley that day; she had already lost him.

Tears crashed against her sobbing cheeks and pooled into her hands. Her heart hardened in refusal to believe she could have ever let him go. Collapsing onto the mattress, Sarah released the suppressed emotions. She folded her arms across her chest, aching for a warm touch of comfort.

Realizing she would soon need to rejoin the others for the reception, Sarah lifted herself from the bed and ran her hands over her goosebump-ladened arms. With a deep breath, she wiped her tears and then practiced a smile with the mirror across the room. Deciding little could mask her insecurities, she darkened her eyes shut. Listening to the sole sound of her body, her breathing stopped at the sound of the door opening.

The latch clicked as a card from the outside pulled from the slot. Steadying to her feet, Sarah crept to the door just as it began opening. The warming smile upon Michael's face on the other side softened the tension in her muscles.

"I thought I'd find you here. What happened?"

"I lost it . . . Seeing the bride. . . I couldn't."

"Do you still love him?"

"I don't even know if that's the problem. There are so many emotions right now; it's hard to say."

Michael gathered Sarah in his arms, kissing her gently on the lips.

Relishing his embrace, Sarah paused upon the taste of his breath.

"Have you been drinking?"

"I thought this would be an eventful weekend, so I brought along my own," he said, removing a flask from inside his jacket pocket. "Care to have some? It'll take the edge off."

Sarah took hold of the canister and sipped the last of which it contained. Shaking the empty vessel, she handed it back.

"Sorry, I started earlier without you."

"You don't seem drunk," she laughed.

"I have a good poker face of sorts."

Michael motioned for Sarah to turn around as he raised his hands to her shoulders and slid the dress cuffs down her arms. His fingers worked along her neck, kneading the muscles before moving to her arms and down her back. "Take a seat on the bed." Following the guidance of his arms, Sarah sat where she previously rested. Turning her to face him, Michael resumed kissing her, while his hands worked to unzip the dress.

Hesitation followed as Sarah reached to secure her outfit. "We probably need to get to the reception, before someone notices we're both gone," said Sarah, standing to her feet. However, Michael caught her wrist tightly, jerking her toward the bed.

"Just a minute," he persisted.

Bouncing backwards, Sarah fell beside Michael, indulging in his forthcoming kisses. Easily, he worked his right hand inside her dress, gripping her thigh before gliding his fingers to the outside of her underwear. "Granny panties, huh?"

"Yeah, so."

He laughed and shook his head as he slid them over and projected his fingers inside. Sarah jerked with a slight grimace of shock and indulgence. Paralysis stunned her body as she sat comprehending what was happening. At first, his presence brought more discomfort; however, giving into the desire from within, the tension in her body soon eased.

Pulling his hand from her dress, Sarah caught her breath while trying to find her words. Leaving her motionless, Michael stood from the bed as he worked to undo his pants.

"What are you doing?" she sighed.

"My turn," he said, holding her shoulder with his hand.

"Michael, we can't. I know I'm a mess, but it wouldn't be right."

His grip moved to her neck as he tightened his clasp, forcing her to focus upward. "I've tolerated your sensitivity all this time."

"Please," Sarah negotiated. "I will later, just not right now." A single tear crested her cheek.

"Do you promise?"

"Yes—"

Michael loosened his hand and rebuttoned his pants. He leaned over, slipping his tongue between her lips, and then pulled her from the bed. One hand hooked around her waist as the other lifted her chin to anchor her eyes on him. "You make me crazy. I get all worked up just thinking about you. I know why he wanted you in the first place now."

"What do you mean?"

"He thought you would be a good lay. And, I bet he's right?"

"Wesley never tried to sleep with me. That's not the type of guy he is."

"Oh please. Every guy thinks about getting a girl naked. And by the way, you're welcome."

"Welcome? For what?"

"You won't be able to look at him the same now."

"What do you mean?"

"I don't believe your goody ex-boyfriend ever made that move. Did he?"

"No, but—"

"Just think, if you would let me, I would give you something to completely take your mind off of him."

"I highly doubt that."

"Quit acting like a prude, when in reality you're no saint."

Sarah batted her hand across his cheek without thinking or hesitation.

"Okay then." Michael raised his hand, slapping her across the face. Sarah covered herself, as if he might try to bash her other side, yet he paused. "You question me, but in reality, you need me more than I need you."

The pain that pounded Sarah's face left her silent, listening to his every word. "I want to be with you. Wesley clearly doesn't feel that way anymore. Get over him before I decide to walk out."

"Why did you hit me?" she asked timidly.

"You've hit me twice now. I figured you needed a wake-up call with your own medicine. Now what are we going to do?"

"Are you going to hit me anymore?"

"Not if you don't provoke me."

"I want to go find Emily and Caroline."

"That's not an option."

"Why not? They are probably getting worried about me by now. Did you not tell them where you were going?"

"I didn't have to."

"That means they'll be asking everyone else if they've seen me."

"I highly doubt that."

"What do you mean?"

"The wedding is over . . . Haley ran out."

"What?"

"She made it all the way to the altar, and just as the preacher started going through his part, she started to pull away. The next thing everyone knew, she was running through the double doors."

"But why?"

"She didn't tell me on her way out, but I wouldn't be surprised if it had something to do with you and Wesley."

"Then why wouldn't she say something before, instead of making a big scene?"

"Why would you come to the wedding, then leave before it ever started?"

Sarah stopped to consider her choice. All the excitement of the wedding might have masked her inner feelings, until withholding them no longer prevailed.

"What about Wesley? Where is he?"

"Is that all you're worried about? He ran after her of course. I told you he loves her, not you."

"That's not all I'm worried about. How do you know Emily and Caroline aren't looking for me?"

"I told them I would find you and make sure you got home safely. There was no need for them to stick around; without a reception, they insisted, but eventually agreed.

"Well, can we head home now?"

"You drove. Remember?"

Sarah checked the zipper on her dress, then slipped on her coat.

"I have the room for the night. Why don't we stay here? You're obviously too upset to drive."

"I rather not."

"Suit yourself. Just don't forget, Haley will be making up this whole day to Wesley tonight. Married or not."

"Why do you insist on telling me that? You don't think I know what they're doing?"

"You could have that too," Michael said, closing the door.

CHAPTER 19:

Within a Field

Sarah lugged the mattress up the stairs as Emily moved the smaller belongings to their original places. With the scheduled therapy sessions completed, Emily sought freedom from the chair by climbing the stairs unassisted and returning to her room.

"You know I don't mind having your bed downstairs."

"Now that I can get up here by myself, I thought it would be better, for when Paul spends the night."

"I just hope I can't hear you two through the walls."

"You won't, but that's better than seeing us singing, isn't it?"

Sarah shook her head as she pushed the mattress against the wall. "Where is Paul anyways? He would be a big help."

"He wanted to, but he has a big test to study for."

"And why do you want to go to the pool after we finish?"

"I've started to enjoy swimming," said Emily. "Besides you get a workout at track, and the few laps I complete in the pool are at least something."

Emily opened the hamper that contained her clean sheets and tossed one end of the bedding to Sarah. As Sarah pulled the corners over the bottom edges, Emily fixed the ruffles on top.

"Have you heard anything about the wedding?"

"No, but I probably will, the next time I go home."

"I didn't want to ask in front of everyone when you got back to the house after us, but where did you go?"

"I got too sick to watch, so I left."

"That bad, huh?"

"And, it only got worse—"

"What do you mean?"

"Michael got upset with me. He thinks I was the reason she ran out, but I don't think so. I barely talked to them, and if she didn't want me at the wedding, then why was I ever invited?"

"Exactly. Besides you didn't do anything wrong."

"I guess he felt jealous. Anyways, he tried telling me what he thought, and the bad part is, he probably was right. I somehow still have feelings for Wesley and it's making me confused . . . Then, he did something to make me forget about him."

"What did he do?"

"He ran his fingers inside me."

"Did it work?" Emily asked.

"Emm!" Sarah said in embarrassment.

"Well . . ."

Sarah sighed. "At first it did, but while he was in me, I started thinking about Wesley. Afterward, he told me that I would never be able to look at Wesley the same, and on some level, I believe him."

"You didn't!" Emily exclaimed.

"It wasn't like I was trying to imagine being with a different guy. That's just where my thoughts went."

"So, what happened after that? Did you, you know—"

Sarah paused for a minute, then took a breath before continuing. "He wanted me to give it up and have sex right there."

"Wait, where were you?"

"That's not important, but a motel. Let me finish . . . He started undressing, and I told him I couldn't do it then. Luckily, he listened, but he expects me to, and soon I'd imagine."

"Why didn't you?"

"I didn't want my first time to be because I was upset. I almost made that mistake before, remember?"

"Oh yeah, sorry. So now what?"

"I feel like I should give in to some extent, but I don't want to be pressured into anything."

"You don't have to have sex, instead just return the favor. He's only looking for the next step in the relationship anyways. I bet if you do that, he'll forget the whole wedding ordeal."

"You think so?"

"I do. Guys are like puppies. They only want attention, and no matter if you're rubbing their ears or their bellies, they don't care, as long as you aren't making them beg."

"Do you make Paul beg?" Sarah teased. "Actually, never mind, I rather not know."

"Ha! There's no begging; I want him as much as he does me."

Shaking her head, Sarah looked about the room, examining their work. "Does this look right?" Sarah asked as she discarded the last of the boxes.

"It does. Thank you. Paul and I will keep the noise at a minimum to return the favor."

"Gee, thanks, Emm. Are you ready to go swim?"

"Yes. Let me change," she said, lifting up her shirt.

"While you're doing that, I'll get mine."

A few minutes later, Sarah returned modeling her suit in the doorway.

"I hope you're wearing something over that?"

"I will, but why? Does it look bad?"

"No, but I feel like racing today, and I don't want you cramping because your muscles aren't warm."

"Oh really?"

"Come on, Sarah," she said, grabbing her hand.

The water failed to lap the sides of the pool, as no other swimmers resided inside. Only the sound of a lone lifeguard broke the silence as he said hello in passing.

"I don't think Michael will be around," Emily said confidently. "If you're that worried, the lifeguard might know."

"It's fine. It's not like we're going to get it on in the pool."

"Thanks for the notice . . . Are you ready or do you need to warm up?" asked Emily.

"How about a few push-ups, just to get the blood flowing?"

"Let's do a starter lap instead."

"That works for me."

Sarah jumped in at Emily's command. Each stayed within view of the other, watching their facial expressions through the goggles during each stroke of their shared side.

As they reached the far end, Sarah turned and pushed from the wall mere seconds before Emily and then slowed her pace enough to fall in sync. She twisted her body through the water, eyeing the line at the bottom of the pool. Only as they approached the start, did she glide in preparation to meet the wall.

Pulling her head from the water, Sarah adjusted her bangs that now stuck to the sides of her goggles.

"I'm ready if you are," Sarah said.

"I feel great. Let's go down and back twice."

"Sure. You can call the start."

Emily situated her grip along the edge of the pool as she turned to Sarah. Her daring smile flashed brightly before initiating the start.

"On your mark, Get set. Go!" Emily exclaimed as her face met the water.

Crashing her head beneath, Sarah's exhale went unseen among the surrounding bubbles. The splashing beside her gave assurance that Emily had not achieved a lead upon her quick start. Hammering forward, she kicked her legs, hoping to edge ahead. Turning her eyes briefly toward the other lane, she noticed another smile as Emily pulled face to face with her. However, with a jolt forward, Sarah began to inch ahead.

The water flowed freely over her skin, and the exertion emulated flying over a distant land with blue ranges of grass below. Her breathing became more systematic, and each stroke found a better rhythm. Sarah reached the far wall before Emily, yet this time, she decided not to slow up on the return.

Sarah quickly regained a full breath as Emily latched her fingers onto the edge and then pushed off. A few strokes later, she could hear Emily following, her presence feeling as though she was within reach of Sarah's toes. Lowering her head under the water and counting off five strokes instead of three, Sarah pulled herself over the water until she could feel Emily fall behind.

As Sarah reached the wall, she instantly turned for the second lap. Emily flashed by as the two passed a few yards apart. A trail of blonde hair was all Sarah noticed in their brief elapse.

The further down the lane she swam, the more distance she felt between them. A slight hesitation warranted her to pause before turning into the homestretch, as something felt out of place. As she thrusted away from the wall, she noticed this time Emily was not coming in from the other side. Having outkicked her came as no surprise but looking ahead there was still no sign of her approach.

Sarah stopped mid stroke and began treading water as she glanced to the adjacent lane, but there was no Emily. Again, she went under, continuing to progress toward the wall. As her eyes refocused, a glimmer caught Sarah's eye. A diamond ring, within a field of dark blue, sparkled from the stray light above. Terror struck her body upon realizing the ring was attached to a motionless silhouette at the bottom of the pool.

Sarah flipped her hips upward and frantically dove to the bottom. The breath in her lungs expanded against her insides the deeper she swam. Realizing the air was pulling her to the surface, Sarah dispelled the oxygen in her lungs, allowing her to sink closer to Emily.

Securing her hands under Emily's arms, Sarah tugged with all her might. She looked above, pleading for Emily to help lift themselves to the surface, but Emily remained limp. As the struggle persisted, her own body grew weaker with each attempt. There would be no way she would leave Emily, but as Sarah considered her own demise, a cloud of bubbles appeared overhead. Two hands stretched out from within the haze, releasing Sarah of the burden. With Sarah free to rise toward the surface, the set of hands tethered to Emily, snatching her from the bottom of the pool.

Sarah broke the surface with a gasp, followed by a cry for help. Seconds later, the lifeguard emerged from beneath, hastily dragging Emily to the edge. He shoved her upper torso over the concrete and then lifted her legs from the water. Frantically, Sarah crawled over the side, as he lifted himself from the pool.

Kneeling beside Emily, the guard tilted her head, assessing no noticeable breath or pulse. Cupping his hands together, he flattened his palms on her chest and pumped his arms as he counted. Pausing, he forced a deep breath into her mouth, then returned to her chest.

Sarah slid across the cement, alongside the two. "Come on, Emily! Breathe!"

"One, two, three," called the lifeguard. "Give her another breath," he instructed. Sarah pulled back her hair and gaped open her mouth following a deep inhale. Her mouth settled over Emily's lips as she thrust every ounce of air into her body."

"One, two, three . . . Again!"

Determined, Sarah cradled Emily's head in one hand while holding her chin with the other. Pressing their lips together, she mustered another deep breath, expelling all she had into the crevices of Emily's lungs.

Sarah settled on her knees as her arms propped her over Emily.

"One, two, three . . . Again!"

Another influx filled Emily's lungs without a response.

"I don't think she's . . . going to make it," said the lifeguard.

"No. We have to keep trying," Sarah insisted. Shoving him out of the way, Sarah threw her leg over Emily. Now straddling her body, she pounded her hands into her chest, trying to force the water out. Giving five hard thrusts, she gave Emily a breath, but still nothing.

Other voices echoed nearby as an arm tugged at Sarah's shoulder. Shrugging them off, she continued to pump her arms. Again, the set of hands tried to pry her away, but instead, Sarah latched her arms and legs around Emily, clutching to the last bit of life she had.

Not budging, two sets of arms pried her clasp lose, raising Sarah to her feet. Suddenly, a loud scream pierced her ears, hammering against her insides. Only when Michael arrived and wrapped his arms around Sarah's body, muffling her mouth, did Sarah realize she was the one screaming.

By this time, a stretcher collapsed onto its wheels beside Emily as a young man checked her pulse. Shaking his head, he checked his watch. They loaded her body onto the cart and pulled a sheet over to cover her face. Sarah wanted to cry out again, but she no longer could find the strength within. Even the urge to sob was withdrawn from shortness of breath.

She strained to free herself from Michael, but he only gripped tighter.

"Let her go," he said. "There's nothing you can do."

Sarah watched as the men rolled the cart away. The wheels bumped against the doorjamb as they swiveled to clear the exit. The last end to travel through was Emily's head, and a lock of blonde hair that dangled just below the sheet.

"Can you take me to the hospital?"

"I don't think they're going—"

"Take me to the hospital!" she screamed.

Michael draped a towel around Sarah's shoulders, urging her to first grab her clothes. Sarah listened only for directional purposes, unable to determine what to do next.

Fumbling the locker open, Sarah jerked her clothes from the gym bag. Her now shivering body trembled as she worked the pants over her drenched legs. The denim bore harder as it conformed to her body, barely riding over her hips. Disregarding her hair, Sarah flung on a shirt and raced to the pool.

"Let's go," she directed breathlessly.

Seeing her disheveled attire, Michael draped his jacket around her. "I'm parked in the back."

Sarah began running as Michael followed behind. Despite everything she had seen and her own effort to revive Emily, hope still loomed in her mind. She had lost Emily once before, and she couldn't bear the thought of doing so again.

Reaching the car first, she jostled the door until Michael reached across the seat to pop the lock. She sat silently as they sped through the parking lot and toward the hospital. The lifeguard's words drummed tauntingly inside her head. "One, two, three . . . breathe. One, two, three . . ." Sarah counted again and again, hoping to reinstall the breath into Emily's lungs. Sarah closed her eyes, yet again trying to pray for Emily's life. No matter the urgency with which she whispered the petition, only the trailing thoughts of trying to revive Emily meddled with her mind.

Pouring out her heart, the hope for peace that everything would be fine failed to come. Unlike the prayer by Emily's bedside, there was no reassurance. This time there was only dread and despair.

Sarah's eyes opened to a blur of tears. Wiping them away, the view of the hospital focused into vision, and she knew it was too late.

As Michael pulled along the emergency entrance, Sarah leapt from the car and ran toward the now empty ambulance. A paramedic closing the doors met her with concern. "Where is Emily?" But the man could only shake his head and look to the double doors of the hospital.

Running inside, Sarah paused as she realized she knew not where she was going. "The girl . . . they just brought in. Where is she?"

"I'm not sure, miss; have a seat and I'll see what I can find out."

Sarah paced the floor, unable to settle in a chair. She hovered near the wing where doctors and nurses occasionally appeared to converse with families. However, there were no doctors that called Emily's name. Only the lone conventional clock could be heard ticking: one, two, three.

The moments to follow were neither of a conscious nor unconscious state. Michael at some point arrived after parking the car, but spoke only in drones, to which she gave no response. Pulling a hospital card from his pocket, Michael disappeared behind the doors, only to emerge a few minutes later. At that moment, Sarah no longer could deny any feelings or accounts. Michael braced her shoulders, guiding them to two accompanying chairs.

"I just spoke with the nurse . . . Emily's . . . gone." The new words rolled inside her, ratcheting her gut. Sarah buried her head into Michael's shoulder and wept through his shirt. Her best friend was dead. In a matter of minutes, the lovely smile and sarcasm, which displayed Emily best, vanished and was clouded under an ocean of water. *How?* The second chance to renew their friendship proved to be one of the best gifts she had ever received, but sitting in a familiar hospital, there would be no third.

"Do you think I can at least see her?" she said, raising her head.

"I wish you could, but they've already turned her over to the coroner. Maybe you should start trying to get ahold of her family."

There was no phone call she dreaded worse, but someone would have to convey the heartbreaking news. Rising on her quivering legs, Sarah humbly walked to the nurse's station.

"Can I borrow the phone, please? I need to call Emily's parents."

"Local or long distance?"

"Distance," she mumbled.

The nurse unhooked the phone from the receiver and pressed zero. Sarah transferred the number for Emily's parents and waited for the long rings to end. Her mother's voice was the one to crackle on the other side.

"Ms. Ellis. It's Sarah . . . I'm afraid it's Emily . . . No, it's not. Maybe you should sit down . . . There was an incident at the pool today . . . and," Sarah gave a hard swallow, "She was swimming one minute, then I found her under the water . . . We tried to save her . . .

but she's . . . gone," she cried. A long pause ensued as a shout of terror echoed through the phone. Sarah remained silent until Cora's voice lowered to a muffled cry. "I know. I can't believe it . . . Yes . . . I'll see you when you get here . . . I love you too. Goodbye."

Sarah handed the receiver to the nurse, as she coiled the cord into place. Slumping to Michael, she refrained from his gesture to sit. "We need to go find Paul," she said, pulling his hand.

Sarah propped against Michael as they walked to the car. Her damp hair now lay cold upon her scalp, causing the frost to nip at her ears until the heat of the car warmed them.

"Just show me the way," Michael instructed.

Sarah broke from her conceived conversation of how to tell Paul only to indicate turns; however, no practiced conversation would ever soften the blow.

Telling Cora had felt difficult, until faced with telling Paul in person. Upon doing so, he fell to his knees, graveling at Sarah's legs, as if pleading for her life.

"This can't be!" he screamed. "She was going to be my wife."

"I know, Paul. It doesn't seem real."

"You don't understand, Sarah," he said, looking up from the ground.

"What do you mean? She was my best friend. I loved her just as much as you did—"

"No, that's not it," he sobbed.

"What, Paul? Why would you say it like that?"

"You may have lost your best friend, but I lost my best friend, my wife, and . . . and—"

"And what?"

Paul choked back the outburst of emotions long enough to convey his last thought. Sarah collapsed to the ground on top of him. Aside from fainting, she felt the darkest and coldest she could ever remember. Unbelief drained her body of will and life. How could this all be true? A dream surely, or a nightmare that she soon would awake from, she hoped. However, the pain struck too fierce and bold. There were no dreams to awake from and this was reality.

Michael and Sarah helped Paul inside, hoisting his almost lifeless body from the ground. She couldn't fathom leaving him in such shape, but with soaked clothes and no car, she had little choice.

"Come with us," she pleaded.

But he shook his head, unable to form any words.

As Michael pulled in beside Sarah's car, he turned, giving a deep sigh.

"Are you going to be okay?"

"I don't know . . ."

"Is there anything I can do?"

"I don't want to be alone right now . . . It's just too much."

"You know I'm here for you."

"Michael. I can't go back to our apartment. Not right now. Can I stay with you for a while?"

"Of course," he said, looping his fingers around her hand. "As long as you want."

"Thank you."

"Sarah?"

"Yeah," she said, finally acknowledging he was looking at her.

"What was the last thing Paul said? About a best friend, wife, and something else."

Sarah curled in her shivering lip. "He said a baby. Their baby."

CHAPTER 20:

Life After

Beneath the swaying leaves of the willow, the black dress flapped in the spring air. The sun brought the only warmth upon those gathered, with soothing rays that went silently through the crowd. Soft moans arose as disbelief became reality to the one person resting alone among the congregation.

Settling on the row opposite of the family, Sarah and Michael stood alongside Paul as his trance fixated on the casket. Looping her free arm through Paul's, Sarah leaned her head on his shoulder. His jacket, which soon was spotted with her tears, was only salvaged by the blotting of her handkerchief.

Across the aisle, Cora braced against Carter until she found her legs too weak to stand. Other relatives could be seen in attendance, but with Emily being the only child, there was no other immediate family.

Sarah's parents stood lamenting a row behind her. Hearing her own mother cry, mixed with the screeches from Emily's, exacerbated the feeling of losing a child.

Sarah looked up to Paul, but his eyes never deviated from the silent Emily sleeping in front of them. Following his stare, she focused on the preacher who now stood above the casket. He quoted a familiar Scripture, reading the words, "If the tree fall toward the south, or toward the north, in the place where the tree falleth, there it shall be." Upon finishing the text, his voice quaked, and soon his utterance changed from mere words to preaching.

A leaf broke from a nearby tree, finding its way from the branch to the white dress that adorned Emily. Harboring just above her folded hands, another breath of wind flickered the leaf free to rise back into the air. The question that had pondered Sarah's mind returned briefly at the end of the sermon, before being pushed aside by a sudden upheaval in Paul's appearance. Shaking ensued alongside his short breaths before he broke from his stance. He fell to his knees and graveled his way to the casket. Pulling up on the rim of his bride's bed, he bowed his head on Emily's chest. His pain-ridden cries were only muffled from her body.

Sarah eased forward to Paul's side, sliding her arm around his waist. He lifted enough to secure his left arm to her back, pulling her tight to the casket. Sarah leaned into his ear. "Paul, I know she loved you. I've never seen her so moved by one person." Paul stifled his groan and finally eased away from Emily. He rubbed his hand along her belly, as a smile of what could have been trickled through his thoughts. Still sliding his fingers over the dress, he leaned over, kissing her a final time on the lips. Slinking away, Paul left Sarah standing alone by her friend.

She looked upon Emily, unsure of how to say goodbye. The first time felt easier. There had been time, or so it seemed. However, the days following her drowning were a blur. There had been no time for visits, only a crowded room lined with visitors for the viewing. The only time they had spent alone was by Cora's request. The nail polish Sarah brushed while they discussed Emily's intimate night with Paul had long faded. Looking at her fingers now, Sarah questioned how she ever inked the blue along her nails properly while standing in the frigid morgue.

Emily's soul was long gone, leaving her with nothing to say. Previously, she could feel Emily still breathing, hear her heart beating, and hope she was listening. Now all was vanity. Knowing nothing else to say, she followed Paul, bending over to kiss Emily on the cheek. As she rose, Sarah took a final look at the blonde hair that flowed down beside her face. Fishing her hand into her purse, she pulled out the almost empty bottle, placing it inside the casket. "It'll be your turn when we get to heaven," she whispered.

Turning away, she paused slightly upon realizing Paul did not return to his seat. Instead of rejoining her family, Sarah continued down the aisle. Eyes watched as she passed, but she hung her head to the ground, eyeing the blades of grass below. Upon reaching the cars, Sarah found Paul's truck, where he lay hunkered against the steering wheel.

"Paul, you're in no shape to drive."

"I can't do anything," he stammered.

"I know. But she's gone. We have to realize that."

"They are gone," he insisted.

"Sorry, they."

Silence ensued until Sarah managed the courage to ask her own question. "How far was she?"

"It was early. We just found out. That's why we didn't tell you."

"Does anyone else know?"

"No, and I think we should keep it that way," he said turning his face toward Sarah.

"What about her parents?"

"No. That'll only crush them more."

"But what about the medical report?"

"What about it?"

"Neither me nor her parents believe she accidently drowned. Something happened. And when they finish the autopsy report, it'll show she's pregnant."

Paul shrugged his shoulders. "What do you want from me?"

"I don't want anything. I want to help. And trust me, they would be better off hearing the news from you than from someone they don't even know."

"I suppose . . . We agreed to tell them together, in a few more weeks."

"Would it help if I go with you?"

Paul shook his head. "I think it's best if I do it alone." Sarah took his hand, stroking her fingers in his palm. "Sarah," he continued.

"Yeah, Paul."

"I know she didn't drown."

Sarah raised her brows, "What do you mean—"

"Sarah! There you are," interrupted Michael, as he appeared alongside her. "I told your parents I'd find you."

"Hey. I wanted to make sure he was okay," she said before addressing Paul. "Will you be alright if I head back with Michael?"

But Paul offered no audible reply.

Sarah placed a kiss on the top of Paul's head while wrapping her arms around him.

"I'll be there in a second, Michael."

"Alright, I'll let them know."

As he left, Sarah leaned away from Paul. "What were you saying before?"

"I'll talk to her parents."

"I mean about Emily not drowning?"

Paul shook his head and frowned. "It was nothing, just frustration."

"Okay, I'll be back when the ceremony finishes, if you still plan to be here."

"Yeah. I need to talk to Emily's parents anyways."

Sarah smiled, "Don't forget, Carter and Cora love you too."

"They're going to be crushed though."

"I know, but you either tell them now or they'll start grieving again later."

With those final words, Sarah slowly walked across the grass to join the rows of seats. Rounding the end chair, Sarah stood eyeing the casket that pulled her focus straight ahead. Some of the friends and family turned their heads as she began walking down the aisle. Her march through the middle of the crowd was marked by all black, instead of the bright colors she would have expected when joining Emily at the altar that summer.

Sarah flattened her dress as she returned to the seat accompanying Michael. A foreign hand stretched across Michael's lap and clasped on to her arm. Sarah leaned forward in search of the person to which it belonged. Abby's auburn hair glowed in the sun, but her radiance was overcome by the concern on her face. "Is Paul okay?" she mouthed silently. Sarah gently nodded her head in response.

Reaching the end of the eulogy, the preacher paused before continuing. "At this time, would any of the family like to say a word?" Sarah looked to Carter and Cora, but Emily's grief-stricken parents fell silent. Continuing, the man glanced over the tear-filled faces, "Or any friends at this time?" Sarah's heart fluttered, aching. Her breath escaped her, despite knowing she needed to say something. However, as her voice found silence, so did everyone else's. The preacher looked to the coroner as if to proceed with the burial. Without a voice, Sarah instead found her feet beneath her. "Yes, Sarah. Would you like to say something?" he turned in acknowledgment. A nod was all she could muster as she addressed Emily's parents. Her peripheral vision grayed, as her sight bore solely on them. Her heartbeat pounded into her head, and a quaky voice sounded from her lips.

"There was a time when Emily and I first met. The memories of that day flourish now as I recall the first time we spoke. A scared freshman, with no friends and a new town to call home, Emily found me, sitting alone on the first day of practice. The acceptance in her voice when she first spoke bound us together. 'I was wondering where you went,' Emily had said. As if she already knew me and was concerned enough to seek me out. Honestly, if not for her, I don't know how I would've ever made it this far in college. Even during the toughest of times, whether I knew it or not, she never left my side. Till this day," she continued while quivering and stammering with love, "Emily was the friend I needed. She added to everything we did together, most of which I would have never been secure enough to venture on my own. Life, heartaches, and uncertainty, all battled me; however, Emily brought a light to each. I'm so blessed to have had the opportunity to thank her these past few months. Sitting with her day by day, I hoped and prayed she would come back to me. Begging one night by her bedside, I was given assurance she would be alright. Not assured she would recover from the wreck, but that she had a home in heaven." Sarah withheld her tears enough to look around at Emily's pristine blonde hair. "And, I'll always love her."

With the last words spoken, the coffin lid was lowered over the soft dimples etched on Emily's face. The last part that Sarah saw of her friend, however, was not the dimples, nor the white dress, not even the blonde hair, but the last glimmer of a diamond ring.

Sarah watched as they lowered the casket into the opening below. Megan, Cliff, and Michael joined her, offering solidity, while everyone else retreated to their cars. Shovel by shovel, the dirt covered the shimmering top until the borders disappeared. Yet, Sarah stayed.

Only once the last of the mound had been pressed in place, did she budge. Only then did she leave her stance to join the comfort of her own mother's arms, taking a final look at the friendship she once had.

Arriving at Michael's after a prolonged goodbye to her parents, Sarah dropped her purse on the floor as she entered the guest's bedroom. Almost a week had passed since she started staying with Michael, yet the unrest of knowing a second home still pained her mind. However, the newness of the room brought no familiarity nor notions of Emily. As such, the accommodations left her unwilling to return to the apartment for any extended time.

As her thoughts drifted, Sarah contemplated how much work remained for both school and track, but today would fail as means of production. Shedding her black dress, Sarah closed her eyes and fell across the mattress. Unable to force herself under the covers, she pulled the comforter across her body.

At that time, a knock at the door gave way to Michael.

"Are you going to sleep?"

"No," Sarah grumbled. "I'm just resting."

Michael walked to the bedside, waiting for her to acknowledge his presence. However, as she remained still, he continued.

"I've been thinking."

"About what?"

He flipped the comforter off her, then pulled at her hands. "Do you always sleep in your underwear?"

"That's what you were wondering?"

"No . . . I want you to see something."

Sarah conceded to the tugging of her arms but insisted on dressing before doing anything else. Michael waited for her to finish before leaving the room. A few moments later, Sarah wandered into the hall, where Michael stood outside his bedroom. Smiling, he opened the door.

"I rearranged my stuff," he said, pausing to wave her inside. "I want you to move in here with me."

"Why? I have everything set up already in the guest room."

"Because couples sleep together, not in different beds."

Sarah inspected the layout, but the accommodations appeared unnoticeable.

"Michael, I rather not."

"Come on," he insisted. "We both know you're not going back to your apartment." He grabbed her arm and ushered her alongside the bed. "Lie down . . . This mattress is much better than the rock in your room."

Unsure why, Sarah listened to his command. Lying down, the cushioning indeed proved more enjoyable than the springs she currently tossed on. The bed shifted as Michael lay beside her, butting his chest against her back. He gently stroked her hair, then ran his hand down her chest. As she leaned into his body, Michael lowered his hand in between her legs.

Flattening herself on the bed, Sarah found her lips greeted by his. The simple kiss quickly escalated as Michael found her fingers with his free hand and positioned them over his zipper.

"Let's break in this mattress," he said, unbuttoning her pants.

Sarah paused, retreating her lips. Undeterred, Michael began to undress himself, tossing his clothes to the side. The silence of her voice only broke as he started to straddle her with his naked body.

"Now isn't the time," she said.

"That's what you've been saying. When is the right time for you?"

"I don't know, just not right now."

Frustrated, Michael stripped Sarah's pants and underwear from her bottom in one swift jerk.

"Please, Michael. I don't want to."

"Don't worry. I'll do all the work."

Sarah began propping up on her elbows as he pulled a condom from the nightstand.

"Just a minute," he instructed, tugging her legs as to flatten her on the mattress.

"Michael, please. Can't you hold me like before?"

"You still owe me. Remember?" The change in his tone struck fear to her body, rendering Sarah motionless. "The first time will be better if you relax."

As he reached to position himself, Sarah began to push away. Quickly, Michael worked to restrain her hands, leaving Sarah to helplessly clinch her legs together. She squirmed and tossed, but with his strength, the fight was useless. Budging his knees between her thighs, Michael pried her legs apart.

Desperate, Sarah summoned the mucus from her throat and spit in his face. Immediately he stopped, and upon doing so, she realized her mistake. Forgetting her arms and legs, Michael slapped her across the face, reddening both cheeks. Sarah worked to protect her head, but only to open her stomach for a well-formed punch. Crippling to the side blow, she gasped for air.

"Stop!" he demanded. "You're making things worse than they should be. You need to enjoy this."

Her body quivered, giving into the reality of what was to come. She arched her back, trying to stretch her lungs for air. Michael began fumbling again as he waited to mount her.

"Wait," she gasped.

"What? Are you going to help?"

Sarah nodded, provoking a grin over his face. "Alright then," he said, sliding up her body. Sarah anchored onto her elbows and looked up into Michael's eyes. "Go for it," he said.

Grasping him, Sarah gaped her mouth open and sighed. With a final look, she was met by a forceful stare. Shamefully, she lowered her eyes. Pausing before going further, Sarah inhaled a deep breath . . . then closing her eyes, she constricted her grip, sinking her nails into the thin skin. A loud yell echoed above her as he fell to the side of the bed. Hastily, Sarah rolled to the floor. A sharp pain pinned her side as she scurried from the room. Charging down the hall, she vanished into the guest room, slamming the door behind. With the lock fastened, she painfully maneuvered a chest of drawers from the wall to barricade herself inside.

"Sarah!"

Michael's cry was soon followed by his pounding fist bombarding the door.

"Let me in!"

"No! I'll never let you in," she muttered, still cradling her aching side.

"You're just mad it's not Paul or Wesley trying to stick you. Open this door. Now!"

"Go away."

"Sarah, I've been putting up with your sorry life for too long. It's time you treat me like a man." With no reply, he continued ranting between rattles of the doorknob. "If you won't, I have other girls who are always willing."

Curling into a ball along the floor, she trembled in fear as to what Michael might do if she let him in. She lay quietly, waiting; waiting for the yelling to stop, waiting for the pounding to cease, endlessly waiting.

She had failed to see him for whom he really was. The caring guy she met along the dirt course months earlier was not the same guy who now harbored outside her door. Or if he was, the mask he wore had fooled her and everyone else.

Sarah's refusal remained strong, and even hours after his departure from the door, she didn't move.

An endless night followed as she never retreated to her bed, nor departed for the bathroom. Instead, her head rested on the coolness of the floor. Only when exhaustion overcame her, did Sarah possibly momentarily fall asleep.

When she awoke, the glimmers of a new day poked through her window. After gathering her belongings in a suitcase, Sarah stood at the door, calming her breath before leaving the room.

As she walked from the hall to the living room, Michael awaited in the kitchen, making breakfast. Seeing her face and luggage, he dropped the spatula, rushing to meet her before she reached the door.

"Sarah, don't go. I'm so sorry about last night. It'll never happen again—" He reached to hug his arms around her but Sarah pulled away. His body emitted the scent of a long night of drinking following their fight.

"You're right," she said with a smile. He eased his stance as if to gather her in his arms. "It won't happen ever again, because we're done."

"Sarah, please," he said, pulling her hand as she turned to the door. "I'll tell Isabel and the other girl from the restaurant that we're done hooking up."

Turning once more to Michael, Sarah looked long into his mournful eyes. "Forget you."

CHAPTER 21:

For Her

A warmth brought by the late spring air lifted Sarah's spirits as she stepped inside the track. The gape of her neck felt crisp and red from exposure to the sun. While tufts of hair swayed from her bun, teasing the burn, Sarah concentrated on relaxing her breath.

The lightness in her legs carried across the track and into the field. Sarah exhaled as she stopped and wrapped her arms around Abby.

"Are you ready?"

"Ready as I'll ever be, but how about you, Sarah?"

"Yeah," she said, pulling a golden cross from inside her shirt. "This race is for Emily." Despite seeing Abby's smile, Sarah reassured, "But we are in this together."

"Thanks, Sarah. I think we'll hold our own today . . . Do you want to get in a few more laps?"

"Yeah, maybe it'll calm my nerves."

Leaving her bag behind, Sarah and Abby started across the track. As they passed the pit, Sarah caught herself twisting around to affirm a lasting glimpse. Standing along the runway, lifting her pole high into the air, awaited Jenna for her vault. Unsure if her eyes were playing tricks, the lingering glance brought affirmation upon spotting Nigel, who watched as Jenna took to the air.

Abby, noticing the confusion, interrupted her thoughts. "Sarah—"

"Was that Jenna?"

"It was."

"But I thought . . . Everyone said—"

"Yeah, me too. Until today. I saw her with Nigel, so I started asking around. We'd all heard the Jollins girl was pregnant. However, what we didn't realize was she has a sister."

"A sister?"

"Yeah. Anna. I guess that was where the confusion lied. Everyone thought it was Jenna, but apparently, she just overexerted her shoulder. After Jenna was cleared to vault, the coaches kept her recovery hushed, in hopes of gaining a leg up on her competition. She's been practicing during the mornings." Sarah dispelled her breath. "I'm sorry, Sarah. I was going to tell you after the race."

"It's alright. There was no way of knowing without asking Nigel. There's one thing that bothers me about the situation though."

"What's that?"

"I assumed Nigel was sleeping with her this whole time. Now I'm not sure. Maybe I misjudged him too quickly."

"From what I gathered, all the rumors circulating Jenna were about her sister. Apparently, she isn't the loose cannon, but the reserved one."

"Have you ever seen her sister? I haven't noticed anyone pregnant around campus."

"Neither have I. Although, last semester, I think I had a class with her. But that was before track, so I never realized the difference."

Sarah continued running in silence, allowing the news to settle in her mind.

"What are you thinking, Sarah?"

"I'm not really sure. I thought I knew a lot of things, but I'm finding out I don't. I told you what happened with Michael. You haven't told anyone, have you?"

"No, of course not. But you're not going to see him anymore, right? That could be dangerous."

"Absolutely not. I just mean to say, I should've realized sooner, but I let it continue until it was almost too late. Since leaving, I haven't spoken to or seen him. Luckily, he's stayed away."

"Do you think he's afraid you'll get him in trouble?"

"Maybe, but after graduation, I won't have to worry about him anymore. I'll move away and that'll end all contact . . . That's not to say I won't come back to visit you," she encouraged upon noticing the sadness that accompanied Abby's reaction.

"I was about to say," she laughed.

"Here's what I'll do. I can drive up on a Friday, watch you race that Saturday, and spend the day together on Sunday."

"Really, you will?"

"I promise."

They continued their loop until a second call was issued over the loudspeakers. The time had come for her redemption. The top two from each final would be given the chance to compete at nationals, while everyone else would pack their bags until fall.

Sarah took hold of Abby's hands as they waited on the side. She mumbled a small prayer; not for strength, speed, or victory, but that all would go to God's plan. Amen was the last word she consciously heard, as her body settled into the movements as the starter called them to the track.

Given the waterfall start, Sarah and Abby were not seeded on the inside as the top ranked. Instead, they were positioned toward the middle, leaving Natalie to claim the far inside as the favorite. The last time Sarah had run against her was at the end of cross-country. The two girls exchanged looks upon each of their names being announced. The few runners in between meant nothing to Sarah. In her mind, that would have been where Emily was seated. In fact, they were the only three girls whom she considered part of the race.

The race director approached each runner, examining them along the line. As he paced by Sarah, he back stepped.

"You'll have to remove that chain," he instructed.

"But it's a cross," she explained, pulling the emblem from her shirt.

"Either you or the chain goes," he insisted.

So that's how it's going to be.

Sliding the gold over her head, she rushed to the side, handing off the cross to Cavlere. She wasted no time in explaining, but merely jolted back to the start. Again, the director passed across the girls, then drew his starter pistol from its holster.

"There'll be a two-command start. I'll say on your mark, then the gun. Let's have a good race, ladies."

Under Coach's suggestion, Sarah only had the mile to contend with. Abby on the other hand placed third in the two mile the night before, coming up short for nationals. Sarah took a final look at Abby, nodded, and refocused on the starter.

"On your marks," he exclaimed as the girls hastily toed the line. "Pow!"

The explosion rung in Sarah's ears as she felt her body jolt forward with the wave of girls. Pushing her way to the inside, her spikes hammered into the track as she fought for a position. As before, she found Natalie cutting to the front in an effort to break early from the pack; however, Sarah hastily followed.

Coming through the first lap, her legs had settled into rhythm, but the burn of an up-tempo pace left her body questioning the amount of exertion. *I'm already committed at this point,* she thought. *There's no reason to turn back now.* Sarah knew if she let off the gas, that would be the end of her college career. Ending with a loss had proven devastating enough the prior semester. Lose this time and she went home with nothing to show; but win and she would keep her drive alive.

As they raced around the backstretch, the burden to stay with Natalie proved unconceivable, until being replaced by the encroaching desire to pass her and strive for a win. *One, two, three . . .* she heard amidst her thoughts. Upon hearing the last of the numbers, Sarah felt her legs take hold and increase the pace.

Soon she found herself pulling alongside Natalie. *Breathe . . .* She looked up toward the sky and exhaled hard. *This is for you, Emily,* she thought, bearing hard into the curve. Despite pulling ahead enough to take the lead from the outside, Sarah stayed with Natalie throughout the bend. As they emerged, Sarah again increased her positioning before cutting to the front.

"Two laps to go!" they heard upon reaching the line. Sarah ignored the voice and the timer, but heeded to the craving to press on. She knew the last lap would require a full out kick, meaning she needed to create space now more than ever.

Entering the backstretch, Sarah closed her eyes and focused on Emily. The pain, the tears, the fear that had consumed her since Emily's death fueled her desire. Each step felt as though Natalie was falling off, but still Sarah pressed on. The impending bell lap was something she had dreamed about her entire college career, and now she was ready.

"Ding, ding, ding!"

The roar of the crowd overflowed the pandemonium onto the field. Sarah's skin trembled in excitement as she transitioned to her first kick. Her legs glided beneath, falling in line with her command. The urge to look around for the other girls had vanished, as she knew this was her race now.

Streaming past the spectators, Paul's voice reveled from the crowd. "You better go!" he cried. Foreign footsteps caught her ear as she met the two-hundred mark. Unaware Natalie was still within reach, Sarah started her final kick sooner than she anticipated. Rolling into the homestretch, the distant steps and breaths pulled in closer, yet Sarah dared not deviate her focus from the finish line.

Losing any momentum at this point meant forfeiting the race. *Emily, Emily, Emily . . .* she thought, pouring out the last of her energy.

Looking long upon the approaching finish line, Sarah closed her eyes and exhausted the last of her will, until she felt the tape stretch against her chest. As the plastic broke, she turned and clasped onto the body that followed behind her. The two girls stumbled to the grass before tumbling to the ground. Sarah gasped, unaware her eyes remained closed.

"We did it, together," she heard. Opening her eyes, Abby's bright smile emerged in front of Sarah. They had done what they claimed they would do, for Emily.

Sarah rolled over the grass on top of Abby. Laughter was followed by tears, then bursts of excitement. Four years had come and gone without any sight of nationals, but on her last possible attempt, she had made it alongside the best girl she knew to journey with.

Lifting to their hands and knees, Sarah and Abby saw Coach sprinting across the field from the two-hundred-meter mark. The rare aspect of his teeth-lined smile would have provoked a joke due to the lack of his seriousness, but this time they just embraced his hug as the three jumped for joy. "I've never been so proud of you ladies. Overcoming so much, just to make a stand when it mattered the most. Emily would've been proud too."

Even the sound of Emily's name brought no sadness. The few times in life where rejoicing meant more than any sorrows was truly a treasure, and there was nothing that could steal Sarah away in the moment.

"It was all Sarah," Abby explained. "She knew what we needed to do, and I followed her like she insisted."

"Abby, I honestly thought you were Natalie nipping on my shoes."

"Ha. You did? I passed her before the final lap."

"It's a good thing I didn't look around, because if I'd known, that last lap would have been much different, but I'm glad it wasn't."

Sarah glanced to the side where an anxious Paul awaited to greet them. "Come on. Let's go see Paul."

Running across the field and around the fence, Sarah jumped into Paul's arms. He hoisted her from the ground with a consuming hug that almost tumbled them both to the ground. "Sarah, you're amazing. I didn't know how you'd pull off that upset with everything you've been through, only that you would."

"No. Everything we've been through," she corrected, looking from Paul to Abby. Paul lowered Sarah before hugging Abby, who was already enthralled in Ralph's arms.

"Ralph, how about we take these girls out and celebrate tonight?"

"And, Ralph," Sarah added, "Mr. Two Miler Runner Up."

"I'm ready to celebrate anything," he joked. "Just imagine, we'll all be heading to nationals together."

Sarah looked to Paul, as if to offer her own sympathy. "You're coming with us."

"You know I wouldn't miss this for the world."

"Has anyone seen Nigel?" Ralph interjected. "We can't forget him. He's the champ after all."

"There he is, with Jenna," directed Paul.

"Nigel!" Ralph yelled. "Come here."

Hearing his name, Nigel mentioned something to Jenna, ensuring his quick return, before running to join the others.

"Hey! Great job, ladies. That was some feat. And, Sarah," he said transitioning his eyes from Abby, "you really meant business once you took the lead."

"Thanks, Nigel. I have Abby to thank for pushing me through."

"We're going to dinner to celebrate," Ralph interrupted. "Do you and Jenna want to join us?"

Nigel took a brief look at Sarah before considering what he might say. Trying to feign indifference, Sarah gave a nod of agreement. "Umm, yeah, let me talk it over with Jenna, but I think that would be fun."

"Great, say eight o'clock, at the usual."

As the group turned to gather their bags, Sarah's own name caught her attention.

"Sarah . . . Can I speak with you for a minute?"

"Sure, Nigel. What is it?"

He waited a moment before the others realized he wanted to speak to Sarah alone. As they continued on their way, he broke his silence. "I know we haven't talked much this semester, and I'm sorry about Emily."

Sarah stopped him, lifting her hand. "I know this isn't about Emily. So just say whatever's on your mind."

"I just wanted to make sure we are cool. If not, Jenna and I don't have to show tonight."

"Nigel, if there's one thing I've learned from Emily, it's to not ever hold a grudge. You taught me a lot about myself that I probably never would have learned. Although I wasn't happy at the moment,

I don't want to hold any hate toward you. Life is too short to hate someone, especially someone you once felt so close to."

"Thanks, Sarah. You're an amazing girl."

"Thanks, Nigel," she said, wrapping her arms around his neck. "I guess I should be careful though. I don't want Jenna to get the wrong impression."

"No, Jenna's pretty cool. But I guess you two haven't really met."

"Not in a 'get to know you' kind of way."

"Well, if you like, we can work on changing that tonight."

"Perfect."

"Alright. Tell the others I'll see everyone there."

Sarah watched as Nigel trotted back to the bleachers where Jenna awaited. *Could two sisters really be that different?* She pondered the question as she made her way to her gym bag and joined the others for a ride home. For the first time in a long time, her heart felt warmth and love. Looking around the car, she could see a slice of Emily in everyone there: Paul with his sweet compassionate side, which she only saw in Emily once they started dating; Ralph with his jovialness, making light of any situation while not afraid to take on anything new; Abby with her true friendship that helped fill the void with Emily's passing; and even herself. By being a part of Emily's life, Sarah had grown to be like her. The brashness and strength she now showed would have never developed if not for Emily. Defending herself against Michael, comforting Paul while losing her own best friend, and forgiving others for the past sorrows, all correlated with realizing she could be happy by herself.

Much had changed in the days following her departure from Michael's place. Foremost, she discovered that even though Emily no longer would be with her physically, parts of her remained within herself and her friends.

Sarah had also discovered peace with her past. Talking with Nigel wielded a certain clarity and humbleness, which proved to be the right thing to do. As for Michael, she cared not to see him again. Writing him out of her life, however, proved less than easy. The night that followed her departure, she spent alone in the abandoned apartment, crying, hurting, and longing. Wishing for Michael to comfort her only brought more tug into the confusion she endured. She cared deeply for him, yet at the same time his harsh hands smacking across her face and grabbing her neck never said love. The lingering feeling of no self-worth and brokenness followed as Sarah prayed to God for peace. She never wanted to hate Michael, and honestly, she still did not.

After mulling the situation over, Sarah easily convinced Abby to spend the night, allowing her to adjust. With no intentions of disrupting Emily's bed, Abby curled up with Sarah for three nights before Sarah found the answer she had prayed for. Her friends were there to help her through; however, Michael was not going to be one of those friends. He had played a special role in her life, and now that time had passed. Yet, no hate, nor regret, flowered from their relationship.

Once Abby had returned to her dorm, Sarah prayed a new prayer, one for Michael, that he might see the harm he caused and change his ways before it was too late; not for her sake, but for the next girl's.

All the recent thoughts filtered through her head, but as night approached, the heartfelt glory of the race still swooned inside her. Such thoughts only ceased as a knock pursued from the door. Sarah abandoned the mirror to meet Paul, Ralph, and Abby downstairs. With their greetings, no sorrows filtered their voices, but the hopes of a new dawn instead filled their lungs.

As they stepped into the Mexican restaurant, Nigel and Jenna waited at a table. Beside Jenna sat another girl, whom Sarah recognized, yet had no prior conversations with. Greeting the others, Nigel was quick to introduce everyone. "And, this is Macie. She qualified for pole-vaulting, so I invited her to celebrate."

"Nice to meet you, Macie," Sarah replied with a smile.

With Ralph occupied between Nigel and Abby, Sarah found herself conversing mainly with Paul. Curious about the girl that sat just to the other side, Sarah tried to include Macie, who gave little in reply. How could Jenna be friends with someone so different, or were they more the same than she thought?

As Jenna referred to Macie, she would smile and only add to the story when necessary. Finding the situation seemingly odd, Sarah almost gave up on including her until a passing thought changed her mind. She too was once put off by the inclusion of an unknown large group. Too many questions, uncertainty of others' impressions, and holding your breath to feel like a part of the team, all resurfaced the memories of her freshman year before Emily came along.

"Paul," she nudged, "can you switch places with me?"

"Umm sure. But why?"

"Just because," she insinuated with her eyes.

Unsure of her purpose, he stood from his chair as Sarah slid over. She was not sure herself, but one thing she did know was that Emily would have done the same thing.

CHAPTER 22:

For Me

The hotel lobby echoed with excitement as teams from all over poured through the main doors. Outside buses lined the curb, and attendants hustled to move bags as the next wave of athletes arrived. The heat from the engines amplified the heat from the noonday sun, leaving sweat to bead shortly after unloading from the bus. If it was hot now, the track would be much the same.

Coach Cavlere stood amidst the lobby, waiting for everyone to collect their bags and gather around. For the first time since Sarah could recall, he was smiling before a race. Knowing they had progressed this far was proof enough to the testament of what they had overcome, still everyone maintained focus on what Nationals meant.

"Is everyone here?" he questioned the group, as he searched for missing faces. "Where's Jenna?"

"Here she comes with Macie," said a girl.

"Okay. I think we have everyone," he continued, counting the tops of their heads. "Yes. We're good; now listen up. The events will be staggered across three days. I'll constantly remind you of each competition's time, but you must be on your A game and warm up beforehand. Also, multiple schools share our colors, which adds to the confusion and may cause some of you to get separated. That said, each day we will meet here at nine, noon, and five. No events are scheduled during those slots, so no excuses."

Sarah trailed her attention from Coach to Abby, as they would room together for the weekend. Without surprise, she was standing alongside Ralph. Veering her eyes to the other teammates, Sarah realized Paul was nowhere in sight. However, discovering his presence behind her shoulder conjured an embarrassing screech.

"Keep quiet while I issue everyone's room keys. Remember, this isn't an excuse to party, and you'll all be expected in your rooms by nine each night and asleep by ten. Sarah, you and Emm . . . I mean Abby, will be together. Here's your key."

"Just the one?" Sarah asked.

"Yes, that way I know everyone is sticking close to their roommate."

No thoughts of wandering off without Abby troubled her mind; however, the childish provision bore little surprise. Heeding to his words, Sarah placed the key in her pocket before joining Abby in search of the elevator.

To Sarah's astonishment, the door opened to a cozy yet spacious room that trumped anywhere they previously stayed. A vast window painted an outline of the city in its panes, which included a distant view of the track. A few men could be spotted cutting the grass, raking sand, and disposing of any trash in last-minute preparations.

The grandeur of the stage superseded any state or regional course. No matter the size, luxury, or distinction, she needed to resettle her thoughts on new goals. College running had always circled around reaching this point, and despite Coach having already installed the movements and expectations inside their minds, she needed to prepare mentally. Region had served as a race for Emily, which proved she could return in triumph alongside her friend's spirit. However, this time would be different. This time, the race was for herself.

Lying across the bed, Sarah noticed Abby unpacking her running shorts. She closed her eyes momentarily before raising her head.

"What are you doing?"

"I'm going for a light jog to loosen my legs. Do you want to join?" she asked, skittishly changing into her sports bra.

"Yeah. If I don't, I'll regret it later."

As Sarah broke from the bed and found her own running clothes, Abby worked on retying her laces.

"Did you catch what Coach said?"

"I did. That's just one of those things I imagine we all will find ourselves doing from time to time."

"How are you holding up, Sarah?"

"I'll be alright," she said shortly as she slipped on her shoes. "But let's put that out of our minds this weekend. Emily would expect us to give this race everything we have, and worrying about the past won't get us anywhere fast."

Abby trailed Sarah to the lobby and through the double doors. Whether by intention or just wonder, halfway through the run, the two found themselves circling the stadium. Reaching the far side, they noticed a lone gate, which remained propped open. Without a word, the two turned inside the wrought iron gate and through a tunnel that led to the field. As the concrete overlay retreated for the sky, the significance of them not being the only ones there vanished. Mounds of risers and steps surrounded the nest of what had all intents and purposes for track usage. Rivaling a massive football stadium, the structure brought the wonders of how the race might feel.

Sarah swung open a lose gate and led Abby onto the track. As they circled, Sarah soaked in all the vastness of the site. The next time she would find herself on this track would be at the race, at which point, there would be no time to gawk and daydream. She turned to Abby, who now ran beside her. "Are you getting nervous yet?"

"A little, but I'm more excited to be here. How about you?"

"The same. I just want to enjoy every moment."

A subtle breeze formed along the back stretch, but only enough to cool their skin without hindering their stride. Sarah looked across the pretend crowd, imagining them cheering as they entered into the final stretch. She could envision Paul standing beside Ralph, with Nigel joining them for the final lap. Nothing felt more relaxing and right. As they turned the curve, Sarah watched the blank clock, not looking for minutes and seconds, but focusing on her Coach who would be standing nearby.

Upon crossing the manifested finish line, Sarah turned toward the side where they entered. "Let's head back. I want to shower before dinner."

As night settled over the city and the team parted their ways, Sarah bid the guys goodnight before heading to her room. However, with the race two days away, the rush remained too intense to fall asleep.

She lay in her bed, gazing at the dark ceiling as Abby flipped off the bathroom light and crawled into the other bed.

"Good night, Sarah."

"Night, Abby."

As she continued to lie awake, Sarah said her prayers silently. Only upon finishing, did she notice Abby had fallen asleep. Sarah cradled her head in the pillow, hopeful to drown out any noises from the street or hallway, but the silence proved just as bothersome. Flickering her eyes open and close, she settled with them closed, yet listened to the faint noises in hopes they would soon dwindle to silence.

Forgoing the insanity of wrestling with her sheets, Sarah pulled the key card from the nightstand, and with a final check on Abby, she snuck into the hall. Despite what she heard from inside, once the door clicked shut, the corridor appeared eerily silent. Each step and breath formed as if intended to wake anyone in the neighboring suites. Unsure which rooms hosted whom, and pessimistic that she might bump into Coach, Sarah continued sneaking to the elevators.

Riding down the shaft left little causation to be conspicuous as the bell dinged between floors. Forgoing any further attempt of concealing her late-night walk, Sarah left the doors in stride as they opened.

A breakfast bar that traversed the far side of the common area struck her appeal, yet the only accessible food was cookies and cartons of milk. Pulling a small chocolate chip from the jar, Sarah wandered to a dimly lit couch that sat apart from the rest of the seating area. However, as she eased around the arm of the couch, she paused just short of sitting on someone's head.

"What're you doing down here?" she asked.

"I could ask you the same," Paul replied.

"I'm too excited to sleep, but I doubt that's your reason."

"Yeah. I'm on a foldaway bed, and this couch is much comfier."

"Do you mind if I join you for a bit?"

"Not at all," Paul replied, lifting his head. As Sarah sunk into the welcoming cushions, Paul retreated his head onto her lap. "Sarah?"

"Yeah, Paul."

"Do you remember when we were talking, and I was going to tell you something?"

"I do, but honestly, I forgot. What was it about?"

"Emily . . ." A long pause ensued to ensure speaking of her was okay.

"I thought so," she said, stroking his hair. "It'll take a while for the pain to subside. I keep fearing that reality hasn't sunk in yet, and then one day, I'll just lose it."

"It definitely feels real to me now. It's like I look for her everywhere I go, then realize she's gone."

"Me too. The only difference is the whole thing feels like a dream."

"Sarah, there's something I've been meaning to tell you. Actually, Emily and I both should have, but I guess that falls on me now." He dispelled a deep breath. "Here it goes," he said, adjusting his neck backwards to catch her eyes. "Emily didn't drown. Despite what anyone else thinks, or if you feel like you could have done something, you couldn't."

"What do you mean, Paul?"

"After the wreck, the coma, and Christmas break, Emily went in for a follow-up test. They wanted to make sure there was no damage from the coma. When they scanned her brain, they found something. She had formed a small hemorrhage. At the time, there was little worry because the bleeding appeared to have stopped. However, one thing they warned her about was the possibility of randomly bleeding again. Unfortunately, they couldn't say much else. They did advise she could suffer issues while doing physical activities, or even while she was asleep. At that point, the problem could consist of a slight bleed like prior, or a massive brain aneurysm. Given the situation, Emily decided to live as normal of a life as possible. She told me, if she was going to die, it would be on her own terms, and not her body's."

A tear dripped from Sarah's eye, catching Paul on the cheek. "Why . . . Why didn't either of you mention this before?"

"There was no reason to. Nothing could be done to prevent the issue, so telling you would only cause a turmoil of emotions."

"Oh, thanks. I think I'd learn to handle it."

"I know, but that was Emily's final say. I just felt like you needed to know. For a while, I was afraid you felt at fault, since you were . . . with her at the time."

"You're right. I did. It was hard not to. I tried everything I could to save her, but nothing worked. I'd never felt so helpless in my entire life. Lying on top of her motionless body, trying to put my own life into hers . . . and nothing."

Paul reached his hands up to Sarah's face. "I'm sorry. I should've told you sooner." He lifted his head, sitting up beside her. Looping his arm around Sarah, Paul cradled her head on his shoulder. "And Sarah, that's why everything else happened."

"Everything else?"

"After hearing the report, we decided to go ahead and get engaged. Seeing that time may not be in our favor, it was almost natural for us to start having sex. I always thought I would regret sleeping with a girl before I got married, but in this instance, I'm glad we did. Doing so, I gave Emily something she really wanted. Something she never would have known, felt, or lived if we hadn't."

"A baby—"

"Yeah. I don't think Emily was far enough to form a fully developed baby; however, as soon as we found out, she lit up with excitement, as if she'd received the greatest gift life could offer."

"I'm glad she got to relish that experience. Some people never do," Sarah sniffed, unable to hide her word's true meaning.

"Sarah? Why do you say it like that?"

She unhid her eyes from his shadow as he lifted her chin. "Paul, I found out this semester that I probably won't be able to have kids of my own."

"Sarah. I feel terrible. Here I am talking about something long gone, thinking it'd help, but it's only crushing you."

"No. I'm glad you told me about Emily. And, that's why I was honest with you."

"I appreciate your openness."

"Well, there's something else . . . Emily was kind enough to offer herself as a surrogate," Sarah snickered. "Can you imagine her having someone else's baby for them?"

"If it was yours, I could not be more excited."

Sarah touted a smile of happiness, but still broke with tears. She guided her lips to Paul's as he tugged her closer. Her body confined to his as their lips parted with gaping kisses. He pulled at her leg, allowing her to slide over him. As her thighs straddled his, she ran her fingers into his hair. Paul arched his chest closer, while passing his hands from her breast, down her legs, and onto her bottom. All forms of grief, agony, love, and passion steamed their bodies. Lowering his mouth from her lips, Paul worked along the side of her neck before reaching the top of her chest.

Sarah opened her eyes, becoming aware they were still in the hotel lobby. With slight relief, there was no one else to see them in the shadows. Still enjoying the caressing of Paul's lips, Sarah twisted her body, suggesting that Paul lie on the couch. As he pulled away, he tugged at her waist to reaffirm her body against him.

Sarah's leg edged between Paul's as he grazed his hand from her knee to the inseam of her shorts. Panting, Sarah slid her hand along his leg to the same point and waited. They looked long into each other's eyes, breathless and restless.

"Are you okay?" Paul broke.

Sarah nodded her head as she summoned her eyes closed. Biting her lips together, she felt Paul's lips meet hers again as his hand slid the remaining way up her leg. Just as she found the courage to grasp her hand around him, she stopped, pulling away.

"Paul, we can't do this."

He lowered his eyes. "I just . . . I mean—"

"You still miss her too much. And it's not fair for either of us, or to Emily."

Realizing she was right, and strung with emotions, Paul reclined flat against the sofa. Sarah laid her head upon his chest, counting the beats of his heart.

"I love you, Paul. I want you to know that."

"Sarah, I hope you already know how much I love you. And, I'd never try to replace Emily. I love you both, and I'm just struggling with where to go next."

"I understand, but for now, we need to slow down and take the time to be friends. And I think it's important to remember, if you're with me, then children are likely out of the question."

"Sarah, if I was with you, you're all I would ever need or expect."

Sarah raised her head, kissing him again on the lips. "I think that's why I know I love you. You always understand and care about me. But for now, I think we should wait. Give us both some time."

Paul slid his face closer for a final kiss. "I'll wait, if that's what we need."

Sarah snuggled closer, escaping from the world, and settling into a love she longed for immensely. Unaware of time and place, they dozed off in the warmth of their bodies.

Only at the beep of her watch, did Sarah raise from his cradling arms.

"What's wrong?" Paul muffled, almost naturally expecting to wake up with her.

"It's one in the morning. We should probably get to our rooms."

"I already told the guys I was sleeping here. I can walk you to your room if you like."

"If you don't mind . . . I'd stay here, but can you imagine if Coach caught us?"

"I rather not," said Paul, raising up from the couch. Grabbing her hand, they walked through the darken lobby to the elevators. "What's your room number?"

"507."

As the doors closed, Paul turned Sarah's body into his and laid his head on top of hers. The ride to the fifth floor seemed to linger between floors, yet the gap in time felt short in comparison to falling asleep on the couch.

With a final ding, the doors slid open. Sarah walked with her head on his shoulder until she pulled the key from her pocket. "I guess this is it?" she questioned.

"For now. I guess so."

Sarah contemplated asking him to stay the night with her, but with Abby and Coach, she would have more explaining to do than she could possibly handle. So instead, she wrapped her hand around his, feeling the brashness of his skin. "If it's meant to be, it'll be."

Paul sighed, then stepped away. Sarah watched with the door ajar until he disappeared around the corner. Her heart sank. *Would love, life, and possibly marriage always be this complicated?*

The door shut, issuing a click that penetrated the room. Tiptoeing to the bed, Sarah pulled the covers over her shoulders, listening for any disturbance in Abby's sleep. She considered that night with Paul would be unexplainable, yet she fought to decide if their actions were wrong or right. She thought what Emily would think, she thought what Emily would tell her if she was still here. Maybe she should tell Abby to ease her conscience. Or maybe she should let the night be just that, a night full of love and a special connection.

Relaxing, Sarah dozed between consciousness and retreating to her dreams. She knew that no matter what, there would always be a connection with Paul. It was just a matter of if he was the right one.

CHAPTER 23:

Graduation

Arriving home from a national stage entailed more than what Sarah left with, as the happiness of reaching the final apex of her college career was replaced with nostalgia. Now hinged around her neck sat a bronze medal. The placed finished proved more than she ever hoped and dreamed for. Unsure of how she could ever manage the kick of the fastest girls in her league, she smiled with a sense of accomplishment. Every athlete dreams of finishing on top, but a gold medallion would have no greater meaning.

As Sarah stood over the headstone of Emily's grave, she showed the medal as if to share the accomplishment. "That was some race, Emm . . . I wish you were there though." Sarah removed the ribbon, placing it on the stone for Emily to hold.

"You wouldn't believe what happened. At the start, everyone went out quicker than expected. Based on the pace of all the top girls'

PRs, we were ten seconds under on the first lap. Abby hung on like a champ though. On the second lap, the nerves finally settled into place, and we landed where I expected to hit for splits. After that, the girls quickly broke apart. Two runners from the same region split from the pack; Abby and I tried to follow, along with a few others, but we also figured they'd crash before the final lap. Maybe that was their plan, but it never happened. They finished thirty meters before everyone else, which left me, Abby, and four other girls fighting for third. When we lapped around for the final two hundred, someone passed me from the inside, breaking my stride. I've never been so upset while running, feeling like I was getting pushed out of the way. Emily, I'm done with being treated like I don't matter. I thought of you, why I was even at this race, and what everything meant to me. I've lost so much this year, and yet gained something new in return. I decided if she was going to steal the race from me, I'd make sure she didn't forget who I was. I didn't wait until we cleared the curve, but swung wide and poured out every emotion I had bottled up this year. I think if we were fighting fist to fist," Sarah laughed, "I would've socked her good in the nose. When I reached her side, the tone of her breath sounded of frustration, like I was trying to start something. Nonetheless, I intended to finish it. We battled the entire homestretch. I wish I knew how fast we were going; I can't recall ever breaking the line with such speed. Right as we approached the finish, a jolt ran through my body, giving me enough push to edge her out."

Sarah gathered the bronze medal from the headstone and stuck it into her pocket. "I was so proud of Abby too. She finished fifth. Next year, all the other girls will be on the lookout for her." Sarah grew silent, anticipating her next words.

"Emm . . . There's something I need to tell you. I just want to say, I feel like a terrible friend, and I can't begin to explain what I was thinking." Sarah sighed intently. "Paul and I . . . kissed. Well, more than just kissed, but I'm so sorry. I know losing you took a toll on us both, but I can't say I didn't feel something between us, because I did. We both did."

She waited for a response in silence before continuing. "What should I do, Emm? We said it was too soon for anything, which only makes sense. At least I think."

"Oh, Emily, please forgive me. I know he's yours, and his heart will always belong to you. I don't think that'll ever change. We love you more than we'd ever love each other. I'll let him go. Just tell me."

With no resolve or contentment, Sarah left her apology with Emily as she laid a rose at the base of the grave. Sarah rubbed the smoothness of the rock as she gathered herself to her feet. Disbelief grew at how quickly the weeks passed since Emily's death. If not enough had changed, she finally considered the bereavement was settling inside her.

Departing the graveside, Sarah headed to Yemington. The entire drive, the long-awaited graduation drummed in her head. Following this ceremony, she had always planned to return home and begin her life as an adult. Despite talks with Emily, no arrangements or promises of living together after college were mentioned. Either the distance between them or the reality that sooner or later, their time together would cease caused the question to never arise. Half thankful for the lapse, Sarah recognized she needed to start anew. The memories of college would surely fade, but there would always remain those times that crossed her mind, good and bad.

Yet, one piece appeared to be missing before she could transition. Graduation previously showed promises of Emily and Sarah posing for pictures, modeling their gowns, and celebrating their final days of college. None of which would ever come true, neither would the possibility of Emily cradling her or Sarah's baby. Life would continue, while Emily's story stood still. She would never know the cry of her newborn, the love of a husband and children, or even the glories of grandparenthood. All these experiences Sarah wanted for Emily, but the desire was in vain, and the thoughts were mere considerations of what at one point was possible. Not by choice, but by life, she would face all blessings and adversities without her best friend. Coming to her grave helped with mulling over the troubles, but what would she do when searching for reassurance in the middle of the night from miles away?

Sarah eased the car to the shoulder and lowered her head to the steering wheel. She prayed for love, help, and guidance, everything she once found in Emily. Would she ever discover such charity again, or would life remain cruel?

An ache throbbed in her heart before a slight glimpse of peace arose. Amongst her sobs, a soft and gentle voice, akin to Emily, whispered, "Time, time, time." The voice departed as swiftly as it arrived, provoking Sarah's pain to merge with anger. "Time? How much time does it take to heal? How long do I have to suffer?" she choked, giving in to the perception that nothing came in her own time. Nor when she tried to make choices to steer her life better, did such paths pan out. Waiting anxiously did not present the answer either. Clearing her mind, Sarah decided no matter what, she would endure such discouragement to seek a happy life, for happiness would come. Anything else would leave her broken, alone, and sad.

Shifting the car into drive, Sarah continued along the road to school. No radio, singing, or other noise occupied her thoughts. Instead, Sarah prepared for a life of uncertainty. She had changed this year more than ever. Many times, her actions felt wrong and contrary to her beliefs. In a sense, they were, and who knew what life would have surmounted to if she stayed the perfect girl. Perhaps the reward would have manifested into a loving and caring relationship. Perhaps Emily would still be with them. Perhaps she would be the one planning a wedding. Then again, those mistakes provided lessons she might never know, or the strength that only develops through facing adversity. Perhaps the new path would foster a grand and more appreciated future. Or what if, by some chance, they all led to the same destination? What if God's plan was formed to lead her to the right man, the right career, the right everything, and she was the one who decided if His desires unfolded through a trail of ease, or a path of difficulties. She would never know the answer, nor was she supposed to.

Sarah's hands loosened their overbearing grip from the wheel. Past choices were far removed from her control. Living in the past, good or bad, would only bear a heavy heart, with questions without answers that she most desperately craved.

Arriving at the apartment, Sarah spent the remainder of the day packing her room. Emily's parents had long departed from their morning visit to remove her belongings. With no remaining items to trigger thoughts of Emily, the apartment emitted a welcoming sense. At first, the packing bore dreadful, imagining leaving the town she truly loved. However, the home they shared quickly retreated into the empty apartment they first saw a year prior. Recalling when they chose rooms and signed the lease brought memories of excitement.

A final box fit snug against the wall, leaving only her bedding, a change of clothes, and the gown she would wear to graduation. Sarah combed the tassel connected to her cap between her fingers. Her parents would arrive that night for the ceremony and then dinner to follow. Laying the cap aside, Sarah shed her clothes before searching for a towel. Realizing they were stuffed away in one of the boxes she had moved to the living room, Sarah descended the stairs in search for a box marked "bathroom."

Alongside the couch, she spotted the cardboard container. Sitting gingerly along the edge of the cushions, she quickly realized her mistake. Pricking through her undies, a sharp pin poked at her skin. Jumping, Sarah turned to realize the cause of her shock. Cradled on the couch appeared two earrings. Besides the now slightly bent post, the studs were unmistakably those she gifted Emily. Upon examining the jewelry, Sarah noticed one of the backs was missing. Sarah slid her hand between the cushions with no avail. *Perhaps one fell out and she simply removed the other? But why hadn't she searched for the backs?* Sarah lay along the couch, still holding the earrings in her hand. A faint scent trickled through her nose as the smell of Emily was emitted from the cushions. She inhaled deeply, feigning her head was in Emily's lap. But as she enjoyed the fond remembrance, an unsettling sensation followed upon recalling the story of Emily and Paul having sex on the couch.

Sarah jutted her head upward, imagining a fabricated laugh from Emily, poking at the well-played joke. The earrings had not fallen out by chance, but from entangled and passionate love making. Noticing one had fallen out, Emily likely paused long enough to remove the other, placing them on the couch before moving to her mattress. Sarah shook her head in disbelief and amusement. The earrings were all that remained from what likely was the last time Paul and Emily ever had sex, the last time he would run his hands through her hair while their bodies lay pressed together, the last time he would ever know her in that way.

There would be no other time, just the ones of the past. Looking at the couch, Sarah smiled in gratitude for finding a lingering part of her friend.

As she returned upstairs, Sarah hunted for a place to store the pieces. With all her belongings packed, Sarah unhooked her bra and placed them in the cups until she finished showering. Then, she would look for a more permanent home.

A steady stream drenched her body as Sarah soaked under the shower head. Years of laboring, mixed with late nights and high aspirations, all conjoined at this apex in her life. Within a few hours, she would walk across the stage to receive her diploma, marking her last official act as a college student. Leading up to that point, her life seemed clear, planned, and purposeful, but all that had changed. Despite the promising teaching job, and the ability to move to her parents, the mystic of being grown bore little appeal. Much like a race, she trained arduously, felt accomplished with the finishing of each class, and adjusted well to all the adversities she met along the way. However, unlike running, where the big finish line depicted a time full of joy and celebration, breaking the tape meant the beginning of a new chapter for which she was unsure of how to turn the page.

Rinsing her hair, Sarah looked to the drain as the suds passed out of sight. She had not considered any plans following dinner with her parents, aside from meeting with the landlord the next day. At that moment, she realized an evening meant to be one of the most special in her entire life would resolve in isolation. Perhaps her mother might offer to stay the night, but why?

Water dripped from the spout as Sarah retrieved a towel from the hook. Blotting her face, an alluring thought penetrated her mind.

What about Paul? He was also graduating, and obviously in the same boat. Sarah's body urged her to invite him over, but again why? She already realized their previous night alone was a mistake. And to boot, Paul's plans after graduation were unbeknownst to Sarah. At best, they might forge a long-distance relationship.

Sarah unfolded the towel from her hair and stood looking in the mirror at her bare body. A jolt of passion tingled her chest as she imagined one other possibility. What if . . . What if they finished what they started? Would they have sex? Maybe. Would she be alright with that? Did she care anymore? Paul loved her and she loved him. From Emily, she had learned the shortness of life and how precious opportunities were. However, Paul was no longer a virgin. To her reasoning mind's point, he had already made love to another girl; she would not be his first, but he would be hers. Was that more bothersome than knowing he loved the other girl? The other girl? The other girl was Emily. Why was she thinking of her best friend as someone else?

Unable to consider the situation further, Sarah wrapped the towel around herself. Removing the earrings from her bra, she threaded them through her ears. As for the one missing a back, Sarah held the stud in place using the bend she formed. Satisfied, she looped her arms through the bra straps and clipped the hooks.

The dusk of that evening brought the arrival of her family. While she finished dressing, Sarah's dad helped in loading boxes. By the time Sarah joined them in the living room, all the large ones had been packed away, and everyone awaited her by the stairs.

The black gown swayed elegantly as she carefully traversed the stairs. Her knees showed through the split in the gown, barely hinting at the hem of the white dress below. Hitting the final step, she gleamed with a smile. "How do I look?"

"Absolutely amazing," offered Cliff.

"I can't believe my little girl is all grown up," Megan sniffed. "It feels like yesterday when you started your first day of elementary school."

"Mom, don't start crying or I will, and I probably won't be able to stop."

"Come here, Liv," she said, opening her arms for a hug. "You look beautiful."

With Matty leading the way, followed by her and their parents, they headed to the cars. As Sarah locked the door, she noticed an enthusiastic Matty standing by her passenger side. "Can I ride with you?"

"Yes, but I'll have to drop you off with Mom and Dad."

From that moment on, the night felt like a dream. Standing in line alphabetically left her surrounded by those she never became acquainted with. A few fellow runners fell in line above and below her, but none within talking distance.

Even after receiving her diploma and eating dinner, the daydream never lifted. Half thankful for a dreary emotionless state, Sarah sighed as she hugged her family goodnight. Emily had failed to cross her mind the entire evening, so to her hopes, the pictures she took were likely full of smiles instead of sadness.

Watching as her parents drove away in the opposite direction as they left the parking lot, Sarah aimed the steering wheel toward her apartment. However, as she reached the four ways, Sarah found herself headed in a different direction. Watching her body override her mind, she stayed conscious only to make sure she was on the right road. When the car came to a halt beside a lone car, she put the shifter in park.

The intense heartbeat throbbing in her head quickened the closer she moved to the door. Ringing the bell, she contemplated leaving before the door finally opened.

"Sarah, what are you doing here?"

"Do you mind if I come in, Paul?"

"Of course," he said, gesturing a welcome.

Sarah stepped inside, watching as the door closed behind.

CHAPTER 24:

A Rising Summer

Throwing the final box on the carport to burn later, Sarah returned to her bedroom. Most of the belongings fit in their original spots, with a few new exceptions. An overstuffed hamper and her college furnishings were the main exclusions.

With summer vacation leaving the teaching position to start in September, for the first time in her life, the next few months would develop without shape or structure. Now cradling an old photo album, Sarah contemplated what to do next.

Within the process of graduating and moving home, the reason and longing to run had slowly escaped her life without notice. A pair of worn running shoes beside the dirty laundry sought her attention when she looked up from the photos. Closing the cover, Sarah fetched a pair of running shorts, shirt, and bra from her drawers before she could reconsider a run. Without pausing for socks, she knelt for her shoes and quickly started outside.

Summer always arrived hot and humid, with a touch of drought. Often a mid-day run brought scorching weather and a need to carry water. Today, Sarah found the same to be true, but instead of bearing the heat along the roads, she wandered down to the old trails. A longer run than expected always pursued while in the woods, but remaining inside all day failed to appeal either.

The sun followed until she reached the cover of the trees. However, the coolness of the shade brought little relief to the humidity. Sweat clouded her eyes and slowly drenched her shirt. Sarah tugged the tee over her head, tossing it on a limb for collecting upon her return.

Each passing tree branch personified a memory that accumulated over the past year. Seeing each one enter and leave her view brought clarity not only to the run but also to life. Among losing her best friend, Sarah found Emily's presence in other people. She also saw through Michael and the accompanying blindness and disbelief. And now the stance of another relationship showed clear.

After leaving graduation, the drive to Paul's house felt automatic. As she walked to the door, the desire to wrap their bodies together fluttered her thoughts. The passion continued upon entering and climaxed as he shut the door and led her to the living room. However, in an instant, those bottled emotions faded. The rare fire to throw her morals aside and enjoy a lone, heated night with Paul vanished, all for one very peculiar reason.

As they sat together, she waited for him to make the first move before her deeply crazed desires fluoresced through an unseen vail. However, he stopped her after their first kiss. "I want this more than you can ever know, Sarah, but it's not right. And more importantly, I know that's not who we really are."

Whether from spite, shame, agreement, or a mixture of the three, Sarah's passion dissolved. Never did she consider herself a bad person until that point. Even with Nigel, she considered the forgotten night as a mistake for which she was ashamed, but that moment when Paul cited her for the actions they were taking, she harbored new feelings. Upon hearing those words, she rose from the couch in silence and headed toward the door. Paul quickly followed, seeing a cause for concern. As he questioned why she was leaving, or what he had done wrong, she turned tearfully and spoke assuredly. "Goodbye, Paul."

The shame weighed too great to withstand. So, instead of confronting the situation, she left. Looking back, it may have not been the best choice, but Sarah remained firm in the decision. Life changed too quickly, and at no future point did she want someone who reminded her she may not be good enough. Sarah knew very well what her past entailed and harbored enough self-hate for those occasions. Instead of scrutiny and judgment, she desired understanding. In that moment, the pain inside bore heavy enough, and for that reason, she could not stay.

Sudden breezes and glimmers of sunlight amongst the branches brought renewed delight to her run. In the weeks that followed graduation, Sarah had unknowingly begun to discover the joy she desired. A new start in her hometown left the past where it belonged. Each day, the darkness and pain trailed further in the rearview mirror, allowing a better future to clench her life.

Edging the path's end, Sarah crossed over from the river trail on her return to the house. A refreshed body and mind fluttered her soul as she came to a walk in the drive. The short absence from her long friendship with running was starting to rekindle at the perfect time. There would be months ahead to focus on what life would look like, but for now, this would be the only acquaintance to occupy her time and effort.

The morning run faded as Sarah showered and got ready with her still damp hair for lunch. Entering the kitchen, she was caught by surprise to see her mother, as if expecting no one to be home.

"What are you doing today?" asked Megan.

"I thought I'd take the time to clean out the old stuff I've collected in my room."

"Are you going to throw out a bunch of things?"

"Maybe. It depends on what it is. I don't need many of my college belongings anymore."

"What if you get your own place after you start teaching?"

"I'll keep the furnishings that might come in handy, but like old papers, worn out running shoes, or anything like that can go."

"Liv, would you mind doing me a favor today?"

"Sure."

"I need you to run to the store. Your dad's birthday is tomorrow, and I'm going to make the cake before he gets home from work."

"I need to find a present for him as well. And, while I'm gone, I'll stop and fill out the paperwork for the next school year."

Sarah finished her sandwich before returning upstairs to change into a pair of jeans and a blouse. In sight of signing her contract, she thought it best to look a step above casual. Examining her hair, Sarah blotted her head with a towel to remove the moister while combing the strands to portray a kempt appearance. Satisfied, she gave a smile in the mirror before turning off the lights.

The drive to the schoolhouse felt familiar from her childhood days of being dropped off. However, with no children and only a few faculty, the building favored a tax office more than a school. Seeing the secretary, she waited as instructed outside of the principal's office. As she flipped through the papers, a familiar voice filled her ears.

"Sarah, is that you?" Peering up, Sarah was greeted with a warm welcome from Caroline's mom. "I heard you were teaching here next year, but I'm surprised I got to see you so soon."

"Ms. May. I'm just as surprised," she said, laughingly.

"Please, call me Judy . . . I know. I transferred here last year after ten years at my previous school."

"Really? How do you like it so far?"

"I love it. The ladies and the few gentlemen I work with are my second family. Don't get me wrong, the other school was amazing, and it was a tough choice to make. Eventually, it resided on trying something new before retiring. The recurring ten-year itch, I guess you'd say."

"You aren't retiring now, are you?"

"Oh goodness, no. I still have at least five more years before I can consider that . . . Rumor has it that you're coming to first grade. Is that right?"

"Yes, or that's the last I heard. I'm going to be filling Ms. Kites' role. Has she moved out already?"

"Oh, Sarah! We're going to be neighbors. Yes, she packed up her belongings slowly over the past few weeks. I think it helped her process retirement easier. Would you like to see your room?"

"That's amazing! I would love to, but I've got to meet with the principal."

Judy peeked a glance through the office window. "She's on the phone and must have just received a call since she was in my room ten minutes ago. You'll probably have another thirty minutes to wait. Come on. I'll walk you down for a quick visit."

Sarah looked to the door before following after Judy. Timidly traversing the hall, she noticed a few teachers remained packing the last of their rooms before disappearing into summer vacation.

Stopping outside of her own room, Judy commented on her schedule before continuing to the next classroom. Jiggling the handle, the door opened into a darkened room lined with desks. The lights flickered as Judy flipped on the switches, casting away the ghastly image inside.

"What do you think?"

"This is the room where I spent first grade," she laughed. "I love it though. I couldn't fathom a better place to start my career than where everything else began."

"I have plenty of posters and anything else you might possibly need. So, if you forget something or want any ideas, feel free. I bet you won't have any trouble decorating though."

"There are so many possibilities running through my mind right now. I'm not sure if I can wait until fall."

"Usually, they let the new teachers come in before everyone else. That way they don't have to hit the ground running. When you sign your paperwork, just be sure to ask if that's alright."

Sarah walked around the room, only to stop halfway down the middle row. "Ms. Kites never did change. When I came to visit, it felt like stepping back in time. Even this desk sits in the same spot as when I was in her class."

"Are you going to keep the same arrangement?"

"At first, I will. It'd be difficult to rearrange after all these years, but who knows."

"I'm sure that'll be the last thing on your mind once you have a class full of children. I love my kids, but they keep me on my toes," she laughed. "Are you ready to see Ms. Donavan?"

"Yes, we should probably head to her office. I'd rather be the one waiting for her."

Upon Sarah's arrival, Ms. Donavan placed the receiver on the hook. Walking to the door, she exited with a delightful cheer.

"Sarah, it's nice to see you today. Come in and we'll get started."

Sarah sat across the large oak table, crossing her legs under the signed papers as she waited for Ms. Donavan to pull a file from the cabinet.

"I spoke with Judy earlier; I believe you two know each other?"

"We do. Her daughter, Caroline, and I were teammates in high school. She stopped me when I came in. Will I be in the room next to hers?"

"Actually, you will. If that's alright."

"Absolutely. It'll be nice to have someone with her experience close by."

"I'm glad to hear it. I assign mentors to teachers in their first year, and Judy was who I had chosen."

Sarah nodded in agreement, imagining what working together would be like.

"Alright, here we are," said Ms. Donavan, sitting down across the desk. "If you can sign all these additional documents, and fill out any new information, such as address changes, we should be set for you to start in September. Do you have any questions?"

"Yes. Well, just the one. Can I access my classroom during the summer? I want to make sure everything is ready for fall."

"Of course. The building will be open from nine to noon every day."

Leaving the school brought a new perspective to life. Sarah not only realized her new purpose but also could now fill the summer void. Adding a few items to her list, ideas and visions of what the school year would behold danced in her head as she drove to the store.

As the glass doors rolled apart, Sarah reached for a basket rather than a buggy. Knowing her excitement might get the best of her, she focused on not overspending the first day. To calm her nerves, she visited the baking section first. Baking soda and another bag of flour were the two ingredients her mother requested.

While the flour sat along the bottom shelf, the soda resided on the top, nearly outside of her reach, causing Sarah to arch on her tiptoes. She angled her body a few different positions before giving a slight jump to clinch the can in her hand. Looking around, there was no one to offer help, but also no awkward stares watching her silly attempts.

Looking over the list, Sarah found her way to the school supplies. Between banners, cardboard cutouts, and name plates, the basket soon became full. Sarah eyed the scribbled words again to assure nothing she would need firsthand was missed. *Markers.* To her surprise, none of the shelves housed markers, except for a few of the permanent kind. Gathering a set of those, she turned in search of the water-based sort.

"Excuse me," she asked, seeing a stocker at the end of the aisle. "Where would the colored markers be?"

"Over on aisle eleven, across the store."

"Thank you."

Realizing she was wasting time pondering over supplies, Sarah hastily followed the main walk to the rear of the store. It had been years since she needed markers, and the store had been rearranged on multiple occasions since then.

Reading each sign as she passed, Sarah zipped down aisle eleven scanning each shelf. Kneeling halfway down the row, she chose two boxes. Uncertainty interceded as she dismissed the thought by placing the ten pack back on the shelf. *All set*, she thought, proceeding to the checkout.

Roaming the front of the store for a fast lane proved unsuccessful, as all the lines were crowded with mothers pushing overloaded grocery carts. She would have no choice but to wait in line to claim the ingredients her mom needed.

Slowly, the lines budged forward, leaving Sarah in the midst of a daydream. Many children accompanying their mothers looked to be nearly six years old. Would some of them be in her class next year?

One boy caught her watching him as he allowed his toy crusader to fly between a shopping cart and a neighboring candy holder.

"Do you want to meet my friend?" he asked, with a certain proudness.

"Hey. Who do you have there?" she asked, bending to his level.

"This is Major Lee. He doesn't normally fly, but Mom says I can't play on the floor here."

Hearing his voice, the lady beside him turned and smiled.

"Well, she sounds really smart. And, what's your name?"

"She also says I shouldn't tell strangers my name."

"Fair enough."

"This is Bradley," the lady interrupted, "and I'm Susan."

"Nice to meet you both. I'm Sarah Mills."

"Oh, Cliff and Megan's daughter?"

"Actually yeah," she laughed.

"It's been years since I've seen you. And now you're all grown. What are you up to these days?"

"I was actually just hired to teach first grade in the fall. Is Bradley in that age group?"

"He is," Susan said with rolling eyes. "Whoever has him next year will likely be in for a surprise. Bradley," she said, catching his attention. "Did you hear that? Ms. Mills might be your teacher?"

Bradley stopped and threw his arms around Sarah, nestling his head into her chest. "I love her already," he exclaimed.

Sarah found herself hugging the young boy in return, while trying to subside the emotions he drummed up inside her.

"Well, there are two teachers, but likely I'll see you either way." Sarah raised up as Bradley returned to his toys. "Hopefully, I will though. I think we'd get along great."

"If he gives you any trouble, don't hesitate to call."

Sarah suppressed a laugh. "I appreciate it."

The line inched forward, and Susan began unloading her groceries onto the counter. However, among the excitement of school, Sarah had nearly forgotten to find a gift for her dad. "You'll have to excuse me. I forgot to grab something. It was nice meeting you both."

"You as well, dear."

"I'll see you this fall, Bradley," she said, weaving away from the line.

Walking to the other side of the store, Sarah headed to the men's department. She had not the slightest idea of what she might find, but it would serve as a good enough place as any to start.

She combed the two aisles dedicated to men's shaving and hygiene before noticing an assortment of colognes. Popping the cap off the sampler, she sprayed the first onto a sheet, only to quickly dismiss the brash smell. Again, with a second, she paused only briefly before deciding that cologne might not be the best idea.

Searching once more her eyes landed on a box that read, "Beard Trimmer on the Go." Sarah flipped the package over in her hands, reading the advertisement. Half satisfied with the gift, she proceeded to leave before another idea struck her thoughts. *A trimmer might not be best,* as now she considered something else. Returning to the trimmers, Sarah replaced the box before heading to the outdoors section.

Between the back and forth, Sarah grew accustomed to the latest layout, and with little effort found the department unassisted. Noticing her shoe had come untied, Sarah kneeled next to a shelf to fix the laces. Only as she heard her name, did Sarah realize she was not alone.

"Hey, Sarah . . ." She looked up to the familiar voice while rising to her feet. Despite not having talked since the wedding, one look at his hopeful smile was all that was needed to alleviate any doubt of the feelings they still shared. Relief slowly consumed her body with each step as she moved closer to him. Meeting the embrace of his arms, all prior pain and tears faded. Knowing her prayers were being answered, Sarah snuggled her head along his chest. "I always imagined we would be together later on in life."

Acknowledgements

It's not too often we can chase our dreams, but one thing I try to tell myself is, remember who helped you along the way. A book is not worth its weight in paper without a beautiful cover. I'm so proud of my mother's work in creating the amazing artwork that is displayed on both of my novels. Inside, the many drafts that have taken shape were revised multiple times, but without the support of those who read the manuscript first, it would have been a tough task to complete. Thank you: J. Major for your constant support, friendship and advise, J. Peacock for your kindness and feedback, and C&A Cross for your willingness and support, and them all for being beta readers. I would also like to thank my dad, mom, and sisters for all their love and support over the past years while I was writing. This amazing journey is nothing short of trying to follow a feeling I had a few years ago. The years since have been challenging and exciting, and I think God for all of them.

- C.S. McKinney